PENGUIN BOOKS

LAURENCE FEARNLEY IS A NOVELIST and non-fiction writer. In 2015 she worked alongside mountaineer Lydia Bradey to write *Going Up is Easy*, a climbing memoir that was a finalist in the Banff Mountain Literature Award. Her previous novel, *Reach*, was longlisted for the 2016 Ockham New Zealand Book Awards, and her 2011 novel, *The Hut Builder*, won the fiction category of the New Zealand Post Book Awards and was shortlisted for the international 2010 Boardman Tasker Prize for mountain writing. Her novel *Edwin and Matilda* was runner-up in the 2008 Montana New Zealand Book Awards, and her second novel, *Room*, was shortlisted for the 2001 Montana New Zealand Book Awards. In 2004 Fearnley was awarded the Artists to Antarctica fellowship, and in 2007 the Robert Burns fellowship at the University of Otago. Laurence lives in Dunedin with her husband and son.

The

quiet

specta

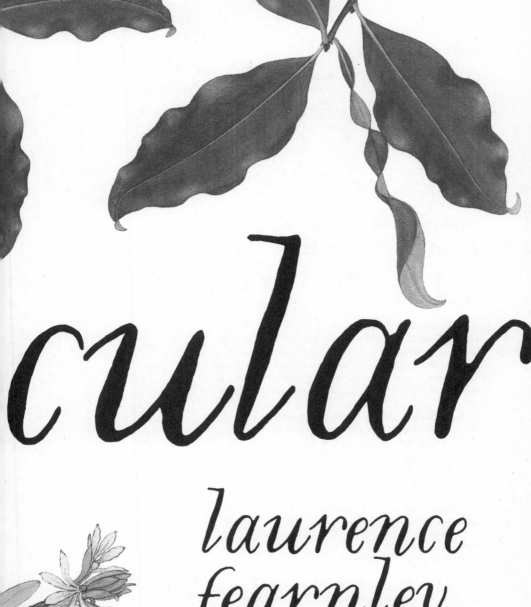

cular

laurence fearnley

PENGUIN BOOKS

PENGUIN

UK | USA | Canada | Ireland | Australia
India | New Zealand | South Africa | China

Penguin is an imprint of the Penguin Random House group
of companies, whose addresses can be found at global.
penguinrandomhouse.com.

Penguin
Random House
New Zealand

First published by Penguin Random House New Zealand, 2016

10 9 8 7 6 5 4 3 2 1

Design by Carla Sy © Penguin Random House New Zealand
Botanical illustrations © Audrey Eagle
Author photograph by Graham Warman
Printed and bound in Australia by Griffin Press,
an Accredited ISO AS/NZS 14001 Environmental Management
Systems Printer

A catalogue record for this book is available from the National
Library of New Zealand.

ISBN 978-0-14-357415-6
eISBN 978-1-74-348724-2

The assistance of Creative New Zealand towards the production
of this book is gratefully acknowledged by the publisher.

ARTS COUNCIL OF NEW ZEALAND TOI AOTEAROA

penguin.co.nz

For Pip Adam

etta

L oretta reversed the car into the shade, shut off the engine and sat with her hands resting on the steering wheel. A long, slow sigh escaped her lips, and she reached down for the catch on the driver's seat and pushed backwards, stretching out her legs and kicking off her slip-on shoes. Her left hip and knee ached. All day she'd been crouching and standing, arranging and reshelving books at Caroline Freeman High library. Following the end of school, she'd driven the fifteen-odd kilometres from the South Island city where she worked to the satellite town where she lived, and where her son, Kit, attended intermediate. On the journey from one side of town to the other, she managed to refill the barbecue gas bottle, return a stack of DVDs to the video store and collect the repaired sandwich-maker that had been ready at the electrical shop for the past two weeks. She closed her eyes, hoping that when she opened them it would be Friday and that the week ahead had somehow vanished.

It was still Monday. She glanced across to the clock, turned on the ignition and registered the time: 4.44. She was sixteen minutes early for the end of orchestra practice and twenty-five minutes early if she factored in the additional time it took Kit to pack up his gear and make his way out of the school gate to the supermarket car park. If only he was here now. He was still young enough to get a kick out of spotting number arrangements on digital clocks and odometers. Being the nerd he was, he would work out that the sum of three fours was twelve — the age he would be at his next birthday.

In any given week Loretta spent hours in limbo, stuck in the unwieldy between-time that filled the space between dropping off and collecting Kit from various activities: orchestra, water polo, gym, art class, chess club, Magic the Gathering and visits to the homes of friends. Recently, she had begun to show signs of being borderline obsessive about time. To make it pass, she adopted a convoluted system whereby she systematically checked the car clock against the time on her cell phone. Then she compared the time on her cell phone with the time announced on the radio. Finally, she tested the radio time against her watch. Typically, she ended up with four variations, none of which truly mattered, given that she was always early and Kit ignored any schedule not governed by his own slow-running internal clock.

In the glove box was a packet of wet wipes. Loretta took one and ran it over the dashboard, creating a clean stripe through the thin layer of dust. She continued to clean, wiping and turning the tissue-like square until it was dark grey and grimy. She took another and wiped down the steering wheel, and then, catching sight of the back seat in the mirror, turned around and took in the discarded clothes, sports gear and empty drink bottles on the back seat. Scrunched-up tissues spilled from the cup-holder, and trapped beneath the central armrest itself was an open book, one of its pages dog-eared. Loretta's mother had taught her never to fold over page corners, and now, partly as a result of that initial training, Loretta could not stand to see any book treated with so little respect.

She reached back, grabbed the book and lifted it to her knee, absently passing the wet wipe over its title: *The Dangerous Book for Boys*. Loretta had seen copies of the book many times, but now, for the first time, scanned the dog-eared page and registered an image of a go-kart. Gently she unfolded the corner and closed the book. She wiped it again, and then, seconds later, opened it at random. As she flicked through the pages, she was surprised to register a faint sense of yearning. She studied the page more closely and tried to fathom what the book was telling her. Little by little, the yearning took shape, and formed two words: freedom, adventure. Instead of making her smile, they caused her to flinch. And then she looked at the book's title once more and said something out loud that startled her: '*The Dangerous Book for Menopausal Women*.' Before she could give it any more thought, however, she spotted Kit across the car park. Though he was some distance away, she knew it was him from the way he held the handle of his guitar case with both hands, elbows bent, the instrument in front of him, horizontal across his body. With each step his knees bumped against the case and as he came closer he tripped and stumbled, but righted himself without falling. The back door swung open and Kit shoved the guitar and then himself onto the seat.

Loretta looked at him in the mirror. 'How was orchestra?' she asked.

'All right,' said Kit.

'I missed you,' said Loretta.

Kit nodded, fastened his seat belt and then, glancing up, smiled at her reflection. 'Love you,' he said.

'Love you more,' she replied.

And then Loretta started the engine and headed for home.

'I WAS WONDERING', SAID LORETTA, 'what I'd put in a book called *The Dangerous Book for Menopausal Women*.'

Her friend Shannon looked puzzled, then shifted uncomfortably on the wide concrete step at the back of the real estate office where they were both sitting. 'I didn't know you were menopausal.'

'I'm not. I mean, I could be — but I'm not sure really. It's not like I've been given a sign. There have been possible hints in that department and, on top of that, a couple of weird things have happened recently.'

'Like what?'

Loretta took a sip from her coffee and checked her watch. It was okay, she still had thirty minutes before she had to leave to collect Kit from water polo.

'Well, I've noticed that young assistants turn down the music when I walk into shops. And at the supermarket recently a woman called me "dear" and offered me a free sample of incontinence pads.'

Shannon snorted. 'How old do they think you are?'

'I don't know, really. Forty? Seventy? Somewhere between the two?'

Shannon rolled her eyes as she fished for a cigarette and her battered Zippo lighter. 'You took them, though? The free pads. You took them?'

"Course I did,' said Loretta. 'I figured they'd make someone a lovely present. You know, a special gift for a "hard-to-buy-for" best friend.'

'Yeah, nice. Appropriate, too.' Shannon narrowed her eyes and inhaled on her cigarette. She allowed the smoke to drift out of her nostrils, then picked a shred of tobacco from her teeth. 'Stick them in the Secret Santa at the end of year party. That's what I'd do.'

They sat in silence for a moment, Loretta examining a grease stain on her new red sweater, Shannon prodding a large dirt-filled terracotta plant pot with the toe of her patent-leather loafer. Originally the pot had housed a pōhutukawa, a leaving gift presented to Shannon on her last day as part-time school secretary. She now ran her own real estate company and the tree that had once flourished and flowered had long since shrivelled and died; in its place were half-smoked cigarettes and lipstick-stained butts.

Loretta cleared her throat. 'So, getting back to *The Dangerous Book for Menopausal Women*. Any ideas?'

Shannon thought for a moment, then replied, 'You could have a chapter on hair and make-up.'

'Why? What's wrong with my hair and make-up?'

Shannon looked at her friend and scowled. 'Nothing . . . much. Regrowth suits you.'

Without thinking, Loretta ran her fingers over her temples, gently pulling at the uneven tufts with her fingers. She trimmed and dyed her own hair and was pretty satisfied with the result. 'But that's not really *dangerous*, is it? Most women would file hair and make-up under "upkeep", wouldn't they?'

Shannon shrugged. 'Up to you — it's your book. But from where I'm sitting the entire beauty industry is completely psycho and dangerous.'

Fearing a lecture, Loretta asked, 'Any other ideas?'

'You could have an affair.'

'What? Who with?'

'I don't know. There must be tons of desperate weirdos about. Take your pick.'

Loretta shook her head. 'Nah. Not interested. Anyway, I'd have to go through that whole sad process of buying matching underwear and shaving my armpits, and I can't be bothered.'

Shannon chuckled and took a drag on her cigarette. 'I don't know. Take up smoking. That's dangerous.'

She held out the cigarette and Loretta took it, examining the stain left by Shannon's red lipstick before placing it gently between her own lips. She held the smoke in her mouth a moment, then exhaled, coughing as she did so.

'Don't waste it,' said Shannon, holding out her hand. 'They're bloody expensive. Give it back.'

Loretta shifted her weight and checked the time on her phone, before pushing up her sleeve and looking at her watch. The old self-winder had stopped, and so she slipped her nails around the crown and pulled gently, adjusting the time. She gave the crown a few turns and drew the watch up to her ear, straining to hear the steady 'tick-tock' that always made her think of her childhood, and the occasions she had curled up on her grandfather's lap. She knew she should think about leaving but she liked hanging out with Shannon and it was nice to sit still and relax for a minute.

'The other day I was waiting outside chess for Kit when I had a massive brainwave. I decided I should buy a campervan. Then, whenever I have to wait around I could stretch out, relax, read a book, make a cup of tea, or have a snooze.'

Shannon nodded. 'That's a great idea.'

'Yeah, I reckon. It'd be like my secret hidey-hole, you know?'

'You should do it.'

'Yeah,' agreed Loretta, 'I will. I'm going to.'

'Good. I know.'

They both laughed.

The door behind them opened and a young woman slipped out of the office and asked Shannon to shove up, before taking a seat on the step. She glanced towards Loretta and smiled, proffering a packet of dried apricots before taking one herself.

'Jess, Loretta. Loretta, Jess. Jess is my new office manager.'

Jess gave a little wave and leant back, shading her eyes.

'Loretta was telling me about her mid-life crisis and how she wants to start living dangerously.'

From the corner of her eye Loretta saw Jess sit up a little and turn towards her.

'Sad but true,' said Loretta.

From the slight frown on Jess's face, Loretta got the feeling she was being weighed up, appraised and rejected as a candidate for danger. For her part, Jess looked about thirty, slim, with long hair pulled back into a ponytail. She wore rimless glasses that lent her face a certain gravitas.

'Jess knows all about danger, don't you?'

Jess drew back, puzzled. 'What? Don't think so.'

Shannon raised her eyebrows and took a final puff on her cigarette before grinding it out on the rim of the plant pot and flicking the butt onto the dirt. 'Gotta go. Second viewing,' she said, before giving Loretta a quick hug, and disappearing through the door.

Loretta glanced at her watch; she still had several minutes before she needed to leave. She was determined not to be early.

'How long have you been working for Shannon, Jess?'

Jess screwed up her face as if making a mental calculation, and then said, 'Three or four weeks, about.'

Loretta wasn't very good at small talk, but in order not to appear rude she ploughed on with another question. 'Where were you before?'

Now that Shannon had gone, Jess seemed uncomfortable, as though desperate to be left in peace. 'I was overseas for a couple of years.'

Loretta nodded. 'Australia?'

'Close. West Papua.'

'What were you doing there?'

Keeping her eyes fixed on the bag in her hand, Jess replied, 'Just IT and admin. Pretty much what I'm doing here.'

'Must have been interesting, though.'

Jess stretched and stood up, 'It had its moments.' She gave a brief smile and said goodbye, before disappearing through the door.

———————

The smell of chlorine hung over the foyer, tickling Loretta's nose as she waited for Kit to emerge from the boys' changing room. One after the other, his teammates wandered out, and several minutes later Kit appeared. He looked as though he hadn't bothered to dry himself. His hair was wet and plastered to his head; drops of water glistened on his face. His school shoes were untied, slipped straight on to his bare feet. His sweatshirt was back-to-front. But when he saw Loretta he gave a slight smirk, and waved as he sauntered towards her.

'How was it?'

'Terrible,' he said.

Loretta took his swim bag and grabbed his towel, giving his hair and ears a quick rub-down.

'What was the score?'

'Dunno. I think we lost. Maybe 22 to 7. Something like that, I think.'

Loretta wished there was something she could say to make Kit feel better, but she saw that he didn't appear too disheartened. The pang of disappointment was hers alone. Nevertheless, she ruffled his hair and in an attempt to cheer him up said, 'I'm thinking of buying a campervan.'

Kit stopped and looked up at her, his eyes widening with pleasure. 'Really?'

Loretta realised her mistake, and felt sorry for having made the suggestion. 'No, not really. But it would be cool, eh?'

'Why don't you buy one?' pressed Kit. 'And then we could go on lots of holidays.'

'Love you,' said Loretta.

'Please?' said Kit.

'I'll think about it.'

They walked in silence back to the car.

THE HOUSE SEEMED EMPTY, as it often did when Kit was away for a night. It wasn't only Loretta who felt his absence — Hamish did, too. He tended to become restless, moving through the house, picking up random items belonging to Kit and examining them carefully before returning them to the shelf where they belonged. Loretta imagined that when Kit left home it would be Hamish who would resist making major changes to their son's room. He formed such strong emotional attachments to objects, specifically objects that had never really belonged to him in the first place — like Kit's Lego collection, for example. She could picture Hamish sorting through the boxes of books and junk in Kit's room and insisting on keeping all the old, discarded items, just in case.

'In case of what?' Loretta would demand.

'In case he needs them, obviously.'

'You think he's going to need that piece of wood decorated with four loose nails and bits of coloured wool some day?'

'Yep.'

'Really?'

'Yep.'

'Really?'

'Absolutely.'

'You know it's missing the glitter and the spray-painted silver pine cone that was PVA-ed onto its end?'

'I did know that. But I can replace it.'

'Oh, so you're an art conservator now, are you?'

'Just one of my many talents.'

Fortunately Pete, Loretta's oldest son, had left home before Hamish came on the scene. Pete had been seventeen and ready for independence, and his departure from home had felt both natural and timely. By contrast, Edie's decision to leave, at fifteen, had come as a total shock. Loretta had vivid memories of her daughter bursting into tears and sobbing uncontrollably as she tried to explain that she wanted to leave home and move in with Martin, her dad. It wasn't that she didn't love Loretta, that wasn't it at all. It was simply that she was fifteen, and she felt she was missing out — or, rather, that she needed to be somewhere else, somewhere bigger, even if it was only Auckland. The shame at her betrayal, visible to Loretta, had been almost unbearable.

'I'll probably hate it once I'm there,' Edie had gulped. 'I bet I'll want to come home after a few weeks.'

Listening to her daughter, Loretta had felt her chest tighten and it was all she could do to speak calmly and assure Edie that moving north was the right decision, that everything would work out all right and that she could always change her mind and come home, any time.

'Auckland's only an hour or two away,' she soothed her child.

'By plane!' Edie wailed.

'Well, yeah,' said Loretta. 'I wasn't expecting you to walk.'

'I'd have to swim Cook Strait as well,' sniffled Edie, attempting to smile.

'Yeah, there's that too,' replied Loretta. 'But you could always hitch a ride on a boat or something. You know, improvise.'

Edie began to laugh and tiny bubbles of snot appeared at her nostrils that she quickly wiped with her sleeve. 'I might fly,' she gulped. 'You wouldn't mind, would you? If I took a plane? It's not too extravagant?'

At any other time Loretta might have snapped 'For God's sake, Edie, take a helicopter for all I care', but instead she soothed and reassured her daughter until, in the end, Edie was persuaded to feel better about leaving and Loretta was left feeling guilty for letting her go, for encouraging her to make the leap, and for the ugly stab of envy she experienced as she imagined her daughter's new future.

Kit was in his first year at primary school when Edie left. No one ever said as much but Kit had been the result of a last-ditch effort by Loretta and Martin to make their marriage work. He was conceived in a back paddock on the night of Martin's youngest sister's wedding. It wasn't the brief sexual act itself or the sudden sobering up, followed by horror, that stuck in Loretta's memory, but the fact that afterwards, while taking a short-cut back to the marquee to avoid the awkwardness of walking alongside Martin, she had negotiated a wire fence and got a shock. In conversations with her friends she blamed the sharp jolt of electricity for stimulating Martin's sperm in the right direction, towards her old eggs. But she had nevertheless been pretty happy to discover she was pregnant once more. For the past few years she'd been looking for a way to cut back on the number of hours she put in as manager of the medical school library, and having a baby appeared to offer a way out, in the short term at least. There was, though, still the problem of her marriage to contend with.

Martin's response was straightforward: he urged Loretta to have an abortion. When she refused, however, he didn't argue but quietly suggested that it might be best if he left her to it. He didn't want to make life difficult for her, and he certainly didn't want to upset the kids, so he proposed to take care of her financially for a year until she was back on her feet. All he asked in return was joint custody of Pete and Edie, with regular weekend access. And, somewhat surprisingly, Loretta thought, he insisted his name be on the unwanted baby's birth certificate. And so, not long after the twelfth week of the pregnancy, they split up.

The gratitude Loretta felt towards Martin was genuine and it prompted her to immediately question whether she had made the correct decision in calling an end to their marriage. Maybe they should give it one more go? They could make it work, couldn't they? For several months following Martin's immediate departure Loretta felt miserable and torn, unable to believe that she had acted rationally, let alone wisely. Seeing Martin often, during the weekend handover, filled her with such anguish and uncertainty that once or twice she asked if she could keep Edie and Pete company and join them all at the bach. Despite Edie's support, Martin didn't think it was a sensible suggestion and, although he remained civil and courteous, he never gave Loretta any cause to believe that he wanted her back. He didn't say it out loud but it was clear that as far as he was concerned they'd spent twenty years together, and of those twelve were great, five not so good and three miserable. Now it was time to move on. Deep down, beneath the thick layer of fear, Loretta felt exactly the same way.

The most unexpected outcome in the whole story was the speed with which Hamish came onto the scene.

'He's the removal man! I paid him over $2000 to move my furniture out, not to . . .' Martin couldn't bring himself to finish the sentence. 'You're pregnant, for God's sake. You can't go around flaunting yourself in front of strangers.'

Loretta's protest that she *hadn't* or rather *hadn't planned to* were cut short.

'I haven't even got a house yet, my furniture's in storage, I'm living with my brother, and you're already— Jesus, it's revolting.'

'It's not revolting! It's not like that. You're exaggerating. I haven't done anything . . .'

'Yeah?'

'. . . wrong. Wrong. I haven't done anything wrong. You never let me finish.'

Martin made a huffing sound. 'I'm basically funding your new relationship. I'm the sucker who practically gave away the family home and handed over a brand-new car. My car! It's done less than 10,000 k's. Talk about being taken for a ride. And what about Edie? And, for the love of God, you're going to have a baby.'

Loretta couldn't bring herself to tell her mother about Hamish. It sounded so tawdry whenever she rehearsed the phone conversation in her mind. It looked even worse when she committed rough notes to paper:

1. *Had unprotected, desperate, drunken sex with husband of twenty years and immediately regretted it.*

2. *Got pregnant and through mutual agreement separated from husband/father of child.*

3. *Bought out husband and kept family home and one car — the smaller (but newer) one.*

4. *After several long months husband got his act together and booked removal truck. I took day off work to oversee proceedings.*

5. *Removal men arrived 9 am. Made lunch and cups of tea for removal men. Made mental note that they were rather slow at their job.*

6. *Collected Edie from school.*

7. *Discovered that Hamish, one of the removal men, liked Talking Heads.*

8. *Offered to lend Hamish my Talking Heads albums (most of which are really Martin's Talking Heads albums).*

9. *Hamish smiled shyly and suggested we could listen to them together.*

10. *Aaaaarrrgh.*

11. *Days later Hamish visited after dinner and we played 'Cross-eyed and Painless' seven times in a row. Giggled like a teenager.*

12. *Nothing happened. Told myself to take things slowly as I don't want to cause trouble with Martin or do anything to upset kids.*

In fact it was true that 'nothing happened' — if the definition of 'nothing' referred to full-on sex rather than falling in love and spending every available moment in Hamish's company. Perhaps, if she hadn't had two kids and a third on the way, things may have moved a little more quickly on the sex front, but as it was she was careful. They finally got around to it three days before Kit was born. She gave in because Kit was overdue and she was being driven mad with waiting. She was tired from lack of sleep, suffering from lower back pain and wanted something to take her mind off things. Sex had made her laugh and afterwards, when Hamish stroked her back and called her beautiful, she felt better than she had for weeks. As he held her, she settled into him, almost as if she was a bird on a nest. 'You are my nest,' she said, and it was true.

FOR THE PAST SEVERAL MINUTES Loretta had been watching a flock of seagulls chasing and battling across the sky above the supermarket. One had a scrap of food in its bill and the others were intent on getting it for themselves. The pursuit seemed relentless. The chased gull climbed, swooped, twisted and altered course in its attempt to lose its attackers but they held on, coming at it from above and below, beating their wings furiously as they all but collided with it. Loretta couldn't figure out why the first seagull continued to fly. Why didn't it land and swallow its food? Why did it keep flying? There had to be a reason.

When she was a child, living in Christchurch, she had been

a member of a bird-watching club. The clubhouse was called the Misty Moors, and Loretta was in charge of keeping the tiny structure tidy. She was the only member of the club. She'd started it while at primary school and had expected her friends and some of her classmates to join, but none of them did. So she sat for hours inside the little hut her father had built out of bits of plywood, and made notes of the birds she could see through the door opening. Because her hut was located in a garden in Shirley, the variety of birds was limited to sparrows, blackbirds and starlings. Very occasionally she might spot a duck or a cat, or one of the neighbour's fantail pigeons, but nothing more exotic than that. The lack of rare birds didn't diminish her desire to see something out of the ordinary. On her small bookshelf were various guides: books about trees, plants, fossils, fish, planes and birds. She frequently dreamt about the day she would see a mangrove swamp, a piece of obsidian or a white heron, or something truly extraordinary like a sunfish, a Concorde or a bittern.

Once she turned twelve, she was allowed to go off by herself at weekends to 'study' birds. She would bike into the easterly headwind, down the long length of Linwood Avenue towards the estuary, where she would find a sheltered spot close to the exposed mudflats and make a tally of all the birds she recognised: oystercatchers, stilts, black swans, godwits, pūkeko and three kinds of seagull — black-backed, red-billed and black-billed. Keeping a record of the birds made her happier than almost anything else in the world.

The birds above the supermarket were all black-backed gulls. They were still charging and diving, and the longer she watched the more anxious she felt. She willed the pursuing birds to find something new to attract their attention. There was an entire car park — surely somewhere, someone had discarded a half-eaten pie or a bag of chips.

A few days before, a woman called Valerie Mansford had gone missing from this same suburban car park. She had parked her car at the rear of the parking area and was last spotted by the mailboxes, posting a white envelope. And then, apparently, she had wandered off. Police had questioned staff in the post shop, the chemist, the bank, the tearooms, the bakery, the butcher's, the bottle store, the pizza restaurant, the op shop and the pet shop, but had found nothing to indicate where the forty-five-year-old woman had gone. Her description resembled that of many, many women: about 168 centimetres, medium to heavy build, shoulder-length brownish hair, last seen wearing jeans and a floral sweatshirt. Her bag, containing her wallet and phone, was found in her car.

Loretta had read the story closely. Valerie Mansford was around her age, and the location of her disappearance was so familiar that Loretta could envisage walking along every alley, street and green space, creating a map of routes the missing woman might have taken. It was astounding how far Loretta could travel in her mind before reaching a dead end.

It had been noticeable that the report contained so little information beyond the woman's last movements and physical appearance. The only significant fact was that the police were very concerned but had ruled out foul play. They didn't say why. Often, Loretta thought she remembered, missing people were described as 'confused', 'depressed', 'on medication' or experiencing relationship or financial problems — anything that gave some explanation for their disappearance. But there had been no such information in the newspaper account

Loretta had seen. Though the police and media were keeping things quiet, the community Facebook pages were full of comments and speculation, ranging from accusations that Ms Mansford had stolen money from her employers and skipped the country through to theories concerning alien abduction. So what happened to her? Why would she disappear? Where was she? And then, by extension, Loretta wondered, Where would I go if I wanted to disappear?

She could see Kit ambling towards the car. As usual he carried his guitar case in front of his body, angling his torso and side-stepping to negotiate a narrow space between the parked vehicles. He could have gone around the cars but, for some reason, he chose to go between them, knocking a mirror in his attempt to sidle past. Loretta could see that he hadn't spotted the ute reversing from the parking space in front of him. She'd warned him before about taking care but he never seemed to notice what was going on around him. He was pretty lucky, though.

The rear door opened and Kit shoved his guitar case in, paused a moment, then clambered in after it, his school backpack still on his shoulders. Loretta watched him in the rear mirror as he tried to fasten his seat belt over the pack.

'Did you notice the seagulls flying over the car park?'

'No,' said Kit.

'Oh, they were amazing. One had food and the others were trying to steal it . . .'

'What's for dinner?' asked Kit.

'Food.'

Loretta could see that Kit was settled but she didn't feel like leaving. She wanted to wait until she saw the seagulls again. Just to get a sense of finality, to find out what had happened to the lead bird.

'Where would you go if you wanted to disappear?' she asked to fill in time.

'I don't know.'

'If you wanted to disappear,' repeated Loretta, 'where do you think you would like to go?'

Kit shrugged. 'What time would I need to be home by?'

'No, you're trying to disappear.'

'Why?'

'I don't know.'

'Well, I don't know, either. So why are you asking me?'

Loretta heard herself sigh. Lately she had a feeling, more and more often, that she was incapable of making herself understood. Somewhere along the line the cable connecting her inner thoughts to her outer expression had unravelled, and ideas that made perfect sense inside her head were often misunderstood or misinterpreted once committed to speech. She turned around in her seat and faced Kit, and then smiled reassuringly. 'What do you know about the missing link?'

Kit shook his head and shrugged again, his lips clamped tightly shut, signalling he wasn't in any mood to answer. Through the rear window, behind his head, two seagulls flew into view. Unlike the birds she had been watching earlier, they appeared to have no purpose in mind. Loretta followed their progress, shifting her gaze to the passenger window and then to the front, as they soared gracefully above the trees in the gardens and then dropped towards the ground, disappearing from view.

'WHAT'S THE MOST DANGEROUS THING you've ever done?' asked Loretta a day later.

'Me?'

Loretta rolled her eyes. Apart from Hamish, there was no one else in the room. 'No, I was asking the guy on the radio.'

Hamish wasn't due to leave for another hour, and Kit wouldn't be ready to collect from town until nine that night. It was Saturday, and despite her intention to spend the afternoon working in the garden, Loretta was sitting at the kitchen table trawling through online news reports of the still-missing woman.

Earlier, she'd offered to help Hamish with his overnight bag and make him a packed lunch, but he was so used to spending two, or sometimes three nights a week away from home that he hadn't needed her help. He was onto it. And besides, he planned to spend the night with Loretta's parents, at their home on Mount Pleasant, on the hills overlooking Christchurch. He didn't always stay with them during his stopovers but he had a late start scheduled for Sunday.

'You and Kit could come with me, if you want,' Hamish had suggested the night before, but Kit had wanted to spend the weekend at a special Magic the Gathering event and Loretta didn't try to persuade him to change his mind. The thought of driving all the way to Christchurch and back, at least six hours each way door to door, didn't appeal to her, not with so many chores needing to be tackled. The garden was looking a mess; weeds were choking the beds of tussock she had planted a few years back after tearing out the toetoe and gorse.

'Anything at all?' she prompted Hamish.

'Dangerous? How dangerous?'

Before she could answer, however, Hamish had wandered out of the kitchen, singing to himself as he pottered about in the bedroom. The sound of his Telecaster filtered through the house. It wasn't plugged in but it was easy to identify the tune, The Bats' 'Time to Get Ready'.

Loretta picked up the phone and dialled her parents' number, waiting several minutes before her father answered.

'Hello, it's me,' she said.

There was a pause on the other end, and then Ted's voice asked, 'Who's this?'

'Loretta.'

'Who?'

Calls home had begun like this for as long as Loretta could remember. Even so, she felt a slight pang of disappointment or, perhaps, fear when her father consistently failed to recognise her voice. It wasn't as though he was terribly hard of hearing. For a time she had wondered if he was simply winding her up.

'Loretta,' she repeated.

'Oh,' came the reply, 'I'll pass you on to your mother.'

Loretta could make out the sound of movement and called out loudly, hoping to capture his attention. 'No, I want to talk to you.'

When he came back on the line Ted sounded wary, as if trapped.

'I wanted to ask you something. I want to know what is the most dangerous thing you've ever done?'

There was silence at Ted's end, and Loretta was about to repeat herself when she heard him mumble 'Dangerous?' A sound like fingers being scratched through hair followed and then her father's voice once more, asking, 'Do you mean the earthquakes?'

Loretta shook her head. 'No, I was thinking of something . . .'

'The war?' offered her father. 'Growing up in London during the Blitz?'

Loretta sighed. She didn't mean to sound exasperated, but her father, catching the noise, mumbled, 'Hold on, I'll give you to Connie.' Loretta raised her voice, saying, 'No, it's all right . . .' but she could already hear the sound of the sliding door, her father's voice calling, 'Constance, it's Loretta on the phone. She wants to ask you something . . . about danger.'

In the background she could make out her mother's voice and the mumbled urgency of a conversation, and then her father was back on the line, passing on Connie's answer: 'Being aboard the *Wahine* when it went down?'

This time Loretta laughed out loud. 'You're doing this on purpose, aren't you? You're toying with me.'

And then there was a shuffling noise and Connie was on the other end. 'What's all this about danger? Your father thinks you've gone mad.'

Loretta tried to explain but got stuck in the attempt to arrange her thoughts into sentences and ended up fumbling, muttering something about lions and tigers. There was a pause. 'Lions?' A second passed and then her mother added, 'No, that was your Aunt Avis. And the animal in question wasn't a lion, it was an elephant. But she was nowhere near the tent when it got trampled, so it wasn't really dangerous. Not technically speaking. Though it could have been, I suppose, had she been sleeping inside at the time.'

'Oh, stop!' cried Loretta. 'You're not getting it.'

'Well, I don't understand what you're talking about. Avis spent years in Kenya before moving to America.'

'Stop. Please stop.'

But Connie showed no sign of letting up. 'Well, what do you want? It's not like any of us have been to the moon, or spent months in a submarine. Is that more what you're looking for? Because I thought you said lions and tigers.'

'Please stop, now,' repeated Loretta.

'I'm not the one who started it,' said Connie.

Loretta tried to bring the conversation around to Hamish, telling her mother that he hoped to be with them by 10 pm, but Connie was only half listening. 'Your father's asking if slipping off the roof or falling off a ladder would count . . . He's done both.'

'It's all right, Mum,' said Loretta. 'I think I've got enough material, now.'

'The neighbour's dog? It's not very big but it tends to jump up on me when I'm collecting the post. It's a nasty, ratty thing. Patch. That's its name . . . not very original.'

'Really, Mum, I don't need any more examples. Forget about it.'

But Loretta continued to dwell on the topic. She tried to recall the most dangerous moments of her life, the times when she had taken extreme risks and subjected herself to potentially life-changing moments, but all she could come up with were memories of unprotected teenage sex and several drunken, one-night stands with virtual strangers after student parties. It wasn't the kind of material that would make it into a best-selling book. Her experiences seemed too accidental, far less prescribed than the creative and neatly outlined dangers she had glimpsed on the pages of Kit's library book. Or perhaps she was confusing danger with something else. Maybe that was the problem. Or maybe it was because for centuries history-makers had focused their attention on the wrong kind of dangers?

'Definitely childbirth,' agreed Shannon, later that evening. 'Childbirth . . . unprotected sex . . . that cleaner who used to bail me up in the car park after school. I'm pretty sure he was dangerous. Well, threatening at least. But childbirth is definitely dangerous. It's not going to be much use to you, though … with your project.'

Loretta didn't follow. 'Project?'

'Yeah, project. Like all your other crazy, weird projects. What was that last one? Recreating the map of the South Island? Didn't you substitute all the male place-names with female ones? What did you call our local hills again?'

'You mean Locke and Cooper?'

'That's right. Locke and Cooper. Remind me, who were they again?'

A smile crept across Loretta's face. 'Elsie Locke and Whina Cooper.'

'And your name for this city?'

'Clark. But, strictly speaking, I didn't need to change the old version because it wasn't male to begin with. I also decided to replace my town with "Batham" — even though I didn't have to. I thought, why not? It's better than the official name. Plus, it has a nice, spooky, Gotham City quality to it.'

'Right. Interesting.' Shannon pretended to yawn. 'So, who's Batham?'

'Elizabeth "Betty" Batham, a scientist. She got the marine laboratory going, among other things.'

Shannon yawned again, this time for real.

Loretta lowered her glance, her eyes settling on the mottled skin on the back of her hands. Shannon was right: redrawing the map had been a project. She'd split the map into four regions — Nelson and Marlborough, Canterbury, Otago and Southland, and the West Coast — and then spent months researching and inserting alternative female names. She hadn't been entirely happy with the result, as it was very Pākehā, but she'd done her best and for a while she displayed the map in the Caroline Freeman school library. 'Caroline Freeman' had been one of the few names she hadn't needed to alter — the name had been in use since the school was established back in 1936. But there had been very few female place-names. Most of them were natural features like mountains, glaciers, lakes and rivers, but there was one well-known bridge, Edith Cavell, which was pretty cool.

Shannon cleared her throat. 'So, getting back to childbirth. It's not going to sit very well with your dangerous menopausal project, is it? Menopause and childbirth — not a good match.'

'Does it really have to be a project?' asked Loretta, frowning. She'd regarded it more as a wayward thought that had pretty much run its course. But a project? That implied dedication and hard work. And knowing how random her thoughts were, and how prone she was to digress, it wouldn't be the kind of project that stood up to scrutiny. Not a project, then, but a hobby?

'The other problem,' said Shannon, 'is that women or, rather, *menopausal* women, aren't really expected to do dangerous things, are they? They're — what do you call it? — risk-averse. Unless they're eccentric, selfish or narcissistic. Or mad. Or single. Or all five — like my sister. And menopausal mothers doing dangerous things, well, how does that work?'

Loretta wasn't really listening. She suddenly remembered all the times she had biked no-hands down the hill from her teenage home on the lower slopes of Mount Pleasant to her high school in Linwood. She hadn't planned to take her hands off the handlebars, and in fact she wouldn't have done so except that one morning she got cold and, without really thinking of the possible consequences, attempted to zip up her jacket without stopping. She wobbled, and almost fell off her bike, but at the same time a sense of exhilaration and powerfulness took hold of her, and remained with her throughout the day, right until 3 pm, when she began the slow, puffing journey homeward. It was in an attempt to recapture that joy that she tried to ride no-hands a few days later. Again, she felt a burst of life that was so strong she laughed out loud. From that moment on she attempted to increase the distance she travelled each day, pushing herself to take bigger risks, to be braver, and she stopped only when the winter frost on the road made the descent too dangerous, even by her own low standards.

'Seriously,' said Shannon, 'you should get Hamish to take you pig hunting. I've seen clips on TV and it looks brutal.'

'For the pigs.'

'Well, of course for the pigs. And the dogs. But the men end up with a couple of scratches, too. Plus there's always the possibility that someone will end up with a knife through their leg.'

'Well, that's a comforting thought.' Loretta glanced at her watch; in a minute she'd have to go for Kit.

'Hey,' said Shannon suddenly, 'you know that woman who's gone missing — Valerie Mansford? Well, I've met her a few times. I sold her an investment property, a unit near the University Oval . . .'

'Armitage Oval,' interrupted Loretta. 'Rachel Armitage, first New Zealand woman to get a degree from Oxford.'

Shannon ignored her, took a sip from her glass and continued. 'She bought the place with her cousin, who lives in Australia, and I manage it. As far as I can tell, he's her only relative, but I'm not one hundred per cent sure about that. But, regardless, she was one of the nicest people I've ever dealt with. She sent me flowers when the contract went through. Beautiful lilies. Unbelievable.'

During the past few days notices had appeared in the shopping centre near Kit's school, seeking information and asking for possible sightings of the Mansford woman. In the photo she was smiling. It looked as if the picture might have been taken near a skifield; the background was white and the outline of a snowman-like mound could be made out near the edge of the frame. Looking at the picture, Loretta had felt a deep sadness. This wasn't how life was meant to unfold.

'When did she buy it?'

'Nine months ago, maybe? I've only done one check on it so it can't be more than ten months, tops.'

'And she seemed okay?'

'Hard to tell. But like I said, she was one of the nicest people I ever did business with. Lovely woman.'

'Do you think she's still alive?' persisted Loretta.

'Don't know. But at least it's not murder, by the sound of it.'

———————

Arranged in groups of four, the chairs at Magic the Gathering were taken by boys and men of various ages. Sitting at a table, with his back to the entrance, Kit was one of the youngest present. Across from him was a man of around forty and beside him a twenty-something-year-old in biker's leathers. The chair next to Kit was vacant. Loretta guessed that its former occupant was the large, shambling man she had passed in the hallway.

The men opposite Kit glanced up but said nothing as Loretta hovered in the doorway. Their focus was on the cards in front of them and, Loretta realised, Kit's next move. Oblivious to her presence in the room, Kit stared fixedly at a card that was illustrated with a dragon-type monster. Still unaware of his mother, he placed his card, chatting animatedly and laughing as he did so. It was clear that he believed he had gained the upper hand. The older man groaned, then laughed, and almost immediately scooped up the cards closest to him and began packing them away. 'I thought you were meant to help me beat John,' he joked, indicating the guy in leather. 'And all the time you were out to get me!'

Kit grinned with satisfaction, and then began to explain his strategy for winning the game. His words made no sense to Loretta — he could have been speaking another language — but she took pleasure in his joy. In this environment he was such a confident, chatty kid, nothing at all like the quiet child she knew at home.

It was clear from the warmth of their smiles that his competitors liked Kit. They listened and, when they finally spoke, gave the impression of respecting his skill, despite the age difference. They teased him — then mentioned, as if in passing, that his mother was here. Immediately, still without turning around, Kit started packing up and a second later he was standing next to Loretta, ready to leave. She noticed that he didn't say goodbye to the men. It was as though being in her presence returned him to silence.

Slowly they walked back to the car.

'Did you have a good day?' asked Loretta.

'It was all right.'

'Did you win many games?'

'No, not really,' mumbled Kit.

'Did you do any good trading?'

'Yeah. A bit.'

'What did you trade?' asked Loretta.

But by now the conversation was dead, and even to her own ears the questions sounded like nagging. She forced herself to remain silent until, as they drew closer to her parked car, she happened to spot a $2 coin on the pavement. She pointed it out to Kit, saying, 'Look, you take it.' He crouched down, but when he tried to pick up the coin nothing happened; it was stuck fast to the asphalt. He tried to ease his fingernail under its edge but couldn't prise it off. He frowned, tapped at the coin with a fragment of road chip and then stood up, glancing up and down the street as if expecting someone to step out of the shadows and laugh at them. The footpath remained deserted.

'I'll try it with my key,' said Loretta.

She felt she had to try, for Kit's sake. When the coin failed to budge, she gave up and, opening her purse, handed Kit a $5 bill.

'What's that for?' asked Kit, genuinely surprised.

'Nothing,' said Loretta.

'You sure?'

She nodded.

Kit's eyes widened. 'Thanks, Mum. I really appreciate it. Thanks so much.'

On the drive home, Loretta felt guilty. Earlier, she had planned to buy Kit's favourite, tuna sushi, for tea. But now that she had given him $5 she thought it would be going too far to buy dinner as well. Without meaning to, she had cheated her son.

SUNDAY, AND LORETTA HAD DROPPED Kit off at his friend Angus's house. It was Angus's birthday and pick-up was in four hours' time, from a horse-trekking outfit near Virgin Flat. The birthday invitation clearly stated that all the kids would be dropped back at their homes between 4.30 and 5 pm but, for some unknown reason, and despite the distance from home, Loretta decided it would be 'easier' to collect her son herself.

'Are you certain you don't want us to bring him home?' asked Helen.

'No, I'm planning to be in the area, anyway.'

'Really? Why?'

Loretta managed to come up with a story about wanting to go for a walk — down the river or over by the wetlands, she hadn't decided. Either way, she'd be close by and would come for Kit around four. As she spoke she remembered an old friend from university, Vendela, telling her once that she would never be a parent 'because all parents are dependent on their children'. At the time, Loretta didn't have strong feelings either way on parenthood, but she made a point of disagreeing with Vendela nevertheless. That was the way their friendship worked. One of them would say something, and the other would take exception. They would argue; neither would ever back down.

As she bypassed the airport turn-off, following signposts to a junction that pointed one way to Tinker Wetlands, another to the rifle club, Loretta wondered if Vendela had ever had children. She had lost contact with her friend years ago, probably around the time Edie was born, if she remembered correctly. She should Google her and find out what had happened. Vendela had wanted to become a literature professor, but not in New Zealand: her plans had centred on upper-tier British and American universities, and the Sorbonne. In truth, Vendela fancied herself as a kind of intellectual free spirit. She was the type of person who would express disdain at Loretta's recent musings about danger, and would feel compelled to make references to her own childhood in Czechoslovakia.

Finally, she would upbraid Loretta for daring to romanticise danger and for allowing ignorance to get the better of intellect. Being told off by Vendela usually resulted in a feeling of slight pleasure, a sensation that was even more disturbing because of its vague sexual overtones. It was disconcerting what memories she held onto and recalled after all these years.

The wetlands car park was deserted. Empty cans littered the grass in the picnic area. Ducks pecked at a pizza carton, while, nearby, a sparrow attempted to demolish a finger-length strip of crust. Close by, a black hoodie was draped over the entrance gate. As Loretta passed through, she absentmindedly picked up the garment, checking its condition and size. It looked like something a teenager would wear, and examining it more closely she noticed a dark oily stain on one sleeve that extended across the hem. Without thinking she rubbed her finger over the patch, then raised it to her nose and took a careful sniff. As the fumes hit her nose, she jumped back, dropping the hoodie on her shoe. She kicked it off and then did a little backwards shuffle. 'God, you're an idiot sometimes,' she muttered. 'Who in their right mind touches discarded clothes.' Yet, even as the words came out, another persistent voice scolded, 'It's only petrol. It will wash out. Take it home for Kit.' She no longer wanted the hoodie but was loath to leave it behind. No doubt it would still be there after her walk.

A long, straight, wide track led into the distance. According to the wetlands map, it would take around two hours to make a complete circuit of the area. She glanced at her immediate surroundings — a swamp covered in flax and raupō on one side, and a low hill covered with thistle and gorse on the other — Loretta didn't feel very inspired. She had imagined that she would be walking close to the edge of the lake, but that didn't seem to be the case. Still, she was here now.

As she followed the path she composed a list of all the things she needed to do before work the next day. She should phone her mother, and Hamish's mother, and then, maybe, her brother, and her elderly neighbour, whom she hadn't seen for several days. It was unlikely he was dead but she should probably check — she didn't want to get painted by the media as a prime example of a neighbour who could have done more. The man was such a bore, though. And a moaner. He was the kind of person who would die purely out of spite. She pictured him now, on his deathbed, his trembling hand reaching out for pen and paper. 'See,' he would write, as the ink from his blue biro skipped over the page, 'I told you this would happen — not that you care.'

Chores taken care of, Loretta's thoughts flashed onward, settling on the woman who had disappeared. Reports detailing the police search were no longer posted in the local paper. She had ceased to be news. A duck flew overhead. On the drive to the wetlands Loretta had devised a new make-up trick tailored for middle-aged women. It would do for lips what winged eyeliner accomplished for eyes. A slight upwards flick at the corner of the mouth and never again would anyone be called 'grumpy' when they were simply thinking, or trying to read in peace. The lips would be set in a lasting, but subtle, smile. If she created a matching product, Hamish could leave his job and help her manage the company — from a log cabin overlooking the Remarkables. Loretta stopped and glanced at her watch, then looked back in the direction she had come. The car park was no longer visible. She guessed she might as well keep going. There wasn't much else to do.

She tried to concentrate on her surroundings. The path she followed was raised above the wetlands; it was wide and green, with depressions made by wheels either side of the centre strip. On first sight, the swamp itself had appeared to be untouched by human hand, but now she could see that a great deal of planting had taken place. The area around her was divided into zones: flax and raupō in the wettest areas, and a variety of shrubs and trees ranging from pōkākā through to kānuka, hīnau, cabbage trees, kōwhai and rimu in the higher and drier areas. Semi-circular rows of flax acted as windbreaks for nursery plantings of pōkākā and pittosporum, the twiggy seedlings barely reaching above their individual pale orange-beige plastic protectors. A small brown bird flitted nearby. A sparrow. Female. Back when she was the president of the Misty Moors, she would have made notes of all these things. She had once filled books with useless information about birds and plants, pages of entries, most of which followed a formula:

Weather: Overcast.
Wind: Moderate. Easterly.
Temperature: Temperate climate. Region of 12-25 degrees.
  Higher temperature in sunshine, cooler in shade.
Passerines: Sparrows — male and female. Starlings.
  Blackbirds — male and female.
Ducks: Grey and mallard. Combination of the two.
Other: Seagulls. Red-billed. Black-backed.
Exotic birds: None.
Birds of interest: Juvenile black-backed gull. Possible sighting of
  redpoll.
Unidentified bird-calls: Brrrrip brrrip cooo brrrip brrrrip.
Note: Identify bird-call.
Flora: Glasswort, flax, pittosporum, cabbage tree, p hutukawa.
  Clover. Buttercup. Gorse.
Further action: Check sexual variation in starlings. Return
  in three days with bread for one-legged gull. Note changes.
  Binoculars required.

At times, Loretta remembered, she entered comments about the condition of her bicycle:

Mechanical: Tyre rubbing on rear mudguard.
Action taken: Lift mudguard away from tyre and twist.
Minor improvement. Continue to monitor.
Other: Spoke reflectors grimy. Clean before next outing.

One of the most memorable Christmas presents she ever received was her older brother's thrashed Raleigh Twenty. She could still remember her surprise when she unwrapped it. It was sparkling clean, the frame resprayed a bright lemon-yellow colour. A brand-new white girl's saddle replaced the old Brooks leather one, and a new carrier and saddlebag were attached to the back. Glittering yellow and red reflectors had been fixed to the spokes. A butterfly decal was crookedly arranged on the front mudguard. One of its wings was wrinkled: the sticker had clearly stuck before it had been positioned properly and someone, probably her mother, had tried to peel it off and reset it. Hearing 'It's from all of us!' somehow made the present worse. Still, at least she came out of it better than her brother — he was given their grandfather's old bike: a dull red three-speed with new racing handlebars and toe clips.

It was remarkable that she no longer made field notes or action lists. It was obvious that she had once enjoyed keeping track of her life. Making notes had given her not only a sense of purpose but a feeling of authority. She had been so sure of herself when she was a kid. Maybe becoming a librarian was, after all, the natural progression of all that early note-taking and cataloguing. Of course it was. Why had she never thought of that before?

A plane passed overhead, travelling north on its way to

the airport. It was so low that Loretta could see its landing gear, wheels that looked too small to support its weight. She imagined that someone aboard the plane, a nervous passenger, had glimpsed her from above. That same passenger might also be wondering about the wisdom of placing the flightpath so close to a wetlands bird sanctuary. As if to prove her point, a large harrier hawk floated by.

She had been walking now for over forty minutes, but Loretta still hadn't caught sight of the lake. If she'd been walking for fitness, or jogging, this wouldn't trouble her, but because she wanted to see water and, more specifically, birds on or by the water, she couldn't help but feel a little annoyed. She had come for a show, after all, and if she'd known in advance that it was going to be this boring she would have brought a book to read, or not bothered coming at all. She certainly wouldn't come again. Not unless something happened within the next twenty minutes.

She kept walking, following the path as it headed north. The hills, Locke and Cooper, now lay directly ahead of her. A wooden predator trap lay on the ground beyond the edge of the track. Curious to see if it had caught anything, Loretta squatted and peered inside. It looked empty.

She was now standing beside a low rise. The boundary to the mound was fenced off from the wetlands and a notice wired to a farm gate stated 'Private property — keep out'. In the paddock beyond the gate were several sheep. All white, she noticed, as if filling in one of her childhood exercise books. She decided that walking up the hill had to be more interesting than staying on the track — she might get a glimpse of the water — and then she would come straight back. She wouldn't disturb the stock.

A larger plane flew above her. This one was a jet, its tail markings black and silver. By the time she got to the top of the rise, its passengers would be disembarking, filing across the tarmac and into the overseas terminal, their introduction to the country the smell of grass, a whiff of silage and the sight of a floppy-eared sniffer dog.

If Loretta could choose one super power, it would be to possess a dog's sense of smell. She'd thought about this quite a bit, having been asked the question a long time ago by Kit. He had wanted a laser-beam tummy button. Hamish had asked to be a woman for a day but Kit had disallowed that. He repeated the question, stressing that the answer had to be a super power. Hamish had come back with 'Russia or America' and Kit hadn't understood. It had caused trouble. Kit had become upset, Loretta angry. Hamish backed down and said, 'Captain America', which satisfied Kit.

From the top of the hill, Loretta could see the edge of the lake. Standing between her and the water was an area of low brush: gorse and broom and, further away, mānuka and flax. In the opposite direction, the wetlands path circumnavigated a number of small channels and ponds before reaching a stand of tall poplars and circling back towards the car park, which now looked very far away. Loretta wondered if there was a sheep track leading down to the lakeshore. Despite knowing she should head back to the car so as not to be late for Kit, she hesitated and glanced at her watch. She'd count to twenty and if she heard or saw a bird she'd go back down to the gate and retrace her steps to the car park. At the count of fourteen, a sparrow caught her attention. She kept counting. Fifteen, sixteen, seventeen, another sparrow, eighteen, nineteen, plover, twenty.

The sheep ran ahead and scattered as she crossed the paddock and entered the scrub, making in the general direction of the mānuka and flax she had spotted from the top. Her decision to keep exploring cheered her. Having caught sight of the water, she knew she wouldn't feel satisfied until she made a determined effort to get close. She needed to reach the lake edge. The kids at school had a word for what she was feeling: FOMO. Initially, she hadn't known that FOMO stood for 'fear of missing out'. The Year 9 girl who explained the meaning to her had barely managed to keep from saying 'duh'. Loretta didn't think that her behaviour, now, was completely a product of FOMO. Her desire to get close to the lake was fuelled by curiosity, not fear. It's what any great female explorer would do. Which great female explorer? A voice in her head asked as she battled through dense gorse. Which one? Could she name one?

Easy. Amelia Earhart.

Had the imaginary interrogator been real, she would have heard it scoff, You don't know any female explorers, do you?

I know heaps of female explorers, actually.

Name them.

Amelia Earhart.

You've said that, snapped the voice.

Jean Batten.

Two pilots! Anyone else?

Loretta scrambled for another name. Freya Stark. Gertrude Bell. That Native American from *Night at the Museum*. Saca . . . something. The Lewis and Clark woman.

That's four, not counting Saca Something. Seven billion people in the world and you can only name four . . .

Go away and leave me alone, pleaded Loretta.

Still some distance from the lake the earth beneath Loretta's feet began to grow boggy. With each step her foot sank deeper into sludge, the earth sucking at her shoe as she attempted to move forward. She guessed she must be within fifty metres of the shore but it was impossible to continue. Turning to the north, she skirted the swamp, hoping to reach an area of tall mānuka and pine she could see in the distance. It was hard-going. She shoved and stumbled her way through gorse and flax bushes, her feet disappearing into holes that filled with water. She was running out of time but she was reluctant to give up.

At last the ground grew firmer and she found herself beside a dilapidated barbed-wire fence, on the edge of a forested area. Though she wasn't sure, she had a feeling she had rejoined the boundary between the private farmland and the wetlands sanctuary, and that she was about to cross back over to the latter. Pushing down on the wire strands, she squeezed through the fence and slowly walked on, picking her way past fallen branches, pine cones and boulders. After a few minutes the forest thinned, and to her delight she saw she was on a kind of low promontory, the lake mere metres beyond the edge of the trees. The foliage seemed to have been cleared slightly: beyond a large felled trunk an opening through the trees framed the view. Surprisingly, the sawn-off pieces of wood were nowhere to be seen. This simple fact caught Loretta's attention and, forgetting the lake, she turned back to face the forest, taking in her surroundings with more attention. It was only then that she noticed what looked like a large pile of branches layered over and around a fallen pine. The mound was several metres high and as Loretta approached it became clear that the wood and leaves weren't casually dragged and stacked but, rather, constructed and arranged into an elaborate, igloo-like den.

Instinctively, Loretta looked about as if expecting someone or something to emerge from the forest or from the den itself. She listened, straining her ears for the sound of snapping twigs, shuffling steps or heavy breathing, but her surroundings remained undisturbed and remarkably quiet.

Suddenly, a distant shot cracked the silence and Loretta

gave a gasp. Her heart began to pound. A second shot, and she swivelled around, turning so quickly that she tripped over the toes of her shoes and lost her balance, falling to her knees. Another shot. And then silence.

Calm down, she told herself, as she clambered back to her feet. It's just the rifle range. Stop being an idiot.

The voice in her head taunted her, Not very brave, are you? So much for being a fearless-feminist explorer.

Despite her nerves, Loretta smiled.

The gun fired again, but this time it seemed less ominous.

A pair of ducks flew overhead: the honk of one bird matched in volume by the zub, zub, zub of the other. Paradise ducks, said the voice in Loretta's head. You should know that. You used to see them on the banks of the Linwood Avenue canal.

To counteract the stillness of her location, Loretta mumbled aloud, 'Well, of course I know they're paradise ducks. I'm the one who identified them, duh.'

The voice had no reply and skulked away, leaving Loretta alone, wondering what to do next. She wished Kit were with her. He wouldn't be standing around. He'd already be inside the den, enthusiastically exploring. Imagining her son's response provided Loretta with all the encouragement she needed. Summoning up her own adventurous childhood self, she walked to the den's entrance and ducked inside.

The interior was dark but the space was roomier than she expected. As her eyes adjusted to the dimness she could make out objects, and she started to poke around. A couple of tree stumps were arranged near a small table. Along the back wall was a camp bed, an ancient down sleeping bag loosely folded near an equally old-looking floral pillowcase. Another stump and some old crates rested against the third wall. Inside the crates were packets of tea and Milo, a small stove, a billy, and a cup and plate. Both of these, Loretta noticed, were clean, and further investigation unearthed an old scouring pad and a half-bottle of detergent.

More unexpected than the furniture, the cooking utensils or the food, however, were an ornate ceramic vase filled with kānuka and, lying on its side, face turned towards the back wall, a mud-splattered and grimy life-sized corrugated-plastic figure of Daniel Craig as James Bond. It was difficult for Loretta to know which of these two things surprised her more. The flowers looked as if they had been picked within the last week. Only a few petals had wilted and fallen off, and the feathery leaves were still green. Someone had visited the den in recent days, that much was certain. The James Bond cutout was perplexing for other reasons. The fact that it was even inside the den, and not propped up in the corner of some student flat, was one reason. Odder still was the presence of numerous small bullet holes around Bond's top pocket and the addition of lolly-pink make-up colouring the man's lips, and a black beauty mark on his cheek. The whole set-up was fairytale-like and otherworldly, but unthreatening. There was something peaceful and quiet about the shelter; it brought to mind the happy atmosphere of her old Misty Moors clubhouse.

———

Loretta was late to collect Kit. He was waiting halfway down the long driveway leading from the stables to the road. A smear of mud extended from his left elbow, down his side and along his thigh. He looked tired as he pulled open the car door and climbed inside.

'Where were you?' he asked. Before Loretta could answer he

added, 'I was waiting for hours. The others went ages ago.'

They travelled in silence, Loretta thinking about the den and whoever it was who used it.

'I fell off,' said Kit.

Loretta glanced across at him.

'I almost broke my leg. My foot got caught in the stirrups and I was dragged along the track for miles and miles, and then the horse went haywire, jumped a massive fence, and ran away. Literally.'

Despite herself, Loretta smiled at the addition of 'literally'. 'Were you badly hurt?' she asked.

There was a long pause and then Kit answered, 'No. Not really. It wasn't that bad.'

'Was it a big horse?'

Kit shrugged. 'I don't know. It was white.'

'Ah, they're the worst. Mean beasts.'

'Really?' Kit looked pleased. Seconds later he yawned and stretched, and then, turning away from Loretta, rested his head on his seat-belt strap and leant against the window. He closed his eyes.

The wheels made a thrumming sound as they crossed from the worn section of the road to the newly sealed length. Loretta yawned, too, and felt her eyelids begin to droop. Reaching across, she turned on the radio. Rod Stewart's voice sang, 'We are sailing' and Loretta hummed along. 'Naomi James,' she said as the song finished. That makes five.

Dangerous Book for (Menopausal) Women #1
Naomi James

Loretta underlined the name in her new notebook. She scanned the web on her iPad and then copied the name down again.

Naomi James

Around her adults and children of various ages wandered through the food court, forming lines in front of sushi and curry stalls, standing in groups before the fast-food outlets, chatting together and texting while, seemingly, remaining semi-alert to what was going on in the rest of the basement area.

> *Born on a sheep farm, in New Zealand, 1949.*
> *Trained as a hairdresser.*
> *Left country in search of adventure.*
> *Met future husband, round-the-world sailor Rob James.*
> *Naomi decides to sail solo round the world — 272 days*
> *   (September 1977 to June 1978).*
> *Capsized in Roaring Forties. Thought she was going to die.*
> *Navigated using charts (longitude) and sextant (latitude).*

Loretta took a sip from her hot chocolate, wiped her mouth with a paper napkin and sat back in her chair. She had a faint recollection of Naomi James's feat but after all these years the main image that stuck in her mind was her hair. It was shoulder-length with a side-parted fringe that flicked up over one eye. Naomi James had styled her hair the same way Loretta's school friend Jennifer had worn hers. Jennifer had wanted to look like Agnetha, the blonde ABBA singer, but in reality had resembled the male guitarist, Björn.

Loretta couldn't imagine setting off on her own on a nine-month trip. From her circle of friends, she knew no one who had ever done anything remotely adventurous. Tackling the rail trail or walking one of the major tracks was about as wild as it got. It was as though Loretta belonged to a dull, between generation. Too young to belong to the solo yachtsmen and moon explorers, too old to identify with the backpackers, the round-the-world mountain-bikers or base-jumpers. She was one of the women who channelled the right for equality into careers when they could have been fighting for more free time. Why did none of her friends play? Or have fun? They were all so serious.

Something moved in front of Loretta's face and she started. She'd been so lost in thought that she'd failed to notice a group of girls occupy the table next to hers. 'Hey, hey!' A hand waved and looking up she saw an overweight teenager. 'Hey,' repeated the girl, 'do you need that chair?' A second girl had already started to yank it away from the table, dragging it across the floor. 'Hello, can you hear me?' demanded the large girl, clicking her fingers in Loretta's face. Slightly stunned by the intrusion, Loretta nodded and the girl turned her back, immediately sucked into a huddle of girls, posing for a group selfie. They were all from her school, mostly fifteen- and sixteen-year-olds, the kind of girls who were never seen alone, always in gangs. She recognised some of them but had had little to do with them over the years. They weren't regular visitors to the school library, put it that way.

Naomi James.
Married to Rob James.

She wrote the words as neatly as she could, as if trying to recapture the formality of her italic years, the period when she had been at her most prolific, filling in her bird books.

Ten days before their first child was born, Rob James drowned.

Naomi James has a PhD in Philosophy (Wittgenstein).

Loretta looked up from her page. Earlier in the day she had spent an hour or so trying to track down the thesis but had been unable to locate it. This had annoyed and somewhat shamed her because, as a librarian, she felt she should have been able to access the information she needed. In the end, she'd made do with what she was sure was James's MA thesis, 'Transforming reality: a phenomenology of an event'.

She now entered the title into her notebook and leant back in her chair, watching the girls as they took turns picking chips from a shared cardboard bucket. One took three chips at once, poked them into her mouth and smiled — almost leered. Her friends protested at the sight, calling out, 'What the actual fuck! You are *such* a retard.' The girl with the chips laughed, coughed and spluttered, spilling fragments of potato onto the table. 'Jesus, Gloria!' In a split second the atmosphere surrounding the girls shifted. As one, they drew back from Gloria and stood up, shoving their chairs out of the way as they reached for their bags. Gloria, slow to catch on, grinned and made to stand up too. 'Not you,' said the ringleader. 'You stay here with the other pigs.' Gesturing towards Loretta and the other diners, the big girl turned her back on Gloria and flounced off. The whole incident was over in a matter of seconds.

Naomi James no longer sails, wrote Loretta, as Gloria slowly walked away.

'How was fencing?' asked Loretta as Kit piled into the car.

'Good,' mumbled Kit.

'Did you win?'

'No.'

'Have they taught you the mark of Zorro, yet?'

'No. Who's that?'

'He was in the movies.'

'Oh.'

Loretta tapped her fingers on the steering wheel, and then announced, '"I'm no lady when I fight!"'

'What's that? Is it from Zorro?' asked Kit.

'Nothing. It's a line from an old film starring Maureen O'Hara. She was a musketeer in it.'

Kit let out a long sigh. 'Is this one of those things of yours? Where you go on about stuff that no one's interested in, until you get bored?'

'Yep. You know me. Head full of boring stuff.'

They fell into a comfortable silence, broken only by Loretta quietly murmuring, 'I'm no lady when I change lanes.'

At last, as they stopped at the last traffic light before home, Kit said, 'Thanks for picking me up and taking me to fencing.'

'That's okay.'

Loretta stroked her son's hair. She loved him with all her heart. He was such a great kid.

LORETTA SLUMPED IN THE PASSENGER seat, quietly nibbling the remains of her sandwich while Shannon took a call on her mobile. In the space of ten minutes, Shannon had spent half her time talking to someone else, a faceless voice on the end of the line. This time it was Jess. 'Can't you explain the tender process to them?' Shannon asked. As she listened to the answer, Shannon rolled her eyes and made a face that suggested she was dealing with an idiot. 'Well, tell them to Google it.' To Loretta, she softly mouthed the word 'idiots', and then, addressing Jess, said, 'Okay, I'll give them a call. Anything else? No? Good.'

'I've never understood all that tender business,' said Loretta when she finally had her friend's attention.

Shannon patted Loretta on the thigh and murmured, 'There, there. It's all a bit difficult, isn't it, dear', before reaching into her bag for her cigarettes, lighting one up and winding down the window. A strong, warm wind blasted through the window. Elsewhere in the car park, dust and leaves swirled in mini tornados.

Loretta hadn't told Shannon about the den by the lake. She had been on the verge of mentioning it but something made her stop. It wasn't that she wanted to keep the den secret, it was more that she wasn't sure Shannon would be interested, or would even listen. Luxury hotels were more her line. Three nights at a Queenstown resort villa with a tasting menu at a waterfront restaurant, that was Shannon's style these days. Whenever she spoke of her working-class upbringing it was as though she was describing a glitch in an otherwise smoothly running programme. It wasn't that she was ashamed of her past, merely that it no longer served her needs.

'Have you done anything about Christmas yet?' Shannon asked.

'No. You?'

Loretta knew she should give it some thought but there was nothing to plan. Her parents didn't 'do' Christmas and both Pete and Edie were overseas: Pete working as a chef in Perth, and Edie teaching English in South Korea. Apart from phoning and Skyping everyone, she only had to worry about Kip and Hamish, and neither of them demanded much more than a few presents and a roast chicken.

'I was thinking of helping out at the City Mission,' said Shannon, 'but then I thought, stuff it. What's the point if they won't let you drink or smoke?' She laughed, nudging Loretta in the arm. 'Don't tell anyone I said that.' She inhaled and checked her cell phone, frowning slightly. 'Nah, it's all right. I'll flick them five hundred bucks. Poor buggers — wouldn't wish homelessness on anyone.' She glanced at Loretta, and added, 'No good for the real estate business.' She let out a hacking cough before adding, 'Just joking. I know this government is screwing the poor.'

They sat quietly. Loretta rolled the ball of cling film from her sandwich around in her fingers while Shannon checked her phone for texts. Her neatly polished nails punched out a short message, and she growled to herself as she pressed send. 'Emojis. Look at this. There's this buyer, right? He's a forty-five-year-old man haggling over a commercial property worth over a million bucks and he attaches emojis to his texts. See . . .'

She passed Loretta her phone and jabbed at the screen. Images of a green face and a white thumbs-down were attached to the last line of the message. 'He's an adult!' stormed Shannon. 'Not some ten-year-old kid. What is wrong with these people? They're so infantile.'

Loretta nodded and handed the phone back. In general, she hated phones of any kind. She loathed her own cell phone and barely used it. One of the school rules she was most grateful for was the total ban on mobile phone use during class hours, but just that day she had been forced to confiscate a phone from a student. Three girls had turned up halfway through lunch break and headed to the back of the library, hiding themselves among the rows of history books. From her desk at the front, Loretta could hear them talking and giggling but had ignored them, hoping they'd soon leave and head for afternoon class. After five minutes or so, however, another group of kids had entered and they, too, headed towards the rear of the library. With the arrival of the new group the noise level rose, the talking and giggling replaced by frequent shrill cries and jeers. A couple of kids who were sitting at the workstations looked up from their screens, sending glances Loretta's way.

Loretta knew she was going to have to do something, but for some reason she held back, hoping that the problem would resolve itself without her intervention. To her relief the noise died down, but it was only a lull, and before long the calling out and laughter, in combination with excited screams, built up once more.

Reluctantly, Loretta got up from behind her desk. As she approached, some of the students quickly seized books from the shelves and pretended to read. A smaller set of girls, however, pretended to ignore her. Huddled over a phone, they continued to laugh, cajoling the girl holding the mobile to send a message Loretta couldn't see. She believed her presence alone, on the edge of the circle, would be enough to make the girls look up and stop, but she was wrong. Adopting the tone that she had heard other teachers at the school use, she said, 'I'm waiting.'

One or two girls took notice, shuffling awkwardly with their barely examined history books in their hands. But Loretta had the impression that it wasn't in response to her words, but in anticipation of how the phone's owner would respond. For them, clearly, she was where the authority and power lay.

'I'm waiting,' repeated Loretta, her nerve beginning to fail.

The girls around the phone continued to ignore her. Some of the hangers-on shuffled away, taking up positions at the end of the row, watching to see what would happen from there.

'This is a library,' said Loretta.

One of the girls laughed.

'Give me the phone, please.'

No one moved.

'I said, give me the phone.'

From the centre of the circle the phone's owner said, 'No.'

Loretta could feel her heart begin to beat more rapidly. She realised that if she tried to raise her voice, it would sound not so much authoritative as tinny, or desperate. The girls would laugh at her, ignore her demand and, eventually, mock her. She had no choice, though, but to go on.

'Right, give me that phone now.'

The girl with the mobile faced her, eyes drilling into Loretta's. A faint smile morphed into a smirk, and then she very deliberately turned her attention back to the device and began scrolling.

Loretta watched, willing herself to take action.

'This is what is going to happen,' she began, hoping that she sounded calm. 'You will hand over your mobile and I will put it in my drawer . . .'

A ginger-haired girl interrupted, mimicking, 'This is what is going to happen . . .'

The girl with the phone sniggered.

The students who had been hovering at the end of the row now took the opportunity to disappear.

'You can collect it at the end of the day.'

Slowly the girl looked up and Loretta suddenly recognised her as one of the group from the food court. The girl's expression hardened, and her mouth twisted into an ugly sneer. Her eyelashes, Loretta noticed, were clumped, black and spidery, her eyeliner smudged at the corners. Make-up. Another school rule broken.

'Michelle,' one of the other girls spoke, and the phone girl turned.

'I'm not going to ask you again,' said Loretta. She could hear the wobble in her voice. The combination of rising anger and nerves was getting the better of her. Why did she find teenage girls so intimidating?

Michelle placed the phone in her blazer pocket. She stood only thirty centimetres or so from Loretta, and crossed her arms.

Loretta held out her hand, palm upwards. 'In my hand, now.'

No one moved. In the background one of the younger kids coughed. The sound of whispering filtered through the aisles.

An image flashed through Loretta's mind. In it, her hands clasped Michelle's neck and forced her to her knees. A second image quickly followed the first. This time the roles were reversed. Loretta didn't care about the phone, but this was her library, and the kids who spent their lunch break reading or working on the computers were her kids. They deserved better.

Loretta took a deep breath. To her dismay she didn't know what to do next. In one last, desperate attempt to gain the upper hand, she changed tack.

'You girls,' she said, looking at the group closest to Michelle.

To her relief, one jumped and cast a nervous glance towards Michelle. She's the one, thought Loretta. Work on her.

'You,' she said, pointing to the girl. 'What's your name?'

'Don't tell her,' said Michelle.

'What's your name?'

'Hannah,' said the girl.

Michelle looked angry.

'Give me your phone,' said Loretta.

The girl didn't understand.

'I want your mobile,' repeated Loretta.

'But . . .' protested Hannah.

'Now!' snapped Loretta.

Hannah felt in one pocket, then the other. Loretta watched, her heart sinking. Maybe Hannah wasn't carrying one. It could be in her school bag, or anywhere. Hannah seemed flustered. She kept patting her pockets, pulling out a tissue, some coins, a chapstick.

'Hurry up,' said Loretta.

'Why are you picking on her?' asked Michelle, her voice betraying the first, slight hint of uncertainty.

'In your breast pocket,' ordered Loretta.

'You are so out of line,' said Michelle.

Loretta ignored her. She saw Hannah fumble, pull out the phone and hesitate. Deep inside, her heart went out to the girl. What she was about to do wasn't fair.

'Right,' she said. There was now something firm in her tone, a not-to-be-messed-with quality, and Hannah looked suitably shaken. 'I will look after this phone until Michelle decides to do as she's told. I expect to see Michelle here, in the library, before the end of the day, to apologise. As soon as that happens you can collect your mobile. Understood?'

A chorus of voices rose up, protesting, 'That's not fair' and 'You can't do that.' Only Michelle stood her ground. She held Loretta's gaze and then shrugged. She turned her back, and began to move towards the entrance. She didn't care.

Hannah looked confused. She was left standing alone, after all the other girls filed out after Michelle. Her lips trembled and formed a sideways 'S', and then, remarkably, she appeared to summon some superhuman strength and pull herself together, before marching after the others.

It took some minutes before Loretta stopped shaking.

'Emoticons.' Shannon's voice interrupted Loretta's thoughts. 'The end of civilisation as we know it.' She glanced at her phone and added, 'Yikes, look at the time. Gotta go.' She turned to face Loretta and said, 'Go on, get out. Bugger off.' Loretta felt her shoulder being shoved gently as Shannon made ready to leave. 'See you soon, eh?' called Shannon as she started the engine. 'Don't give up the fight.'

———————

The water polo match was still in progress. Blue- and white-capped heads bobbed in the deep pool. It took a moment before Loretta was able to identify Kit from the rest of the team. He was lower in the water than his fellow players. His upturned moon face barely floated above the surface. When he saw Loretta he tried to wave, and his whole body sank further into the depths. The score, Loretta noticed, was 17–0. Kit tried to wave again but just then the ball hit him on the head and he went under. He came up, coughed, spluttered, and the final whistle sounded. The game was over.

'You did well today,' said Loretta as she walked beside her son towards the entrance of the changing room.

'I got hiccups and almost drowned,' he replied. His eyes were glassy blue, the whites and rims red from the chlorine. A thin trail of watery snot dribbled from his nose and he wiped it with his cap.

'Do you remember the first time you came here, for swimming lessons?' asked Loretta. She had memories of him: swimming nappies poking out from under his togs, his thin, bandy arms almost hidden beneath fluorescent orange bands. He'd hated the water and had clung to her like a chimp, refusing to let go for fear of drowning.

'No.'

'I do,' said Loretta. 'You were a natural.'

Kit looked unconvinced. 'Can we have fish and chips for tea?'

'I'll think about it.'

'Love you, Mu—' He stopped mid-sentence as a group of older kids jostled past on their way to get dressed. One of the swimmers turned and laughed, and then said something to his mates, who joined in. Kit caught the sound of their laughter and blushed, before following them into the room to get dressed.

Loretta stayed where she was, waiting, straining to hear the sound of her child's voice, some cry or yelp, but of course nothing came. An elderly man edged around her before disappearing into the changing room, and Loretta breathed a sigh of relief. He's fine. They're just kids mucking about, she reassured herself.

She missed Hamish. If only he was home. She would like to curl up next to him and tell him about her day. He would be kind, and say the right thing. He'd reassure her that she'd handled the girls as well as could be expected. Hamish would know how to cheer her up. If only he was waiting, and not driving around the country somewhere. These days he was never home.

The Dangerous Book For (Menopausal) Women #2
Mabel Stark

Born 10 December 1889. Died 20 April 1968.
Considered to be the world's first female tiger trainer.

In her photograph on Wikipedia, Mabel was shown wearing a scoop-necked dress, holding what looked like an ostrich feather up to her chin. Her hair was cropped and marcel-waved. There was a soft-focus look about her — pale, flawless skin and deeply coloured, bow-shaped lips. Her birth name was Mary Haynie.

It was odd, thought Loretta, that the tiger tamer would choose Mabel as a stage name. These days, it wasn't a name that inspired images of daring or glamour. But maybe it did back then? She repeated the names to herself: Mary Haynie, Mabel Stark. Mabel Stark, Mary Haynie. Ladies and gentlemen, all the way from Kentucky: the fearless, the daring ... Mabel Stark!

Mauled by a lion in 1916.
Previously mauled by a leopard — twice.
Kept a pet tiger, Rajah.

The short biography stated that Rajah would run up to Mabel, put his paws around her neck and waltz. She'd then throw him to the ground and place her face inside his mouth, before jumping back to her feet.

1922 joined Ringling Brothers Barnum and Bailey Circus.
1925 Ringling Brothers Barnum and Bailey Circus banned all live wild animal acts.
Continued to work in Europe and the United States.

Mauled by her tigers on various occasions.
Worked in the ring with up to 18 big cats at a time.
Wrote about the thrill of working with big cats.
Committed suicide — 1968.

Loretta closed her notebook and gazed across the lake. It had been a great relief to leave her day behind and return to the den. She had almost jogged down the track in her anticipation of reaching the shelter. It made little difference that she would be able to stay for less than an hour. All she wanted was to find a quiet spot to sit comfortably and watch the water and think. In her head, she had somehow managed to reconfigure the den as her own private space.

When she'd arrived, thirty minutes earlier, she'd been surprised to encounter the cutout figure of James Bond lying face down, near the entrance. But Bond's position wasn't the only change since her last visit. A fresh cutting of feathery kānuka replaced the smaller arrangement she had seen during her last visit. Though the flowers had dried, the leaves were a bright, Granny Smith green.

Neither of these changes gave Loretta any real indication of who had visited, or of when they might return, and so she decided to ignore all signs of previous visitors and relax. It took twenty minutes before she realised there was nowhere comfortable to sit. The tree-stump seats wobbled and were too small and low. The bed was too far from the shelter's entrance to offer a view of the lake. She could stretch out on it but she didn't want to spend what free time she had staring at a ceiling of pine and brush. In the end she had been forced to come outside and sit with her back against a tree, as she penned her latest entry in her notebook.

As she was finishing up, a newspaper photo of Valerie

Mansford fell from the pages of her notebook and landed face-up on the ground by her bare feet. As Loretta retrieved the clipping she was once again touched by a wave of sadness. If only Valerie could have followed Mabel Stark's example and run away to join the circus.

The previous evening Loretta had found a film clip of Mabel at work in the tigers' den. Made in 1949, the footage showed the trainer dressed in a shirt and slacks, prodding and poking the tigers as she made them perform for the camera. Every now and again a close-up image of Mabel would fill the screen. Her face was lined, and her eyes struck Loretta as hard, flinty. Her mouth was firm. But it was her hair that most captured Loretta's attention. It was blonde, neatly waved, but rigid, helmet-like. It was difficult to tell if she was wearing a hair net or if she had simply doused it with hairspray. She bore a remarkable resemblance to Margaret Thatcher.

Of course, Valerie Mansford wasn't Mabel Stark. Whereas Mabel had abandoned her nurse's training in order to take up a life of adventure, Valerie had simply disappeared. The posts on Facebook had dwindled; most comments on the community pages now hinted at suicide. There were rumours on several sites suggesting that she had grown depressed after the death of a 'close friend' a few years before, but no one really knew for certain where she was or what had happened. One guy still insisted on alien abduction. The police were remaining tight-lipped, which gave a certain weight to the suicide theory. It seemed doubtful, now, that she would ever turn up.

Loretta had spent part of the previous day waiting for Michelle to come and apologise. In the end she didn't care about the apology. All she wanted was for Michelle to care enough about her friend to retrieve the phone. But by 3 pm it was obvious that Michelle wasn't going to show her face. And so it had been left to Loretta to stand at the school entrance, searching the faces of departing students until she recognised Hannah's face in the crowd. Catching her attention, Loretta beckoned her over and then watched and waited as the girl moved slowly against the torrent of students. At first Hannah appeared nervous. Her relief and gratitude at getting the phone back made Loretta feel newly ashamed. Instead of being kind to the girl, however, she reprimanded her. 'Don't come into the library again until you learn to behave properly and respect other users.' Telling Hannah off made her feel even worse, but it appeared to bring out some hidden depth of defiance in the student. 'Don't worry,' she snapped. 'I wouldn't be seen dead in that dump.'

That morning Loretta had found it difficult to go to work. The episode with Hannah had upset her, but more than that, the girl's retort tainted the library. It had been both a source of pride and a sanctuary, but it now seemed shabby and worn, misused rather than treasured. Loretta remained out of sorts and short-tempered all day. During lunchtime, she evicted three more students and then scolded a boy for bending back the spine of an Asterix book. The poor kid looked mortified and apologised, but Loretta wasn't satisfied. 'If I ever catch you doing it again, I'll give you a detention,' she threatened. The boy was too taken aback to protest, but he had meekly apologised once more and soon left.

At the end of school she had been on her way to collect Kit when she had received a text from the mother of one of his school friends, asking if it would be okay for him to play. She would give him afternoon tea and Loretta could collect him at six. That had been all the excuse she needed to revisit the den. Her den. Now, as it was nearing time to leave, she toyed with the idea of leaving a note for the other visitor — or visitors. What would she say? That she came in peace. That she would respect the property and leave everything as she found it. But such a note struck her as stuffy. Wouldn't something more playful be more in order? After disposing of the kānuka, she carried the empty vase down to the edge of the lake where she picked a bunch of buttercups, creating a new arrangement that she took back to the den. Finally, before leaving, she carried James Bond over to the bed and laid him down with his head on the pillowcase. She stood over him for several minutes, then pulled the sleeping bag up to his chin and left.

––––––––

'Do you like James Bond movies?' she asked Kit once they were strapped into their seats.

'No.'

'Why not?'

Kit made a face, as if the question wasn't worth answering. 'Because they're boring and all the same.'

'Do you like any of them?' Loretta persisted.

'No.'

A year before, Kit had begged to stay up every Saturday night for months on end while all the old James Bond movies screened. It had been his special treat, and he sat glued to the television, oblivious to anything else going on in the room. At one point, Loretta remembered, both she and Hamish had gone to bed before the end of the movie and been forced to leave Kit to turn off the lights. In the morning, they'd found him asleep on the couch, lights and TV still on.

'You used to like James Bond,' she said.

'Maybe. I thought the tanks full of sharks were cool.'

'You used to be quite scared of the villains.'

'Was I?'

She nodded. 'Did you have fun today?'

'No, not really.'

Loretta patted his hand. 'Did you get bored?'

Kit shrugged and then asked, 'Will Hamish be home tonight?'

'Yes.'

'Good,' said Kit. 'I miss that sad old man.'

'Me, too,' said Loretta.

"Course you do,' said Kit.

LORETTA SAT PROPPED UP IN BED next to Hamish. She'd arrived home from work to find him asleep and, with more than an hour to kill before collecting Kit from orchestra, decided to join him and read a book. He slept so soundly that he didn't stir as she clambered over his body, taking up a position closest to the window. When, after five minutes, she decided to make herself a coffee and sidled out of the bed, accidentally dragging half the duvet with her, he still didn't wake. For a split second, Loretta experienced the same rush of fear she used to get when checking on Kit as a baby. Was Hamish breathing? She bent low over him and held the palm of her hand up to his mouth. Of course he's alive, she told herself, but she remained where she was, watching until she was sure that his chest was rising and falling. A thin stream of dribble seeped from the corner of his mouth, confirming once and for all that he was okay.

How on earth did she survive raising three children? At various times throughout their young lives she had convinced herself that they were dead. First, Pete had not been in his cot one morning and she'd assumed he'd climbed out of the open window and fallen onto the concrete path below. He turned out to be in the living room, looking at a book. Edie had overslept, her afternoon nap extending over several hours instead of the usual one. Loretta had woken her up to prove to herself that her daughter didn't have meningitis or something similar. And Kit was a still, silent sleeper. Every morning he looked like a corpse in a coffin, flat on his back, immobile, face pale in the early morning light.

As she came back to bed, Hamish rolled over, knocking the cup in Loretta's hand. The hot brown liquid rushed at the sides of the mug, and then spilled, staining the duvet cover. Hamish groaned and opened his eyes. Seeing Loretta he mumbled, 'Gidday, mate. How long have you been home?'

'Not long. I have to go for Kit soon.'

Hamish yawned, stretched and allowed his hand to drift down Loretta's arm, towards her wrist. He looped his fingers over the back of her hand and gave it a squeeze. And then yawned again.

'What have you got there?' he asked, when he saw the book propped on the windowsill.

'It's about a woman who spent twelve years in a cave.'

'Didn't they make a film about that?' asked Hamish.

Loretta shook her head. 'I think you've got it confused with something else.'

She sipped her coffee and then offered the cup to Hamish. He took it from her, rubbed his finger over the rim and took a long drink. He kept the mug in his hands, blowing the surface of the drink until it rippled, before taking another sip. His eyes,

Loretta noticed, were red-rimmed and his hair stuck up in tufts. The unevenness of the cut reminded Loretta of the old hedge she used to trim at her childhood home. She'd never been able to reach the top of it with her shears, and as a result it had always ended up more lopsided and unkempt than when she started. But, for some reason, her parents never complained or made her have another go at it. They would come outside, praise her and give her $2, which was a fortune back then.

Hamish yawned once more. 'I'm sick of work. I'm fed up with being away all the time, and driving all day. I'm tired of hanging around, waiting to load or unload . . . being mucked around by people. You know, I've been thinking about how I'm not getting any younger and I reckon I should give up work and stay home and look after Kit. Just take a break for a while and make the most of Kit, while he's young. I could grow vegetables, and keep hens and fix the house up. And you could have another baby, if you want. Or maybe we could move further out. You know, get a lifestyle block or something, and barter food.'

Loretta listened quietly and nodded. 'I could be the world's oldest mother and we could live in a cave for twelve years.'

'Yes,' said Hamish, 'exactly. We could live in a cave for twelve years.'

'With your collection of electric guitars.'

'Yes, with my collection of *solar-powered* electric guitars.'

'Why don't you do it then?' said Loretta, calling his bluff.

The sun slanted in through the bedroom window, a narrow shaft that somehow managed to ease past the overhang of the old corrugated-iron verandah. It was such a dark house in summer, built the wrong way around for southern hemisphere conditions: the laundry, bathroom and kitchen were the sunniest rooms. Despite its bay windows, the front living room was dark; the only good thing about it was the large pot-belly stove and the view out to Locke and Cooper beyond the garden. Loretta and Hamish had talked about renovating and double-glazing but never managed to feel comfortable with the cost. Raised by frugal parents, Loretta had a deep fear of debt, while Hamish, who was somewhat carefree when it came to money, was tied into paying off his truck. Every month they contributed to a joint savings account, intending to put the savings towards renovations but, inevitably, once the total reached the $3000 to $4000 mark Hamish would start casting around for a new guitar, locating a 'bargain of the century'. His excitement would be so great that Loretta would be unable to refuse him, and so the savings would disappear and the long, painful process of rebuilding their renovation fund would begin again from scratch.

One day, Loretta hoped, they'd fix the place up, but in the meantime they were happy to have a place of their own, free from landlords and restrictions concerning nail- and pin-holes in the walls. Hammering nails into the living room wall had given Loretta a sense of power denied throughout her life as a student and as a young wife. Martin had always had his eye firmly fixed on resale value, and had expected her to live as if she was a resident in a swanky hotel rather than a mother with a young and growing family. Even Blu-Tack had been banned for fear that it would rip the wallpaper. If it hadn't been for the invention of cork noticeboards, the older children would have grown up in a house with no pictures, not even their own finger-painted and collaged masterpieces.

'We could live on your salary, couldn't we?' asked Hamish. 'If I did make a career change?'

Loretta shook her head. Maybe she could have managed in the old days, when she was still employed full-time at the university, but not now. Not with the wages offered by her part-time position at Caroline Freeman High.

In recent years Hamish had begun to talk more and more frequently about quitting and moving to the country. At first he raised the topic only when he was tired or stressed as a result of a particularly busy period. The conversation about changing their lives would last just a day or so and then, like the echoes of an argument, dissipate and fade for another few months. But these days Hamish's mutterings of dissatisfaction had a more persistent, desperate edge. It was clear he was seriously considering his options, and the possibility of him giving up a well-paid job chilled Loretta. Much as she dreamed about escape, she didn't want her old age to be defined by money problems and anxiety.

'Maybe we should hold back until after Christmas and then figure out what we can afford to do. In the meantime, I can start thinking about another job. Maybe I could find something that's better paid.'

She felt Hamish's hand on her thigh. A hand that was huge, powerful, an archetypal workingman's hand, and yet so light against her skin that it seemed no heavier than a bird.

'Maybe Shannon could find you something? You could keep the school job, 'cause you enjoy that, don't you, babe? But maybe, during the holidays when you've got nothing on, you could do some office work for her, or something? You're always telling me how busy she is now she's running her own company. There's bound to be a part-time position.'

Loretta caught her breath and sat quietly, waiting for Hamish to finish. In her heart of hearts she hoped he might identify some work opportunities for himself, but he never did. He talked about pulling his weight at home, of spending time with Kit, or, if he was especially animated, he raised the possibility of getting a band together or giving the occasional guitar lesson. But nothing concrete. He left that side of things to Loretta.

From her place on the bed, she could see the shadowed reflection from the fishpond on the ceiling. It was a circular ripple, a kind of black hole, above her head. She imagined it expanding, drawing her up into its depths, and then closing behind her, swallowing her completely. A surge of panic rushed through her and she turned her head, nestling closer to Hamish, who was quietly humming to himself.

'I'll see what I can do,' she said. 'I don't want to rush into anything, though. I think we need to be sensible about this.'

'Sure, babe.'

Hamish wriggled his free arm out from around her waist and she felt it keenly, as if it was a withdrawal of affection.

'Kit's getting older, eh?' she said, hoping to change the subject.

'Yep.'

Loretta took a sip of coffee, holding the cold dregs in her mouth before swallowing them back and placing the mug on the windowsill next to her book. The very thought of trying to figure out what to do with Kit if she worked full-time created a low, stabbing pain. Everything about their life was relatively simple now. It *worked*. Much as she loved Hamish, she didn't believe she would be able to rely on him for childcare. Despite his intention to spend more time with them, something would call him away. It always did. He didn't like spending every day in one place. He was the type of person who needed travel in order to enjoy his home and family.

'In a couple of years he'll be old enough to be left alone.' She gave a deep sigh and pressed her palms against her belly, holding in the butterflies. 'We'll work something out, eh?' she added, snuggling down.

'Yep. I can always give guitar lessons from here.'

'Yeah,' agreed Loretta. 'You could even have another go at teaching Kit.'

Hamish laughed. 'He had his chance to learn from the master.'

In the old days, before Kit was born, they would sometimes spend Sunday afternoon in bed. Music would filter in from the living room and they'd read, and take turns putting on the kettle, making snacks or changing the CD. By the end of the afternoon, the bedcover would be covered in crumbs, and dotted around the edge of the bed would be glasses, cups and plates. Neither one of them would want to be the first to get up and leave. They'd play paper, scissors, rock to see who would have to move first. Inevitably Loretta lost. She always made her hand into a fist, and Hamish knew that. Maybe she just liked that final caress, the paper of his fingers hovering against her knuckles, protecting her in the seconds before he playfully kicked her out of bed.

The Dangerous Book for (Menopausal) Women #3
Tenzin Palmo

Aka: Diane Perry.
British.
Librarian turned Buddhist hermit.
Born into the wrong body — wanted to be male. Later,
   glad to be female.
No kids . . .

Of course, thought Loretta.

Reference: Cave in the Snow: Tenzin Palmo's Quest for Enlightenment (1999) by Vicki Mackenzie.

Loretta swiped a crumb off the open page of her notebook and took another bite from her ham and cheese sandwich. So, she thought, Here's a librarian (like me), and a city girl (like me) who becomes a Buddhist and, at the age of twenty, moves to Dalhousie, in northwest India (not like me).

She picked up her pen and wrote:

Diane — Adventurous Buddhist.
Loretta — Stay-at-home atheist.

Loretta had checked out images of Dalhousie during her lunch break. It was all mountain meadows, forests and green peaks in summer. Snow-covered peaks in the winter. It had put Loretta in mind of Switzerland or the Rockies — more locations she had never seen, except in pictures. Dalhousie was the summer retreat of Lord Dalhousie, Governor-General of India during the first half of the 1850s. 'Dalhousie — Good choice,' added Loretta.

She shifted position, tugging her collapsible chair to a small spot of sunshine, out of the wind, near the water's edge. The chair tilted as she sat down, and for a second she was thrown off-balance and almost fell onto the muddy shore. In thirty minutes or so the last of the late afternoon sun would disappear and the entire area would be cast into shade. To her left, James Bond stood facing the lake. From the back, he was nothing more than white corrugated plastic. If she hadn't seen the figure before, Loretta doubted that she would even know the cutout was human in form.

She took up her notebook once more and wrote:

Diane becomes nun (not into relationships, or sex).
Age 33 leaves male-dominated monastery and moves to
  a cave.
Grows vegetables.

What sort of vegetables? wondered Loretta, as she took another bite from her sandwich and continued writing:

Meditates four times a day — for several hours at a time.

She laughed out loud imagining what would happen if she spent hours each day meditating. And then she sighed as she thought about how boring life would become.

Slept upright, cross-legged on a cushion, in a 2 x 3-foot-
  square meditation box.
Austerity.
After nine years of semi-solitude in cave, spent final
  three years in complete isolation.
Resourcefulness and confidence.

Loretta closed the notebook and sat with her hands in her lap. She couldn't remember the last time she had slept alone, in the wild. In fact, not counting the times she had camped out in the Misty Moors clubhouse in her parents' garden, she doubted she had ever gone off by herself in search of peace and solitude — or spiritual enlightenment. Perhaps that explained her lack of resourcefulness. Had she spent more time alone up a mountain she may have been able to process Hamish's desire to move to the country without panicking. She'd be more *confident,* less of a coward. Well, it was never too late to make amends. Hamish would be away at the weekend. Kit could go and stay at a mate's. And she would come back to the den and spend the night contemplating the stars and working on her inner life.

According to her research, there had been a time when Tenzin Palmo was concerned about being attacked, or raped. But she'd got over that fear almost as soon as she entered the cave. In fact, she had felt completely safe. And she didn't even have James Bond to protect her.

Loretta had been a little disappointed to discover James on the bed where she'd left him. The buttercups, though wilted, were still in the vase. She didn't want to meet the other visitor, or visitors, but she enjoyed speculating about who they were. The James Bond figure made her think that a boy, maybe a kid not much older than Kit, was responsible for the building. But the flowers and the orderliness of the den made her believe a girl might be involved. Maybe a thirteen- or fourteen-year-old, someone very much like herself at that age. It could be that the den was created by a brother and sister. Or twins? She could see twins hanging out together after school.

For reasons she couldn't pinpoint, she dismissed the idea that another adult frequented the place to enjoy the peace and quiet. She didn't know why, but she felt certain that the den belonged to someone who was happier playing grown-ups than being one. She decided it was a child's place. That might explain why she felt so safe and relaxed pottering about. It seemed out of the question that some crazy rapist, or the farmer whose land the den occupied, would turn up and confront her. Good vibes surrounded the den; it was marked for happy times.

As she settled back in her chair, the notebook on the ground next to her, she closed her eyes and listened. The wind was blowing from the south and gave the air a chilled quality that brought with it the sweetness of broom and gorse, the freshness of grass and the stink of reeds and swamp water. The sound of planes approaching the airport from the north was muffled, the engines little more than a faint exhalation a long way off. Even those that took off towards the south and flew overhead were too high by the time they reached the wetlands to make much of an impression. The firing range was also silent.

The wind had strengthened in the past half-hour. With her eyes shut, Loretta heard the gusts through the trees and was reminded of breaking waves, the roar and ease of surf. From the direction of the lake a duck called and then, moments later, a clatter of noise as more joined in. Closer by, chaffinches and redpolls. And then, suddenly, a new sound — one she couldn't instantly recognise. Opening her eyes and sitting up, she looked in the direction of the water but could see nothing out of the ordinary. There it was again. A faint voice, tuneful. Loretta strained her ears, caught the first few bars of a song but then the voice stopped.

Automatically, Loretta stood up and pulled her chair back from the bank, then retreated to the edge of the bush, where she could still see the lake. As she watched, a figure in a Canadian canoe paddled into view. No more than fifty metres offshore, the paddler traced the shoreline, cutting in and out of the reeds that spread out into the shallow bay. Although it was clear she had a general direction in mind, it didn't seem as though she was in a hurry. She seemed to be paddling for pleasure, enjoying her surroundings and poking around. As Loretta watched, the canoeist disappeared behind a low rise, leaving behind only the gentle ripple and wash from her vessel.

A woman. An older woman. Maybe sixty?

Loretta stepped out of her hiding place and made her way quietly to the edge of the lake, where she hoped she would get a better view. To her disappointment, the woman was nowhere to be seen. The ducks that had been startled by the canoe finished their lazy circle above and came back down, wings outstretched, hydroplaning as they braked to a standstill on the water.

Then, from behind a dense clump of flax, the woman reappeared. She was no further than a hundred metres away, drifting with her paddle balanced in front of her, resting across the gunwale. Reaching into the front of her lifejacket pocket, she pulled out a notebook, quickly wrote something down and then replaced the notebook. Loretta felt indignant. The child within her bristled. The notebook was my idea! Then the child notekeeper added, Write down what she's doing. You need to make a full list of her actions, for future reference.

Loretta watched as the canoe drifted in the breeze and made a slow circle in the bay. As the boat turned, the last rays of sun caught the woman's hair, ringing her head in a halo of golden light. Then, as the light faded, she pulled up the hood on her windproof and, without looking back, paddled away.

───────────

'Good movie?' Loretta asked Kit when she got home.

'All right.'

Just once, thought Loretta, you could make an effort to answer a question properly.

'Hamish, what did you think of the movie?'

'It was too long.'

'That's why we walked out,' said Kit. 'Hamish said that if we snuck out he would buy me sushi.'

'Provided you promised not to blab to your mother.'

'Oh, yeah,' said Kit. 'Sorry, Hamish.'

'So how much of the movie did you actually see?' asked Loretta.

'Enough,' said Hamish. 'Too much.'

Hamish and Kit looked so happy. They'd had fun and were full of their secret adventure. And yet, in spite of herself, Loretta couldn't stop from muttering, 'Just as well we're made of money.'

Hamish screwed up his face in an attempt to mimic hers. 'Ah, you old grump. What did you get up to, anyway?'

Loretta opened her mouth to respond, then closed it again.

'What?' pushed Hamish.

Loretta shrugged. 'I mucked about and went for a walk.' She waited for Hamish to ask for details but he seemed perfectly satisfied.

'Near the wetlands,' she added.

'What?'

'I went for a walk by the wetlands. Looking for birds and stuff.'

'By the airport?'

Loretta nodded. 'Yep. Watched the sun go down.'

'When I was a kid,' began Loretta as she tucked Kit into bed later that night, 'I used to go off by myself and have adventures. Then, once I left school I stopped doing stuff like that. I went to university and got a job in a library. I worked my way up through the system until I was the manager at the medical school library. I used to watch the students come in, and half the time I didn't know whether to feel sorry for them, or to feel envious. There was a bit of both going through my head. Sorry because they were so worn-out, and envious because they had a drive and confidence that I lacked. Sometimes, I'd just find them irritating because they didn't have a clue about how to use the library. They were too busy to bother with more than the basics.

'Once or twice, when Pete or Edie were sick, but not too sick, I'd have to take them into work with me and I'd stick them in my office with a blanket and a book. It always amazed me that none of the medical students ever asked why there was a child in my room. The office space was open to the circulation desk, so it wasn't as if the student doctors couldn't see them. I remember, one day, feeling offended because Edie had a bad, hacking cough and no one asked if she was okay. She wasn't that sick, but she had a streaming cold and a bit of a temperature. Really, she shouldn't have been out of bed. But I had no choice but to bring her in. I can't remember why, now. Why I had no choice.

'I was feeling tense and quite stressed and I was at the circulation desk, keeping close to Edie, and student after student came up to request help or to secure a book, and not one of them asked, "Is that your daughter? Is she okay? Have you seen a doctor?" Not one. Do you know what? I think that was the real reason why I was so keen to leave that job in the end. It was because I couldn't stand being around such uncaring people any more. I don't think I've ever told anyone that. So, when I found out I was pregnant with you, I was delighted. You gave me the reason I needed to leave that job. I owe my sanity to you.'

'You're welcome.'

Loretta stayed where she was, on the edge of Kit's bed. He was used to her lingering in his room at night. Sometimes she would fold his clothes or pick up his toys off the floor. Other times she would rearrange the books on his shelves. She'd move slowly, quietly, as if stalking a deer. She didn't want to disturb her son. Tonight, for no reason she could think of, she had told him about why she had walked away from the one decent paying job she had ever had. After all these years, she still had mixed feelings about what she had done. Given the state of her first marriage, her behaviour had been pretty reckless.

'I saw a woman in a beautiful canoe today. Out on the lake at the wetlands. She was singing.'

There was no response and she leant in close and pulled the covers up around her son's chin. He turned his face to the wall and she kissed him on the cheek.

'Good night, mate.'

He was already asleep.

LORETTA SPOTTED SHANNON FIRST. As usual, she had her phone pressed to her ear and her gaze fixed on her feet, as she walked back and forth along the footpath in front of the real estate office. Loretta gave a quick toot of the horn and felt strangely satisfied to see Shannon jump. It took several more minutes, however, before her friend finished the call and got into the car.

'So where are you taking me?' she asked, gathering up a pile of Loretta's supermarket eco-bags and tossing them onto the back seat. 'Somewhere good, I hope, because I've had a crap week — literally!'

'Well, I think it's good,' said Loretta. 'But you might not like it.' Even as she spoke, she knew that taking Shannon to the den was a mistake. If she had any sense she would turn back, or suggest going to a café instead, but somewhere deep inside her the childish urge to share her den discovery had taken hold. It was as if she had a chance to finally fulfil the dreams she had once held for her Misty Moors bird club.

From the corner of her eye she could see Shannon surveying the surrounding farmlands with disdain. 'It's not an antique shop, is it? Or worse, one of those country crafty shops, because what I *don't* need is a fake duck decoy or one of those "Keep Calm" posters. Also, so we're clear, I am not interested in anything home-made unless it's ninety per cent proof.' Without looking at Loretta, she let out a long sigh and grumbled, 'What a waste of a week.'

Loretta drove in silence. Why had she brought Shannon? Did the term 'self-sabotage' mean nothing to her? Really, Kit was the one who might have got something out of the den. Or even Hamish. But Shannon? Even as she attacked herself for her stupidity, she had a fair idea that one of the reasons for choosing Shannon was because she was a woman, and for some reason that mattered. Maybe it was because she trusted that Shannon would not try and take over the space, or do anything to it. At best, Shannon would see the den and express appreciation or approval; at worst, she would shrug and turn her back. But, either way, she wouldn't claim the space for herself, or want to change it. At least, Loretta didn't think she would.

'I haven't been out this way for ages,' said Shannon. 'In fact, the last time I came out here was just after I quit the school secretary job and started working in the old office of Prick and Wanker's. It was one of my first big sales and I got caught up in a deal that almost drove me crazy. The buyer was a total hard-case businesswoman, tough as nails despite her laid-back, hippy exterior. You could tell she got a kick from beating us down. It was like the whole bargaining process amused her. I got the feeling that getting a good deal wasn't just a matter of pride but a source of entertainment. She was also one of the first women I'd ever met who was totally indifferent to what people thought of her. I kind of admired her, in a way. She was rolling in money — completely self-made. Ruth something, her name was. Almost had me in tears, though . . .'

'You? In tears?'

'I tell you what, it doesn't happen often. Tears are pretty low down on my list of emotional responses. Outrage and anger are more my thing. This week, for instance, I had an open home: 6 pm on a Wednesday. I arrived at 5.45 pm, met the owner, got the keys and she left. I started to set up, stepped outside onto the deck and the entire area — I kid you not — was covered, *covered*, in dog poo. Not only the deck but the lawn, too. Every dog in the neighbourhood must have shat on the lawn. There was five minutes till opening and there I was, in my skirt and heels, on my knees picking up poo. I was almost gagging. She doesn't even own a dog. She's dog-sitting for her daughter and thought it would be safest to leave the creature on the deck while she was out at work all day. Why didn't she clean up the poo herself? I'll tell you why — and this confirms how disgusting it was — because the dog had worms. The first, and only, time she bent to pick up its crap, a big white worm crawled out, so she decided to leave the mess for her daughter to clean up. Only her daughter isn't due back till this weekend. Honest to God, Loretta, I thought I was going to be sick.'

'You should have left it.'

'You're telling me. What's worse, no one even turned up for the open home! So, basically, I gave up my free evening — my relaxing-with-a-drink-at-the-end-of-the-day time — to hose down a shitty deck and bag poo. Man, I was angry. You have no idea.'

'And I thought I had it tough.'

'Well, yeah, you have your own little shits to deal with. How is Caroline Freeman High these days?'

What could Loretta say? School was the same as always, only worse. The usual counting down the weeks until the end of year malaise was beginning to grip the teachers, while the students were increasingly tired and anxious about exams, or bored and ready to leave. Not all students, mind. She should remember that. There were a couple of library regulars, girls like little Porsche Chance, who made her job bearable.

They pulled into the wetlands car park and Loretta shut down the engine. As usual they were the only ones there, although there were signs of previous visitors: empty cans were strewn across the grass and two plastic bags, containing what looked like household rubbish, lay on the ground next to the gate. Loretta unbuckled her seat belt and shoved open her door, but before she could climb out, she was stopped by Shannon asking, 'Is there something wrong?'

Loretta glanced across to her friend, and answered, 'No. Why?'

Now it was Shannon's turn to look surprised. 'Oh. What are we doing here, then?'

Loretta hesitated, unsure of what Shannon meant. 'Well, we're here.'

'This,' said Shannon pointing at the scene in front of her. 'This? You want me to get out of the car? Why?'

'Cause I want to show you something,' said Loretta.

'Why don't you tell me, instead? And then we can go and get coffee somewhere. It would save a lot of time.'

Loretta laughed. 'Because I want you to see.'

Shannon groaned and slowly opened her door. 'We're not going tramping, are we?' she asked, walking to the front of the car. 'Look at my sandals.' She wiggled her toes and Loretta noticed for the first time that her friend's toenails were painted neon pink. She also saw that the sandals were little more than three thin straps of leather, devoid of any hint of practicality.

'Tell you what,' said Loretta, 'You wear my shoes and I'll squeeze my feet into Kit's trainers. How does that sound?'

Shannon pulled a face. 'Sounds like rubbish.'

It took several minutes to organise the swap. Much to Loretta's horror, Kit's shoes were damp inside, as if his feet had been sweating profusely when he'd last worn them. On top of that, they were a size too small, and crushed her toes. For her part, Shannon appeared no happier wearing Loretta's shoes. She kept glancing at her feet, turning her ankles this way and that and pulling a face. 'What sort of shoes are these?' she asked. 'Are they plastic, or what?'

'It's called vegan leather. I got them from a cruelty-free site.'

'Vegan leather? What's that even mean?'

Once more Shannon pulled a face, but this time Loretta pretended not to notice, striding ahead before Shannon had time to voice any more complaints.

It was the first time Loretta had visited the wetlands in the company of another person, and it struck her almost straight away that she felt Shannon's presence as an intrusion. Whereas she normally felt free to dawdle, to look around and take her time, she now felt obliged to display a sense of purpose, and to her annoyance she was conscious of moving too quickly, of not spending enough time enjoying her surroundings. Worse, the view struck her as disappointing. In past weeks she had grown more familiar with the wetlands and had begun to take a certain pleasure in its somewhat low-key beauty. Unlike a deep-green forest of native beech, the scraggy mixture of flax, native shrubs and exotics wasn't immediately eye-catching or beautiful. In fact, its strength lay in its scrappiness, its refusal to conform to the spectacular. It was the kind of landscape that became beautiful through familiarity; the more Loretta got in tune with its features, the more she loved it. For some reason, being with another person made it difficult to recall the attraction. It was as though Loretta was being asked to see the wetlands through Shannon's eyes, and she could tell by her friend's tense silence that she was unimpressed.

Loretta stopped. To her surprise, she didn't want to carry on any further. She waited a moment until Shannon caught her up and then said, 'I'm not really into this. Are you?'

Shannon said nothing.

'I reckon we should go and have a bit of cake somewhere, don't you?' continued Loretta.

Shannon glanced about and shifted uncomfortably on her feet, resting her weight first on one hip and then the other.

'I don't mind,' she said, 'If you want to show me your surprise thingy . . . We can keep going.'

'Nah, let's flag it,' said Loretta. 'Come back another day. I don't know, I'm not in the mood . . .'

Shannon made one more attempt to reassure Loretta that she was fine, that she was happy to continue on, that it was no big deal. She wasn't *tired*, if that was what Loretta was worried about. After all, she'd been seeing a personal trainer for the past six months, so it wasn't as if she couldn't keep up.

But Loretta was adamant that they turn back, and as soon as the decision was final, and Shannon was sure it wasn't because of her, she beamed and said, 'Phew, thank God for that.' She became chatty as they headed back to the car, and it was only when they were nearing the car park that she suddenly paused and looked around. Raising her hand as if to silence a noisy child, she said, 'Hang on a minute.'

Loretta followed Shannon's gaze, asking, 'What is it?' She couldn't see anything out of the ordinary. There were no birds flying overhead, no people or animals. The place was almost desolate in its lack of life.

'Hang on,' repeated Shannon. 'This is it, isn't it?'

'What?' asked Loretta.

'This is the place I sold. I didn't recognise it.' She turned in a full circle and exclaimed, 'Wow, that's amazing!'

It was Loretta's turn to feel confused. 'What is? What's amazing?' she asked.

'This place,' said Shannon. 'Incredible. This was open, bare paddocks and swamp when I sold it. None of these trees were here — well, maybe those big poplars over there — but none of the smaller bushes. None of this flax or any of those other trees. I remember it now. There used to be cows out here and the ground was churned up. It was a complete mud bath and it ruined my shoes. This is amazing. I hardly recognise it.'

She glanced around once more and whistled softly through her teeth. 'I'm impressed. She must have spent years working like a slave to get it looking like this.'

As they sat in the courtyard of the nearest café, taking turns to break off mouth-sized lumps of cake with a teaspoon, Loretta brought up the subject of Hamish, and the conversation they'd had about his desire to leave work. Shannon listened quietly while Loretta talked, and it was only as the words came out that Loretta understood how anxious she really was about the future.

'He needs to grow up,' snapped Shannon, when Loretta had stopped talking. 'He's got a family, and you're already working your tits off: first at school and then with Kit. I don't know ... where do these guys get off with their demands?'

Loretta was taken aback by the freedom with which her friend expressed herself. At the same time, she felt grateful, knowing that Shannon was acting out of concern and loyalty for her rather than out of hostility to Hamish.

Shannon continued, 'You go and tell Hamish that he can come and see me about a job if he wants.' She stabbed at the cake and laughed. 'You tell him that if he wants to work every Saturday and Sunday and five evenings a week, and pick up dog poo and scrub toilet bowls until they sparkle, he's welcome to go on trial.'

Loretta took the spoon from Shannon's fingers, carefully scraped a lump of cream-cheese icing from the plate and, without thinking, gave the spoon a long, slow lick. As the creamy, vanilla-flavoured sweetness filled her mouth she let out a contented sigh.

'Maybe we *could* move to the country,' she murmured. Her mind filled with images of hens and happy pigs. A grove of olive trees, old-fashioned apple trees, beehives and two dogs — a short-legged Jack Russell and a chunky golden Labrador — filled the middle distance of her imagination. Inside a rustic, exposed-beamed barn, Hamish was hard at work smoking bacon, while in another, smaller room, scented candles and anti-aging products made from pure olive oil filled the shelves. In her mind's eye, Loretta saw the scene quite clearly but, for all its attractiveness, she didn't see herself. Casting her eye further afield she suddenly glimpsed her own image. Far away from the house, alone on a riverbank, a makeshift shelter at her back, a notebook and a pair of binoculars on her lap, she sat waiting for something to enter into view. That was her. Sitting in the bright sunshine, waiting, and counting down the days until it would all turn to crap.

IT HAD BEEN A CRAZY FEW DAYS, and Loretta wanted nothing more than to go home and sit in a quiet room, preferably alone. Instead she was standing on the doorstep of a stranger's house, watching nervously as Shannon tried the lock.

'I don't think I should be doing this,' said Loretta. She looked over her shoulder towards the street as Shannon sorted through the bunch of keys in her hand.

'It feels wrong,' she persisted.

Shannon ignored her and gave the door a push, allowing it to swing inwards on its hinges. 'It's all right. We're here in an official capacity.'

The words failed to comfort Loretta and she hesitated, hovering on the step as Shannon went into the house. Although it was daytime, Shannon reached for the closest light switch and turned it on. After a fragment of a second the eco-bulb in the hall flickered and shone brightly. Shannon nodded with satisfaction, 'Good. Power's still on. They told me it would be but it's good to know.'

Loretta still couldn't bring herself to step inside. She watched helplessly as Shannon made her way down the hall towards the back of Valerie Mansford's house. 'It's all right, Loretta. Come on. We've got to check everything is okay and chuck out any food.'

Loretta took a step forward. 'Don't they have special cleaners to do that?'

Shannon made a sound, half snort, half laughter, 'Where you do think we are? Los Angeles? Hurry up.'

The cousin of the missing woman had contacted Shannon from Australia. He had been in touch with the police and arranged for Shannon to come and do a quick check, and clean out the fridge and cupboards for anything that might go off or attract rats and other vermin. He'd be over at Christmas to do a proper sort-through of Valerie's things, but in the meantime could Shannon have a quiet recce and make sure everything was secure?

'Did he sound upset?' asked Loretta

'He sounded like someone who had been given an extra burden, but one that might pay off in the long run. That's what he sounded like. As far as I can tell, he's Valerie's only relative and he sees her every year or two when he comes over for a ski holiday. He visits for a couple of days and then goes back to Melbourne. But he doesn't seem to know very much about her — the names of her friends, that kind of thing. He's your typical distant cousin, in other words.'

'But those posters around my local shopping centre? Someone must have printed them off?'

Shannon opened the fridge and glanced in. 'Work colleagues, I guess. Man, you can tell she lived alone.'

The fridge was immaculate. It looked as if it had been recently wiped down. All the shelves were clean and there were no crumbs, scraps of vegetables or shelves of half-opened pickle jars. The butter was in the butter conditioner. A near-full bottle of milk was the only item in the door rack. The single-serve packs of chocolate dessert, arranged on the middle shelf, were still within their use-by date, as was a block of Edam cheese in a clear plastic box. In the meat tray, wrapped in several layers of cling film, was a cooked chicken breast. It looked as if a slice had been taken from it. Of all the things in the fridge this was the only thing that looked truly off.

'It's like a motel fridge,' said Loretta. 'Like when you go to a motel and you put your stuff in and the next morning you remove it. It's got that temporary, unused look about it. God, it's sad.'

They disposed of the meat in the rubbish bag they had

brought, and then Shannon washed the milk down the sink. 'You take the chocolate dessert and cheese,' she said.

Loretta shook her head. 'No. You take it.'

'I've decided to go dairy-free,' said Shannon. 'I won't eat it.'

'I won't eat it, either.'

'Just take it.'

Loretta hesitated.

'Look, the police have all but told me it's a case of suicide. The cousin's asked me to clear out the cupboards. They clearly don't think she's coming back.' Shannon held out the food for Loretta, and added gently, 'Do me a favour, please take it.'

The food cupboard was just as tidy as the fridge. Rice and pasta were stored in tall plastic containers on the top shelf. Flour and other baking ingredients in plastic tubs lined the middle shelf. The bottom shelf resembled a child's shop display of tinned food. At the right-hand side, neatly arranged in a row, were five Harrods tea blends. Each came in a beautifully decorated tin — Spring Celebration, Summer Celebration, Autumn Celebration, Winter Celebration and Birthday Celebration — but it was the colourful ribbon decoration scrolling across the last canister that caught Loretta's attention. Her hand went out and she lifted the tin, opening it to take a sniff. Inside, the plastic packaging was unopened. She reached for Autumn Celebration and opened that. The tin was almost empty. The same was true for the winter tin, but spring and summer, like the birthday blend, were untouched.

'That will be okay,' said Shannon.

Loretta jumped, startled by her friend's voice.

'He can deal with that,' said Shannon. 'Tea keeps forever.'

Loretta replaced the tins, arranging them into a straight line. 'She must have got them for Easter, do you think? When was her birthday?'

Shannon shrugged. 'No idea, why?'

Tears pricked at Loretta's eyes. 'I don't know. Just that she went missing around the start of spring, and she hasn't touched summer, and the birthday tin is unopened. I don't know. Everything's so neat and tidy.' She looked around, helplessly, repeating, 'It's so tidy.'

'Yeah, she wouldn't have lasted a minute in our house,' replied Shannon.

While Shannon finished up in the kitchen, Loretta wandered into the living room and took a seat on a white leather sofa by the window. In front of the sofa, on a coffee table, was a neat stack of magazines and a vase of flowers. Only the pink proteas in the centre of the arrangement looked passably fresh. One or two of the lilies had kept their shape and a few roses were intact, but of the other flowers only stalks and random petals remained. More petals and small dustings of pollen circled the base of the vase. She leant forward, pushed her forefinger into a pile of pollen and rubbed the dark orange dust over the back of her hand. She wanted to leave. They had come in separate cars and so she didn't have to stay, and yet she felt compelled to sit still and wait.

On the wall opposite was a painting. A watercolour of a headland and the sea. In the foreground was a cabbage tree. The sky was a soft pinkish blue.

Below the painting was a cabinet, a glass cabinet, and inside were cups and saucers. At least twelve. Highly decorated. Fine china. An Art Deco tea-set of some kind sat on a tray on top. It may have been Clarice Cliff. It was cream-coloured, with burnt orange and red accents.

To the right of the cabinet was an upright piano. The lid was shut. The tapestry cover of the piano stool looked like it was stitched by hand. The colours were burnt orange and red and the design was vaguely Art Deco.

There was no television in the room. There was a small stereo unit but no sign of CDs. Perhaps they were stowed in the closed shelving unit below the stereo.

There were two armchairs. Covered in matching upholstery. Burnt orange and red tones.

A standard lamp. Chrome. Possibly Art Deco.

A vase of dying flowers on a coffee table. A neat stack of magazines. Small piles of pollen.

A woman's life.

Dangerous Book for (Menopausal) Women #4
Clarice Cliff

Aunt Avis collected Clarice Cliff.
Avis = my mother's oldest sister.
Lived most of her life in Kenya.
Visited three or four times.
Hated kids. Loved animals.
I am named Loretta Avis Deans: Loretta and Deans
*   from my father's side. Avis from my mother's.*
Avis nicknamed me 'Lad'.

Aunt Avis, Loretta recalled, had brought reels of Super 8 film with her when she visited. That was what Loretta remembered most — that and being called Lad. They had movie nights.

Loretta's job had been to rearrange the furniture in a loose U in front of the screen. Her mother and Aunt Avis sat on the couch and her dad stood next to the projector. Loretta took the big armchair, the one with the cracked leather upholstery. She sat with her legs draped over one arm. Inevitably, just as she got comfy something would go wrong with the film and she'd have to leap up and turn on the light and wait while her father fiddled with the reel or adjusted the focus. While he worked, Connie and Avis would keep up a steady stream of conversation, seemingly unaware or uninterested in the film itself. It was only as the first jerky shots hit the screen that either one of them fell quiet.

'That's New Mexico last year. That's Carl. Oh, and that's Carl's wife . . . what's her name.'

'Who's Carl?' asked Connie.

'And that's Wayne. He lives on the reservation. Oh, and that's a rattlesnake.'

Avis never answered questions about who or what people were. Such information struck her as dull and unimportant. Not once did she clarify her relationship to the people in the images. And because she was the one who held the camera and made the films, there were never any shots of her. For this reason, all of Aunt Avis's films were boring.

As a child Loretta would never have known that her Aunt Avis collected Clarice Cliff Bizarre ware had it not been for an exhibition catalogue and a set of coasters that arrived in the mail one day from Texas. The large package was addressed to Connie but inside was a postcard for 'The Lad'. The image on the postcard was a Clarice Cliff teapot adorned with crocuses. The message on the back read 'Spring has sprung!' and was signed 'Your one and only, Aunt Avis.'

From 1927 to 1939 Clarice Cliff was regarded as the leading

British ceramicist. She was so prolific that she had to employ hundreds of staff to carry out her designs. In October 1972 she was discovered dead in her favourite chair, with the radio playing, by her gardener Reg Lamb.

Avis met a different fate. She suffered from early onset Alzheimer's and spent the last nine years of her life in an aged-care residence. She was left unsupervised and drowned in her bath at the age of sixty-four.

IN THE MOONLIGHT THE TRUNKS of the mānuka trees appeared silvery, as if brushed with paint. It was so bright that each thin, straight trunk had a shadow and the tops of the trees appeared perfectly silhouetted against the clear sky. There was very little wind, and sounds reached Loretta in a pure, distinct form: the lapping of waves on the shore, the baa of sheep and the almost donkey-like bray of cattle. The soft call of birds: a blackbird followed by the harsher cry of a duck and lastly a plover or oystercatcher — she wasn't sure which. There were mosquitoes, too. The incessant and invisible zzzz that hung around her head, came closer, stopped, started, faded and disappeared, only to be replaced by a second, or possibly the same, mosquito. Behind her, from inside the den, was a scratching noise, then soft footsteps, running, skittering and squeaking. She hoped it was only a mouse but had a feeling it was a rat. She'd turned her torch in the direction of the noise but had failed to see anything. She'd called out in the dark in an attempt to scare the creature away but that hadn't worked. The scratching came back and, with it, the sound of gnawing. And then, from a long way away, the crack of a gun.

She hadn't noticed before this night, but she could see vehicles travelling along the far side of the lake. For the count of three, their headlights would appear. And then they would disappear for twenty-four seconds to reappear one more time, for six seconds. She couldn't make out the tail-lights of cars passing in the other direction. One set of headlights had been stationary for several minutes. She'd been counting the seconds, watching the lights moving in the distance, when they'd suddenly stopped. What had caused the driver to pull over? Was it a phone call, or had they hit something? Or perhaps they were tired or thirsty or needed to stretch or pee? From where she was, she couldn't see any interior light but she imagined one on all the same. She pictured a single occupant in the car, talking on a phone, his voice lowered simply because it was late and dark and anything loud would have seemed out of place. She imagined that the man was Hamish and that he was talking to her, telling her that he would be home soon but that he'd try not to wake her when he came in. He'd talk to her in the morning. They could sleep in. He was just phoning to say goodnight.

In reality, Kit was sleeping at a friend's and Hamish was somewhere on the West Coast. He had deliveries for Westport, and was then going on to Nelson and Blenheim before heading for home via Christchurch. He'd forgotten about his dissatisfaction with his job and was relatively happy once again. It hadn't occurred to him to let Loretta know this, and so she had continued to worry about what he might do, or where she would find new work and how they would live if he suddenly decided to pack in his job. Night after night she had lain awake fretting, and it was only when she finally mentioned how tired she was and Hamish asked why that it became clear she'd been worrying over nothing. 'Oh that,' said Hamish. 'Don't worry about that. It was a bad week. It's fine now.' Loretta was relieved, but also pissed off.

When she'd mentioned that she'd been feeling sick with anxiety, he'd looked surprised and then laughed. He didn't call her silly or crazy, but that was clearly what he was thinking. 'Jeez, babe, it's work. You should know what it's like. It's a busy time of year. Clients want everything *yesterday*. It's no big deal. I'm not going to chuck in my job. Not yet, anyway.'

He'd smiled apologetically and added, 'You weren't really worried, were you? You know I wouldn't drop you in it.'

Loretta had almost laughed. She'd spent evenings looking through their bank statements, wondering where she could make cuts and how long their savings would last without Hamish's income. She'd even gone as far as making a mental list of what they could sell — not that they owned anything of value. But it was all going to be okay, apparently. If she'd been a teenager she might have exclaimed, 'What the actual fuck!' But she didn't. She understood Hamish too well to believe that the whole matter was behind her.

It was getting late and she should go to bed, yet rather than turn in, she decided to have one more cup of tea. She'd placed her flask inside the den's entrance, beside James Bond's feet. He looked different from the last time she'd been here. His ears had been pierced in her absence and dangling from his lobes were coloured eartags, one blue, the other yellow, both with numbers stamped on them. Strung around his neck were a variety of objects: pieces of plastic, fabric, rubber and wood. These dangling ornaments were haphazardly arranged and yet they were strangely beautiful.

It was much darker inside the den than out. The small clearing was bathed in silver, but only a thin shaft of light edged its way through the entrance, past James Bond, reaching the table where the vase of buttercups and violets stood. A small section of the vase caught the light and glistened, and the flowers she had picked from near the shore soon after arriving cast a faint but discernible shadow across the table's surface.

Next to the vase were the proteas she had taken from Valerie Mansford's house. It had been a spur of the moment decision. Shannon was going to dump them, and for some reason Loretta couldn't bear the thought of them being chucked in the rubbish.

To her shame, she had taken something else from Valerie Mansford's house. As she was leaving she'd noticed, on the hallway stand, a beautiful blue glass jar. Inside was a poured candle and, as she lifted it to read the make, a scent like rosemary reached her, and she breathed deeply. She replaced it on the stand and walked towards the door, but then paused and retraced her steps. She hovered for several seconds and then, furtively, grabbed the candle and walked from the house. It was the only thing she had ever stolen in her life, and she felt so bad about what she'd done that she almost stopped the car and discarded the candle in the first rubbish bin she saw. Though it was dark in the den, Loretta didn't light the candle. She'd decided to save it for a special occasion.

She lay on the narrow camp bed and closed her eyes. With her eyes shut, she listened to the noises around her. The wind had got up a little. She could hear it shuffling through the larger trees, and with each gust, cool air brushed her cheek. The scurrying creature was louder than before. She had the impression that it was running along the wall behind her bed. As long as it promised to stay on the floor and not climb up onto the bed, she didn't mind. Loretta's eyes flicked open and she reached for her torch, searching her immediate surroundings for the creature. She couldn't see it and she could no longer hear it. She should have brought earplugs. Her eyes closed, she drew her sleeping bag up over her face, leaving only a small hole for her mouth. Provided the creature only ran over her body, she could cope, but if it ran across her face, she would have to take action. She knew before she got up that it wouldn't work, but she thought that if she drew James Bond closer to the bed, the mouse, or rat, might mistake him for a real person and stay away. It was one of the least convincing ideas she'd had, but it made her feel better, knowing James was keeping an eye out for her. Once more she lay down and closed her eyes. She strained to hear the sound of feet but the den was quiet. It was eerily quiet. Again she opened her eyes.

In her purse was a packet of tissues, and now she tore a thin strip off one, twisted it into a tight wad and stuffed it into her ear. She did the same for her other ear. The external quiet — that belonging to the den — was immediately matched by an internal silence, a muffled quiet that was centred within her. Loretta was now sealed off from her surroundings and, at last, she could relax. She crawled back inside her sleeping bag and lay with her eyes open, looking at the ceiling of branches above her head. The minutes ticked slowly by and she turned on her side, ready to sleep now that she had shut out the distracting lack of noise. The bed was narrow, and slumped towards its centre. Loretta felt for her torch, wriggled out of her sleeping bag and went outside.

She walked to the edge of the clearing and stood by the lake, looking across the water towards the darkness of the far shore. Few cars were on the road now. She took the wads of paper from her ears and tucked them into her pocket. The difference in sound was negligible. Just the gentle lapping of water, the soft burr of wind. Sounds that should relax her. She was wide awake.

Once, as a seven-year-old, she had left her bed at night and gone into the garden in the hope of hearing a kiwi. She had known there were no kiwi in the suburb of Shirley but that hadn't stopped her from wanting there to be. In many ways, she later realised, her need to believe that there might be a kiwi was similar to other kids' hope of being visited by Santa Claus. There was no difference at all — except that she had gone out to search, whereas all the children she knew stayed in bed, secretly hoping that Santa, or the tooth fairy, would turn up on the appropriate day.

She hadn't seen a kiwi but she had felt tremendous satisfaction, nevertheless, that she hadn't missed the chance to look for the bird. It would have been far worse if she hadn't gone outside in the first place. She'd needed to prove to herself that she was not missing out. That's what I'm doing now, she thought. Reassuring myself that I'm not missing out on something that doesn't necessarily exist. What an idiot.

Without noticing, she'd been walking away from the den, in a direction she hadn't taken before. There was no track, as such, but the way through the trees was relatively clear, and in fifteen minutes she found herself at a fence, on the other side of which was farmland. A short distance away, grazing peacefully, were several cows and she mooed softly, calling them. One of the animals lifted its head, then went back to grazing. Loretta mooed again and this time the cow ignored her. She wondered if it was possible to have a cow as a spirit animal and what that would say about her. That she belonged in a herd? Was docile? Too docile for her own good? In her head she heard her Aunt Avis laugh.

It was peaceful listening to the cows pull and tug at the

grass. The slow, soft presence of the animals comforted her, made her feel sleepier than before. Picking a level spot near her feet, she sat down and pulled her cell phone from her pocket. The faint glow of its screen seemed to offer further reassurance that all was well. Slowly she worked her way through her phone and text messages, clearing month-old conversations and deleting names from her contact list. Next she opened her photo album. The first image showed Kit in the diving pool, his upturned face beneath a blue water-polo cap barely above the surface of the water. He was beaming. Loretta flicked forward, stopped at an image of a sunrise and then swiped back to the image of Kit.

He was so lovely. In a few more years he would dump her, just as Pete and Edie had done. It would start slowly. First he would no longer smile and wave when he saw her waiting for him in the car park. Then, if he was anything like Pete, he would fail to acknowledge her presence when he got into the car. He would open the door, throw his bag in and sit down without saying a word. It was only a matter of time before every trip they made together would be done in silence. Finally, he would pretend not to know her. Full stop. If she ever organised to meet him at a prearranged spot in town, he would make sure to spot her first and start walking before she reached him. He would maintain a distance between them, and remain several steps ahead of her, even when he had no clear idea in what direction they were heading or where the car was parked. Somehow, she'd have to catch his attention and indicate a turn here or a road crossing there so that he could preserve the impression of being out, alone. Then, when they reached the car, he would walk a few steps beyond it and look the other way as she unlocked the door and got in the driver's seat. Only when the engine was running would he do a kind of furtive backstep to the passenger door, as if getting into the car was some out-of-body experience that had nothing to do with him.

Loretta figured she had, at most, only two or three more years of Kit the child. Knowing that, she looked at his photo with renewed intensity and, as she had done with first Pete and then Edie, upbraided herself for not making the most of his company. She should have brought him to the den. They could have spent the night together, sleeping out, playing at being castaways or fugitives or whatever else he wanted. He would have loved it.

But — and she hated to admit it — quiet though Kit was, he would disturb the peace. He was too young to be content with doing nothing, and it was possible he would grow bored after an hour or two. The pleasure of being alone, of sitting quietly, of being free from the constraints of attending to someone else's needs, was something he hadn't yet grown to appreciate. She had no doubt that one day he would discover the deep contentment that comes at the end of the day, when, lying in the dark, the opportunity arises to descend into your own thoughts and daydreams, to find yourself free of self-consciousness or examination, to simply be.

Slowly, Loretta rose to her feet and brushed the seat of her trousers where the slightly damp fabric stuck to her legs. She walked to the fence and leant against the gate, her eyes fixed on the cows. They were further away now, bulky dark shadows that shifted as they moved from one spot to the next. The cow is my spirit animal, she murmured. The den is my temple. She cringed at the earnestness of what she said, but that didn't stop her from affirming, 'The den is my own.' A flood of joy hit her, then, and she turned to go back to the strange, dark, makeshift dwelling that made her complete.

R eading aloud made Chance anxious. It wasn't that she was stupid or anything, but there was something about reading aloud that made her feel like she was being tested and that, whatever she did, she would fail. The letters seemed to go all jazzy on her and then they kept shifting, changing direction and making new patterns that she couldn't recognise. In her head an adult voice would yell, Hurry up, get on with it. What's wrong with you? You're not stupid. You can read, can't you? She couldn't make the voice go away, and that made things worse. She'd get flustered, lose her place and retreat inside herself, until her own quiet voice evaporated, leaving a low, mumbling error.

Recently, during lunchtime, Michelle had shoved a magazine into her hands and said, 'You read it.'

Chance didn't want to, but she was scared of pissing off Michelle so she did as she was told. She concentrated so hard on the words that she didn't even notice, until the others went weird on her, that she'd made a mistake.

This is what she said: 'Lorde has more than twelve followers on social media.'

She was already onto the next sentence when she caught the low throaty sound of Hannah's snigger. It didn't last longer than a second or so and then Hannah went quiet. At that point, a freaky thing happened. All the sound was reabsorbed into the atmosphere. It was like God had sucked it up through a straw. While God held the silence, Chance made a noise like she was slurping the last frothy bit of milkshake from the bottom of the cardboard cup. Everyone but Michelle looked down towards the ground and no one looked at her. Hannah had her phone out and was pretending to be doing something important, like scrolling for the number of the emergency services.

Michelle held out her hand for the magazine and went, 'What?'

In her confusion, Chance still hadn't caught up with the exact nature of her crime but she knew that, whatever she'd done, it was bad. So she did what she should have done from the start, tilted her head to one side, relaxed her mouth and smiled like the make-up girls had once taught her to do, and said, 'Sorry.'

She didn't let go of the magazine but rushed her eyes over the page. Something, the cause of the problem, was there — but she didn't know what it was and so she repeated 'Sorry'. Then she tilted her head the other way, slightly, adding, 'What a doofus.'

The magazine began to shake in her hand and the words on the page jingled and jittered. It was like they were nervous and jumpy, too. It took ages before she found the problem, the missing word. She'd not only missed it when she'd been reading aloud but at least fifteen times afterwards, during her reread. It took her that long to read the sentence properly. The word jumped out: 'million'.

'Twelve million! I meant twelve million flowers.' Her body went rigid. 'Sorry, I mean twelve million *followers*.'

Everyone heard her get it right but it was too late. Michelle and the others had already turned their backs. That was how it happened. That was how she lost all her friends in just one sentence.

Her father had similar problems with words but, unlike Chance, didn't care. Books were for idiots who needed other people to tell them what to think or do. Like your mother, he'd add sometimes when Trudy was within earshot and the two of them were having a go at each other via Chance. Whenever her father started on her mother, Chance would glance across at Trudy to see if she was rubbing her wrist. That's what Trudy did when Bruce opened his mouth. In Trudy's eyes, Bruce was like a bad tattoo — something she'd got etched into her skin on impulse when she was young and now bitterly regretted.

There was an inevitability about the argument that would follow. Bruce would have a go at Trudy about books and Trudy would rub her wrist and go quiet for a while but then explode, and start reminding them of the story they all knew by heart. The story that didn't *ever* need repeating. The origins of Chance's real name. It was a tale that served no purpose other than to make Chance feel guilty for being born and for being the cause of her parents' marriage breakdown. This is how it went:

Her mother had grown up among nuns and books. Her father had grown up among cows and go-karts. Trudy loved 'literature', Bruce loved speed. They first met when Trudy did a story about kart racing for the community newsletter. They married when she became pregnant with their first son, seven months later. Trudy named both her sons after characters in books: Ishmael and Higgs. But her favourite character of all time was female. The woman she most admired in all of literature was Portia. From *The Merchant of Venice*. By Shakespeare. William Shakespeare.

Portia was the name Chance was meant to have. But Trudy never wrote it down on a piece of paper because she assumed that everyone, even an idiot like Bruce, had heard of Shakespeare. In fact, although Bruce knew who Shakespeare was, he had never heard of Portia. He had never seen her name on paper. After Trudy's emergency caesarean, they talked about names. Trudy stated her preference, and added her shaky signature to a form, but as she was still recovering in hospital she left the details of the registration to Bruce.

Bruce left the hospital feeling happier than he thought possible. Not only had his wife pulled through a difficult delivery and given him a beautiful, healthy baby girl, but the near-death experience had softened her sharp edges. As a result of her change in personality, she had gifted him with the most wonderful child's name — a name that held special meaning for him. He was overcome with the generosity of the gift and proudly entered the name 'Porsche' onto the registration form. The man behind the counter who took the form didn't question him or ask, 'Are you sure about that name? Do you need to check with your wife?' No, the man behind the counter looked at the name, looked at Bruce's smiling face, nodded his head in approval and said, 'Classic!'

'Porsche', written in ink, entered into the register of names. It was a name that caused her mother to wince whenever she heard it. Chance was the family name. In other words, it was Porsche's surname. Chance had no memory of her mother ever calling her by her given name, even though Trudy could have overlooked the way it was spelt and treated it as it sounded. Occasionally Bruce would pluck up the courage to use Porsche, but only if his mates were around, for back-up.

Among all Chance's family, acquaintances and teachers there was only one person who called her Porsche, and that was the school librarian, Ms Reed. At first Chance figured that Ms Reed hadn't cottoned onto the spelling of her name but was relying on how it sounded. But then again, she was a librarian called 'Reed' so perhaps that had something to do with her decision. Perhaps she found the whole name thing amusing. But if she did get a kick out of it, she never let on.

Once Michelle and the others dumped her over the magazine incident, Chance spent more time in the library. At first she sat by the window and looked out over the courtyard where the make-up girls hung out. Michelle wasn't one of the pretty girls. She sat on the benches around by the netball courts. Whenever a stray ball bounced her way she'd grab it and refuse to give it back. The netballers would plead with her but she'd laugh and say it was her turn, and then she'd slowly stand up, walk to the court, make like she was going to shoot a goal but would chuck the ball over the high wire fence, into the bushes beyond. Then she'd sit back down and watch, sideways as if not really watching, as the netballers walked the length of the four courts, through the gate, back around the perimeter fence to where the ball had gone over, and into the bushes and blackberry, where the ground was boggy, to find the missing ball.

No one, not even her so-called friends, liked Michelle. Yet somehow she managed to gather people into her circle. She was brilliant at figuring out a person's weakness and then, once she identified it, she would offer sympathy and support. That was how she'd lured Chance into her group. In the early days, whenever a teacher asked Chance to stand up and read in front of the class, Michelle would pipe up, 'No fair, it's my turn to read aloud, not hers,' and the teacher would instantly nod and give in. Michelle would take over and do the reading, much to Chance's relief.

Michelle didn't care how many mistakes she made when she read. It was always the fault of the author if a word got muddled up or came out wrong. Authors didn't know shit about anything. Shakespeare was a dick who couldn't spell properly. Mansfield was a lesbian who played with dolls. Poets were too lazy to write a proper book. Michelle didn't even need to waste her time reading books to know what was wrong with them. She just knew it, in-tu-itively.

The only time Michelle ever seemed unsure of herself was when a university scientist came to their Year 10 science class and, during a demonstration, told Michelle that she should be quiet and pay attention to the experiment as it would come in handy one day — when she needed to break out of jail. Chance had accidentally laughed and Michelle saw her. And that was it. The episode with the magazine took place the following day.

The nice thing about the library was that it was sunny. Light streamed in through the roof lights and glassed wall, and if you sat still long enough it was possible to fall asleep. Chance had heard Ms Reed complain about the damage the ultra-violet rays were doing to the books, but even she appeared to prefer the sunny end of the room. Chance was sitting on a beanbag, chewing on a strand of her long, messy ponytail, when she became aware of a shadow falling over her. At first she thought it was a cloud and so she kept her eyes shut for a minute, but then she heard a quiet cough, a clearing of the throat, and she looked up to see Ms Reed standing in front of her. Instead of looking angry, she was smiling.

'Good book?' she asked.

Chance nodded automatically.

'Can I see it, then?' asked Ms Reed.

Chance blushed. Usually she picked a book off the shelves as a prop before sitting down, but this time she'd forgotten. She'd been distracted by the sight of the make-up girls outside and had sat down without thinking. She expected Ms Reed to kick her out and began to get up, but the librarian simply handed her the top book from the stack she was holding, and told her to stay seated.

'Do you like reading?'

Chance didn't know how to answer. It was complicated. 'Sometimes.' She glanced at the book she'd been handed. A book about body adornment from the Pacific.

'Are you reading anything at the moment?'

Chance nodded.

'What are you reading?'

'I've started on *Lolita*.'

Ms Reed's eyes widened. '*Lolita*?'

Sensing she'd said something wrong, Chance added, 'I've done *The Plague*.'

'Oh, wow.'

Chance felt more and more uncomfortable. She didn't want to answer any more questions about books or be forced to talk about the long reading list her mother set her each term. Ms Reed didn't seem in any hurry to get on with her work, however.

'That must keep you busy.'

Chance nodded. She felt miserable, like the idiot she was. To her immense relief, Ms Reed fell quiet and turned her attention to the window, and the make-up girls outside. Three girls, all with high ponytails, huddled around a fourth, watching as she carefully applied lipstick, a small compact held in her hand.

'Ruth Handler,' murmured the librarian.

Chance started at the sound. She didn't recognise those particular make-up girls. They kept to themselves, pretty much.

'I don't know their names,' she said out loud. 'They're not in any of my classes.'

For a second Ms Reed looked confused. 'What? Oh no, not them. Just someone I was reading about the other day.' She paused, smiled at Chance, and said, 'Doesn't matter. It's nothing. Barbie dolls ... their creator, Ruth Handler.'

Chance blushed for a second time. So now she'd made a fool of herself twice over. Once with the books, once with the name Ruth Handler.

'It's nothing,' Ms Reed repeated. 'I've been making a list of women for a personal project of mine and her name came up . . .' She was interrupted by the sound of the bell. 'You'd best get off to class,' she said, holding out her hand for the book.

————

At 3.30 Chance caught the school bus home. The direction she travelled was opposite to that taken by Michelle and almost every other girl in her class. For as long as she could remember, she'd never had an after-school visit with her classmates. Her chores always got in the way. As soon as she got home, she would grab a snack and then either prepare dinner or go and help her parents with the goats.

Her day-to-day routine was so disconnected from that of the other Year 10 girls that she didn't really understand where she was meant to fit in. They all walked to school in groups, or were dropped off by their parents, and on Fridays they made plans to go into town together, or to hang out and have sleepovers at one another's houses. While they were laughing over Instagram shots and sharing pizza, she was in a goat shed, cleaning out and putting down fresh sawdust for the week ahead. They would be listening to Taylor Swift while she was trying to block out the sound of four hundred bleating goats. But, in a way, it wasn't only the lives and experiences of her friends that made her feel excluded. Her mother's books had exactly the same effect. For almost a year her mother had been giving her novels to read, and not one of them, as far as she could remember, mentioned farming, milking or shovelling poo. Her mother's books touched on every type of life except their own.

When she thought about it, only her father and brothers seemed to have a life that made sense. Ishmael and Higgs had enough energy to stay up half the night, but they were older than her, and busy doing their own thing — chasing girls, working and fixing supermarket trolleys on the side, in an attempt to earn extra 'pocket money' to fund their go-kart obsession. Go-karts were their passion. Personally, she couldn't understand why anyone would develop a thing for go-karts. But at least they had one — a 'thing'. A 'thing' would be good.

OUT OF THE BLUE, around ten months before her conversation about *Lolita* with Ms Reed, Chance received a late Christmas present from her great-aunt Betty, a woman she could not remember ever having met. Inside the parcel was a Little Golden Book, *The Poky Little Puppy*. Chance's immediate reaction was one of embarrassment, quickly followed by dread as she imagined her mother's caustic reaction.

Already, in the weeks leading up to that Christmas, Trudy had raised the idea of a mother–daughter book discussion scheme and begun compiling an elaborate reading list. The intensity with which her mother spoke about books frightened Chance. Trudy didn't seem to read books so much as suck the words off the page. For her, reading was a sport, one that required all the skill and concentration of a racing driver. A good reader was obligated to approach a text with the same energy that a driver negotiated a track. Anticipate, focus, attack — these were all key words used by Trudy during the rundown to the proposed long-term programme. 'You have to work at being a reader. It's like everything else in life — that's how you find your reward.'

When permitted to read alone, Chance preferred to be lulled by stories. A good book for her was one where she could drift off and enter another world. Part of her would remain in the room where she was reading; the other half would float above. She could look down on herself reading and look far away, at the same time. She never felt an urge to guess what would happen next in the story; she wanted to discover it. But in her mother's eyes reading for pleasure, or escape, was a sign of a weak reader.

The very first novel, chosen by Trudy, was *The Great Gatsby*. When Chance laid eyes on the book, she breathed a sigh of relief. At least it was short. But her relief soon turned to anxiety.

'This is one of the greatest books of the twentieth century,' said Trudy. 'It's not as good as *Tender Is the Night*. That's one of the greatest books of all time.' She paused, as if daring Chance to contradict her, but, hearing nothing, continued. 'I first discovered this book when I was nine or ten so it's been a part of my life for a very long time.'

Chance flicked through the pages as her mother spoke. Her copy came from the city library, it was a hardback and had the words 'Fiction STACK' attached to its spine. Trudy's copy was also from the library, but was newer, a paperback with a nice picture of a man and a woman on the cover.

'Robert Redford,' said Trudy. 'Played Gatsby in the movie. Before your time.' She gave Chance a tight squeeze. 'I used to pester my mother to do something like this, when I was your age. I hope you realise I'm giving you a gift, one I never had.'

Chance was taken aback by the remark. She couldn't remember Trudy ever bringing her mother into the conversation. Long ago, before Chance was born, Trudy had cut off all contact with her parents, and Chance had never met either one of them. They were a mystery to her, as was Trudy's older brother, Vincent — and Great-Aunt Betty.

Chance applied herself to reading *The Great Gatsby*. Rather than sitting on her bed or on the comfy couch, she sat at the table — where her mother could see her — and did everything within her power to concentrate. She didn't find the book hard to follow; she liked it. But enjoying the book wasn't enough. She knew her mother was expecting something more than a quick thumbs-up. As if discussing the book wasn't enough, Trudy also suggested they select their favourite passages to read aloud. Chance liked the whole novel and couldn't identify any bits that stood out above the others, but she had an inkling that wasn't the point of the exercise anyway. Her mother wasn't interested in her opinion or choices of text. Trudy merely wanted an opportunity to challenge the worthiness and intelligence of her selection. So, without wanting to, Chance had entered a competition — one that her mother was determined to win. As a result, Chance found herself spending less time reading the book than trying to figure out what she needed to do to win her mother's approval. Sometimes, her thoughts became so stuck trying to think up answers to questions her mother *might* ask that she gave up reading altogether. She'd turn to *The Poky Little Puppy* and look at the pictures, sometimes reading the words but often making up her own story as she flicked from one page to the next.

Less than two weeks after *The Poky Little Puppy* turned up, another parcel arrived in the post. This time the package was addressed to Ishmael, and inside was a copy of a hardcover book: *The Dangerous Book for Boys*. Ishmael took one look at the book and cast it aside. A short while later, he returned to check if it had an exchange card but, seeing it didn't, dumped it in front of Chance and sauntered off. From where she sat, Chance could hear him in the kitchen, banging the cupboards and laughing with her father and Higgs, joking that it would be Higgs's turn next for one of the crazy old girl's gifts. 'You've always wanted a bib and rattle, eh? Or maybe you'll get lucky and get a trike.'

In spite of expectations, Higgs didn't receive anything. He didn't care, but was kind of curious about why he had missed out.

'I bet she's forgotten you exist,' said Trudy. 'It's not like we've kept in touch and she is over ninety. I don't think she's met you or Chance, just Ishmael.'

'Why's she sending us presents all of a sudden?' asked Chance.

'No idea. Ask Bruce. She's his relative, not mine.'

No one bothered asking Bruce, however. *The Poky Little Puppy* was given away to the local op shop and *The Dangerous*

Book for Boys joined the pile of humorous volumes stacked in a basket half-filled with toilet rolls inside the laundry-room toilet. Even *The Great Gatsby*, once read, discussed and *attacked*, was returned to the library — albeit after overdue notices — only to be replaced by a long list of novels by Nobel Prize-winning authors and modern masters. The last of these books, *The Plague*, was memorable for the description of the rats on page nine and Trudy's insistence that Chance read three of the five parts out loud.

And now Chance was stuck on *Lolita*. She was up to page sixty-eight and couldn't bring herself to keep going. Earlier in the day, she'd approached one of the smart girls from her English class, a girl whose mother taught at university, and even she rolled her eyes at the mention of the book. 'Just Google it,' she advised. 'There's a lot of rubbish been written about its perverse brilliance and complex morality, and all you have to do is agree a hundred per cent or argue the complete opposite, and call it sexist bullshit. Either way, you'll be right.'

'But what do you think of it?' pressed Chance.

'Depends who I'm talking to,' said the girl, and wandered off.

Chance had wanted to call after her, 'But what if you were talking to my mother?', but she knew she was wasting her time. In all likelihood, Trudy would get Chance to talk first and then do her best to catch her out. There was no way of knowing, until then, which side Trudy was on.

The best thing she could do, thought Chance, was to 'forget' the novel on the school bus. That would at least buy her some time as it would take a couple of days to retrieve the book from the lost and found, if there even was such a thing. If the book accidentally slipped under a seat, it might never be found and then maybe, maybe, she wouldn't have to read it.

Chance sat in the back of the bus on the way home, and

when she was sure no one was looking stuffed the paperback into the space between the seat and the wall panel. Her joy at getting rid of the book was soon overtaken by nerves and the only way she could control them was by getting off the bus as soon as she could, three stops short of her gate.

She stood on the road, watching the curl of dust swirl up into the sky, as the bus pulled away. For the briefest moment, she thought about raising her hand and waving, pretending to call back the driver, but instead she looked up and down the road, plotting her next move and the quickest way home. A kingfisher perched on the powerline caught her attention, and its presence struck her as a good omen. Then, hoisting on her backpack, she set off across the paddock, walking in a straight line towards the distant fence and the boundary of the wetland sanctuary beyond.

The pasture was a vivid green, dotted here and there with small clusters of clover and dandelions. The ground beneath her feet gave a little in places, cushioning her steps as she drew closer to the sanctuary. She figured it would take almost an hour to get home, and she worried what her parents would say if she was late to help with the animals. It wasn't that they depended on her; it was more that she wanted to pull her weight, and give them no reason for thinking she was unreliable.

Her brothers had got away with a lot more. They both had jobs outside the home: one as a security guard at the local bank, the other at a central city supermarket. In the past, they had been able to cover for each other, often taking turns to work in the shed so that the other one could play sport or practise down at the track. The thing about karting, she often heard her father explain and her brothers repeat, as if a mantra, 'is that it takes over your life. It defines you. Gives you a sense of identity. Like being an All Black.'

'Or a drug addict,' said Trudy.

Chance didn't have the luxury of having somewhere else to go. She wasn't even sure if she had an identity. Her father had probably come closest to defining her when he made the quip that she wasn't much of a team player. He didn't bother saying what she was, but had left it open-ended, as if Chance would be able to fill in the gap. But, in fact, Chance could only add to the list of things she wasn't: a team player, a make-up girl, a brain-box, a bully, a go-kart enthusiast or a willing member of her mother's reading group. Once these things were chipped away, she didn't know what was left.

She crossed the fence and edged her way past a double line of trees planted inside old tyres and forty-four-gallon drums. The trees were stunted, burnt by the wind, but still alive. In the distance she could see a formed four-wheel-drive track, and so she started off towards it, hoping she wouldn't get bogged down in the swamp. With every step she noticed the way the thin strands of water, lacing between the clumps of flax, caught the afternoon sunlight and flickered silver before retreating into blackness. She liked the smell of the boggy earth and the fresh herbal scent of the flax. They were fragrances that struck her as vegetal and healthy, unlike the smell of stale milk, molasses and silage that hung over her parents, always present on their skin as if they were both slowly composting. She'd been conscious of the smell of her own body for as long as she could remember. From an early age she spent part of her pocket money on floral deodorants and powder-scented body sprays, anything to cover the smell of goats. Once, during food technology, her group had been set the task of making cheese and throughout the period, Chance had lived in fear that someone would turn on her and say, 'It smells disgusting. Like you.'

A water-filled channel, about a metre and a half wide,

blocked her way. The bank either side of the channel was sloping and made of clay. The far bank was higher than the ground on which she stood, and dotted with various tall bushes and some cabbage trees. The trench extended as far as she could see. The distance would be a stretch but she didn't feel like wasting time searching for a better spot to cross. She hurled her bag across the ditch, hoping it wouldn't roll back into the water. Then, checking the landing spot for any rocks, she took a run up and flung herself across the divide. Her first foot hit the bank with a thud, and for a split second she was okay, but then she started to lose her balance, her body tilting backwards. Instinctively she shifted her weight, but her back foot slipped on the clay and splashed into the water. She grabbed for a tuft of grass on the bank and managed to stop herself from falling further into the trench.

'Nice save!'

The ground was still sliding beneath her and she couldn't look in the direction of the voice, but a moment later she felt a hand grab her by the shoulder and yank her onto her feet.

'Good work,' said the woman. 'I thought you weren't going to make it. Shows how much I know!'

She was smiling, her entire face crinkled with lines and freckles. 'I guess you didn't want to use the foot-crossing, eh?'

Chance's eyes were fixed on her shoe, the black leather all but invisible beneath a film of yellowish clay and mud, while her sock looked as if someone had squirted runny baby poo on it.

'I haven't been this way before,' she mumbled. 'I'm trying to get home.'

She began wiping the side of her shoe on a patch of grass, angling her ankle first one way then the other. The mud and clay smeared, but remained fixed to the leather.

'It'll wash off,' said the woman. 'It's just dirt.'

She was quietly spoken and had a strange, lilting accent. It was difficult to distinguish its origins as it sounded like a mixture of things. New Zealand? British, maybe? American? She was short and lean, but strong-looking, like a retired gymnast or dancer. Her hair was grey, tied in loose plaits that hung to her shoulders. Partially obscured beneath her jacket, she wore a yellow T-shirt with what looked like 'STORM' printed across it. Around her wrists were coloured strings and on her right wrist was a bright turquoise watch. Slung across her back was a faded purple canvas pack.

'You okay?'

Chance nodded. She had stood up and got her bag and was already looking at the land around her, mapping the next stage of the walk.

'Okay then. I'll get back to my traps.'

The woman grinned, and strode away, waving her hand in a slow lasso motion above her head as she disappeared into a stand of cabbage trees and toetoe.

Chance remained where she was, waiting to see if the woman would reappear. When, after several minutes, there was no sign of her, Chance set off in the direction of home but, to her dismay, soon found her way blocked by another waterway, this one too wide to jump. She didn't know which way to turn. One way seemed to lead back towards the road from which she had come, while the other took her further away from home, towards the shooting range. Suddenly tired and thirsty, she felt annoyed with her mother. If she hadn't been forced to read stupid books like *Lolita*, she wouldn't be in this situation. She'd already be in the goat shed, earning the pocket money her parents paid her each week.

For weeks she'd been saving for a sewing machine,

researching online until she narrowed down her selection to a Bernina, an older model but one that still reached $500 on the second-hand trading site. Once she had the machine she would start making stuff. She hadn't quite worked out what stuff but she had an idea she could source second-hand fabrics and then take orders from the girls at school for bags and accessories, whatever they wanted. She planned to take a course at night school and learn the basic skills. If her mother had allowed her, she would have done fabric technology at school, but it had been out of the question. Trudy insisted that sewing was for non-academic kids and that Chance wasn't to waste her time in a class full of dummies.

'But *you* did sewing,' Chance had argued.

'Not by choice,' snapped Trudy. 'I was forced into it by a teacher who couldn't figure out how to fit me into the timetable. We weren't meant to do a mixture of languages and technical. It had to be one or the other.'

'Why didn't you complain?'

Trudy pulled a face that seemed to suggest Chance was being stupid. 'Because it wouldn't have done any good.'

'Why not?'

'Because no one gave a shit, that's why not.'

'But—'

'But nothing.'

There was a rage in Trudy that often took Chance's breath away.

'It's nothing to do with you,' Trudy said.

Chance spent hours thinking about her mother's behaviour, but could never figure it out. It was so random. It was as if Trudy was blindfolded and hurling rocks into the air. But in that case, the rocks ought to represent an attempt at self-defence, rather than attack. And as far as Chance could tell, no one was trying to hurt Trudy. That's why her anger didn't make sense.

'You still here?'

Startled, Chance looked up. It was the woman again.

'I thought you were on your way home?'

Chance nodded.

'Looks like you might be trapped.' The woman smiled, registered Chance's non-comprehension and motioned towards the ditch. 'Want to tell me where you're headed and I'll point you in the right direction.'

'It's okay,' said Chance. 'I can manage.'

'Hungry?' asked the woman, reaching into her bag.

Chance shook her head, no.

'Thirsty?'

Chance took the bottle the woman held out to her. The water had a strange taste but she drank it anyway, and thanked her.

'Keep it if you want. I've been carrying it around for months. Don't know why.'

Without meaning to, Chance coughed and felt the water rise up in her throat and wash against her tongue.

'Yeah, found the bottle in the car park,' the woman continued. 'People leave all sorts of stuff behind. Mostly trash, but not always.' She ran her hand over her face, then rubbed her forehead. 'Sure you're not hungry? I've got half a sandwich here, somewhere.'

The woman rummaged through her bag, pulling out a jar of peanut butter and then a carton of eggs. 'That's not for you,' she mumbled, shoving the peanut butter back. 'That's for Mister Rat. Can't get enough of it. Why's that, do you think?'

Chance shrugged, 'Don't know.'

'What's your name, anyway? Mine's Riva.'

Chance hesitated before answering. She always had a

problem with the question of her name. Should she reply 'Porsche' and risk feeling uncomfortable when it was used, or say 'Chance' and spend minutes explaining why she had an unusual name. At times like this she wished she had a third option, or no name at all.

'Chance.'

'Great. If you come with me, Chance, I'll show you where to cross. Sound good to you?'

For someone so old, Riva moved across the ground with amazing speed. There was a lightness to her step, and at times Chance found herself having to trot to keep up.

'You see those poplars,' called Riva. 'That's where we're headed.'

It took a further five minutes for Chance to reach the gate by the trees and when she arrived Riva was already kneeling on the ground, tugging a dead possum from a Timms trap. 'I have to check them every day,' she said as she stuffed the creature into a plastic sack. 'Can you give me a hand?'

'What with?'

'There's a couple of apples in my backpack, and a small container of flour. And a knife.'

Chance opened the bag and pushed her hand inside. Something soft in what felt like a plastic bag give way under her grasp and she recoiled. 'There's something in here!'

'A rat?' asked Riva.

'I don't know!' replied Chance.

'Well, it's either a rat or a stoat. Don't worry, it won't bite.'

'Are they dead?'

'Yep.'

Reluctantly, Chance returned her hand to the backpack, easing her fingers past the creature in plastic and down further into the depths of the bag. With the tips of her fingers she felt

128

something round and hard and withdrew her hand. A shiny red apple filled her palm.

'Knife?' asked Riva.

Chance nodded and went back into the bag, this time looking inside as she hunted down the knife and container.

'You want to know something interesting about poplars?' asked Riva.

Chance looked up at the tree that towered above them. Its leaves were a yellow-green, and they flickered in the late afternoon breeze.

'In the old days they used to plant them by fords in rivers. Travellers could see them from miles away and know where to cross.'

Riva cut the apple into chunks as she spoke. She reset the trap with one piece, and then offered a second piece to Chance before taking a bite from the third. 'That makes good sense, don't you think?'

Chance picked out a pip from her apple and bit into the flesh. The skin was firm against her teeth and a small sliver caught in the back of her throat. She coughed, choked and then swallowed.

'You okay?'

Chance nodded. At that moment she felt dumb for not even being able to bite into an apple properly.

'There's the foot-crossing,' said Riva, pointing to a narrow plank. 'You'll always know where to find it now.'

Chance watched as Riva replaced the trap in a gap between low branches, then took a handful of flour and sprinkled it around the trap and on the trunk and the ground.

'Bit of flour, hint of cinnamon, nice hunk of apple.' She clapped her hands together and a small puff of flour filled the air. 'Do you like baking, Chance?'

Chance shook her head. 'No, not really. But I cook dinner at home most nights.'

'What's your specialty?'

'Nothing really. Just whatever Mum wants me to cook.'

'Mine's sandwiches,' said Riva.

A phone buzzed in Chance's bag. The ringtone reminded her of a blowfly caught in a web. It made the phone sound impatient and angry, exactly like her mother. The phone rang on, but Chance made no move to answer. She didn't know how she was going to explain being so late.

'Is that your mum?'

'Probably. Trudy — she doesn't like me calling her Mum.'

Riva was already packing her bag, but paused, and watched Chance who seemed rooted to the spot.

'Do you want me to answer for you?'

'No thanks, it's okay.'

'I could explain you're with me.'

A nervous smile touched Chance's face. The phone fell silent.

'Listen, I've pretty much finished here now. Why don't you come with me and I'll drop you home?'

They walked in silence until they came to a wide four-wheel-drive track and then turned in the direction of the group of buildings Chance passed every day during her school commute. At the first building, a small shed, Riva stopped and unlocked the door, dropping her pack inside.

'I'll come back and deal with the bodies after I get you home. Unless you want to take them?'

'What?'

'You might want the skins? I don't know. I had a grandfather who made a jacket out of moleskins once. He used to wear it when he went skating, back in Norway. I saw photos of him. He looked like that guy in that painting . . .'

'What painting?'

'Can't remember its name. Just remember that it's of a man wearing a hat and dressed in black, skating. My mother had a print of it in her room. A postcard she picked up during a trip to England.'

Riva paused, rummaged in the top pocket of her pack and brought out a wallet and a set of car keys. 'You could make a muff.'

'What's that?' asked Chance.

Riva laughed. 'We're not doing too well here, are we? Come on.'

A station wagon was parked beside the largest of the buildings. Its front door panel was a rusty orange while the rest of the car was white. Inside, taking up all the free space in the passenger seat, the back seat and the boot area, were a number of bulging potato sacks and cardboard boxes filled with stacks of empty green plastic seedling containers and tattered paperbacks. As the passenger door swung open, a wave of heat and a strong smell of manure greeted Chance.

'Jump in. Let's get you home.'

Chance looked at the seat and attempted to ease herself in, rearranging a carton of books to make room for herself.

'What's with all the books?' she asked.

'Mulch,' said Riva. 'What goes around, comes around.'

Chance lifted the top book from the pile. It was missing a cover and the paper was yellowed; one corner was slightly chewed.

'What do you mean?'

'It's obvious, isn't it? Books come from trees so it's only proper that they should give something back.'

Chance still looked puzzled.

'I shred them up and place them around the seedlings and

then weigh them down with bark chips and poo so I don't get scraps of paper flying around the place.'

'But they're books,' protested Chance.

'So what? It's all part of the life cycle.'

For a second Chance imagined how her mother would respond to such an end for her own library of sacred texts. Although she shouldn't, Chance smiled.

'And the smell?'

'Horse poo. The Stills let me collect it.'

'They're my neighbours.'

'This side, or the far side?' asked Riva.

'Far side. We're about a kilometre further on from them.'

'Oh, so you're *a* Chance? Sorry, I didn't make the connection.'

Chance felt her skin redden. She was such an idiot for not giving her proper name. 'That's okay. Everyone calls me Chance, but my real first name is Porsche. Like the car.'

Chance lowered her gaze and picked up another book from the box on her knee, pretending to be engrossed in its blurb, which she realised was in Spanish.

'That's so crazy,' said Riva, not turning her head from the road. 'That's really amazing.'

Startled by Riva's reaction, Chance looked up. 'I know, sorry. It was meant to be Portia, like Shakespeare.'

'No, I mean that's so amazing. That pair of hawks over there. Look. Oh, wow, look at that!'

Chance swung around to see what Riva was pointing at.

'The male's got a chick or a mouse. See that? And he's trying to pass it to his mate. See, look!'

They watched the hawks swoop and flutter in front of them, the smaller male flying above the female. With her claws extended, the female came in close, her wings almost colliding with the male's as both birds performed an aerial twist. Suddenly the prey dropped from the male and was almost instantly caught by the female. She gave a beat of her wings and flew away.

'That's something else.' Riva laughed with delight. 'What would you call it? Flight-dancing? An in-flight meal! Now, she'll take the prey back to the nest and feed her chicks. What's the chance of seeing that, eh? That's something to make you glad to be alive.'

Chance grinned. She was surprised by how exhilarated she felt. In the moment when the birds joined and parted, she found herself wanting to cheer. It was exactly like Riva said, seeing those birds lifted some weight from her own mind and made her glad to be alive.

THE MEMORY OF MEETING RIVA and watching the flight-dancing hawks stayed with Chance throughout dinner, and emboldened her. By the end of the meal, she had worked herself into such a state she could no longer maintain her silence. She had to challenge Trudy. She had to.

'You know what?' she said as she loaded the dishwasher. 'I'm really sick of your stupid books. In fact I'm glad I lost *Lolita*. Who wants to read about some dirt-bag raping a ten-year-old, anyway.'

'She's not ten. You'd know that if you actually read the book.'

'That's what I'm saying. I don't want to read the book. I'm not interested in that book. All that stuff about nymphs and nymphets and Lolita and Lo-Lee-Ta. He makes up all those ridiculous new names for her even though there's nothing wrong with Dolores. Like Dolores isn't a proper name for a girl. And all that Dolly crap. If he's so hung up on names, why doesn't he change his own? Humbert Humbert. I mean, really? It sounds like the name of a broken-down car full of pervs patrolling primary schools. He's a dick!'

'You haven't even read it,' Trudy returned. 'You're taking the easy way out, jumping to conclusions, getting your information off websites. Pre-judging . . .'

'That's not true! You don't know anything about what I think. Just because I happen to disagree with you over something . . . And anyway, you're only reading it because it's on some "best book" list and you want to feel superior to everyone else.' She glared at her mother, and took a deep breath. 'From now on I'm only reading books that I want to read.'

Her heart was pounding, but she no longer cared. Her mother had been on her case from the moment she got in: first about being late to help in the sheds, then about failing to get dinner on, and lastly about the lost book and the fact that she hadn't finished it. Trudy went on and on, and didn't once have a go at either Ishmael or Higgs for missing milking because they were out helping the go-kart club president redesign the web page. They probably hadn't even helped him. More likely, they'd been watching YouTube clips and arguing about which was better — modern or vintage machines. Something totally crucial for the future of civilisation.

'Why don't you ever get the boys to read? Has Ishmael even looked at *Moby Dick*? Does Higgs know which book his name comes from? I bet he doesn't.'

Trudy lowered the pan she was holding and placed it gently on the bench. 'Because,' she said, her voice slow and steady, 'I was hoping that reading would be our special thing.

I imagined it would be something enjoyable that would bring us closer.'

'Well, that worked well, didn't it?'

Trudy lowered her eyes. 'I was under the misapprehension that we would both get something out of it.'

Chance felt the ground shift a fraction beneath her. Her mother was doing that thing she always did, twisting everything around so that it always seemed like Chance was the one in the wrong.

'Our house,' Trudy continued, 'is filled with boys and men, cars and engines, oil and grease and all I was trying—'

'Don't,' said Chance. 'Stop it.'

'Books have always been special—'

'I asked you to stop. Please. Don't do that guilt-trippy stuff on me any more. It's not fair. It's not my fault I don't like your books. If you want it to be fun, why don't you let me choose what we read? And why do you always insist I read bits aloud and then criticise the way I speak? You're always sniggering when I mispronounce words, and you spend heaps of time questioning me so you can tell me I'm wrong, and then correct me. It's not fun. It's never fun. It stresses me out and makes me feel stupid and I hate it.'

Chance took a deep breath and exhaled slowly. She was saying what she wanted to say for once, but it wouldn't help. Even though what she said was the truth, she was the one who would wind up feeling bad. She was already aware of the horrible, anxious feeling working its way through her body, taking hold of her. Without looking, she knew her hands were trembling. Without looking, she knew her mother would also be trembling — but for a different reason: in her mother's case it would be anger.

'You know what? I met someone today who uses books for

mulch. To make trees grow. What do you think of that?'

Trudy shook her head in exasperation. 'I don't know, Chance. You tell me. Someone in the world doesn't value literature as much as me?'

'No! Someone in the world doesn't think every stupid book is a sacred object. They're paper, Mum. Paper!'

She stood facing Trudy, their bodies almost touching. For a second they held each other's gaze, and then Chance felt herself slump. It was too hard. Nothing would change. Her mother would continue to fight and then stop talking altogether. After two or three days things would slowly go back to what they were. Chance would give in, read another book from her mother's list, and the feeling of being cheated would grow stronger and stronger until one day, in a few months' time, they'd end up in the kitchen, having exactly the same argument as this one, one that would leave her feeling sick and upset. And that was how their relationship would go on and on and on, becoming heavier and heavier until Chance gave in or left home.

Chance clasped her hands together, and for a moment the trembling stopped. She glanced at Trudy, tried to smile and then caught her mother's gaze and lowered her eyes. Her jaw began to clench and instinctively she rubbed the palm of her hand against her cheek, as if trying to soothe away toothache.

'You do what you want,' said Trudy. 'I can't be bothered. I don't care any more.'

Chance wished she could escape from her mother, but the only room in the house with a lock on the door was the old laundry toilet. It was generally understood that this room was her father's. In fact, Higgs had dubbed it 'the computer room' on account of their father's habit of locking himself in and spending upwards of thirty minutes scrolling through various news, music and social sites whenever he needed time to himself. In general, Trudy left him alone, but there were occasions when his vanishing act would irritate her and she would hammer on the door and yell at him to hurry up. It was more difficult for Chance. If she went into the toilet her mother would probably stand outside the door and yell at her to come out. Trudy rarely left Chance alone after an argument. She tended to come after her, hunt her down and plant herself in whatever room Chance was sitting in. Trudy was the kind of person who couldn't let a subject drop. Even though she said, 'I can't be bothered,' she didn't mean it. It was inevitable that something would enter her head that did bother her and, more than likely, the entire family would be dragged in.

Chance's defiance over the books would take on a new life, and taint the rest of the night. First, Trudy would rage over the collection of disgusting dirty mugs and plates littered around Ishmael's room. Then, she would notice that Higgs's muddy boots had been left in the hall rather than outside on the doorstep, and she'd hoist them up by their laces and throw them into the garden. Bruce's towel that had been on the bathroom floor for the past hour would get snatched up and tossed at him while he relaxed on the couch. Instead of hitting Bruce, the towel would catch his beer, toppling the bottle and contents onto the carpet. Trudy would curse and Bruce would eventually snap and warn her to settle down. She would tell him not to talk to her like she was some old cow kicking out in the milking shed. He would tell her she was overreacting and then, as the conversation grew more and more heated, accuse her of being insane. At the mention of the word 'insane', Trudy would laugh and bring up the name Porsche, and accuse Bruce of being the crazy one. Bruce would tell her to 'give it a rest' and leave the room. Alone in the room, Trudy would continue talking as she wiped up the spilt beer. Raising her voice, she'd call out, 'I don't know why I have to clean up after you lot! But no one else cares about the carpet!' The room would begin to smell damp and malty and that would make her even more angry.

The rest of the night would play out in a series of sound effects: the slamming of the cleaning bucket in the laundry tub. The bang of the front door as Ishmael followed his dad outside. The wrenching of the dishwasher door as Trudy tried to jam Ishmael's dishes into the rack even though the machine was already running. The scuff and thud of Higgs's feet as he headed down the hall, grabbed his brother's boots and went outside to retrieve his own. The rev of an engine as Bruce and Ishmael got to work on one of the karts. The low mutter of stunted accusations and bitter rage once Trudy realised no one was listening to her.

All this is going to happen tonight, thought Chance, because I don't want to read one of her books.

She sat on the wooden toilet lid, looking at a smudge of mould above the door, a stain that looked like soot and had been there for as long as she could remember, because nobody cleaned it away. The whole room was dismal. The yellowish and grimy light bulb, its glow barely reaching the floor. The old wallpaper covered in brown and orange flowers that could be dahlias, marigolds or sunflowers, it was impossible to tell. The lino that didn't quite reach the edges of the skirting board and curled up like old cardboard around the base of the toilet. The ochre-enamelled door, still with the hole where the handle used to be, but now with a crooked hook and eye lock to keep it from swinging open. The dusty wicker basket that had once been brand-new and brimming with toys but now held karting magazines, books and a scattering of toilet rolls. Sheets had been torn from all the rolls in the basket, so they were all half or quarter full, or empty save for the last glued tatter. Not one of them had neatly perforated edges. Frayed and feathered thumb-sized fragments of tissue littered the floor by her feet. An aerosol tin lay on its side; its cap rested in the far corner of the room, the plastic nozzle nowhere to be seen.

The magazines and books, most of them presents from previous birthdays and Christmases, now looked like they'd been scavenged from a free bin outside the local op shop. Opening one at random, Chance scanned the page, reading a list of Latin phrases that were supposedly relevant to boys. She kept leafing through the book and then hesitated, holding her breath, when she thought she heard her mother approach from down the hall. She waited, half expecting to see the flicker of an eye pressed against the hole in the door, but nothing happened so she went back to the book, read a page about skinning and tanning a rabbit, glanced at the diagrams and then closed the volume, letting it rest across her knees, its bulk warming her thighs.

She thought about what to do next and decided to go back to the kitchen, find her mother and apologise. Until she did this the members of her family would remain divided and scattered in their isolated territories. She had to apologise, if only to make it possible for everyone to return to their rooms and get back to living normally, like a family. She would do what she had seen Michelle insist that the protesting netballers do whenever the bully chucked their ball away. She would say sorry. She would suck it up.

'HOW ARE YOU GETTING ON with your reading?'

The voice appeared out of nowhere and Chance jerked, her decoy book slipping from her knee and onto the floor. She looked up and saw the librarian standing over her, a stack of books and magazines tilting in her hands.

'Good, thanks.'

'I was thinking about you, earlier,' said Ms Reed.

'Oh? Sorry.'

Ms Reed laughed and straightened the pile of books, clutching the magazines closer to her body. Nevertheless one slid off the top, and landed on the floor next to Chance's beanbag. Chance picked it up and handed it back.

Ms Reed thanked her, then crouched down on one knee and placed the magazines on the carpet. An image of a possum on a branch covered with red flowers filled the entire cover of the latest issue of *Forest and Bird*.

'Yeah, so getting back to what I was thinking, I was wondering if you'd like help locating something more enjoyable than *Lolita*. That is, if you'd like?'

Chance didn't know how to respond. It wasn't that she wasn't touched by Ms Reed's offer, but she knew the whole exercise would be pointless, and a waste of the librarian's time. Her mother would kick up a huge fuss if anyone tried to take over the book selection process. Choosing the books was almost as important to Trudy as reading them.

'My mum likes to choose the books. She's kind of fussy,' Chance apologised.

Ms Reed nodded. 'Oh well, just a thought.'

Chance felt annoyed with herself. Now it would seem like she didn't appreciate the help, when the opposite was true.

'Um, sorry,' she said.

She watched Ms Reed walk away, then pushed herself

up from her beanbag and went to the shelves. She intended to hide until she could slip out of the library unseen but, to her embarrassment, Ms Reed appeared at the end of the row, slipping books back onto the shelves as she worked her way towards Chance.

'The animal section. Do you like books about animals?' She came closer and asked, 'What are you after?'

'Nothing,' answered Chance. Without looking, she picked up a book from the shelf closest to her and held it up. 'Found it. Yay, this is exactly what I wanted.'

Ms Reed stopped what she was doing and came closer. 'What have you got?' Without waiting for Chance, she gently lifted the cover of the book so she could read its title. 'Wow, interesting. Are you interested in taxidermy?'

For the first time, Chance took a look at the book in her hands, and frowned. 'Yes. It's what I do . . . stuffing animals, and that.'

'Interesting.' Ms Reed flicked through the pages, nodding as she did so. 'Have you been doing it for long, then?'

It took a second for Chance to answer. 'No, not really. It's my latest hobby. I like making things with my hands.' Inwardly she groaned. What else would she make things with, her feet?

Ms Reed's lips quivered. 'That's great. Good to hear. Are you working on anything at the moment?'

Chance took a deep breath and skimmed the book. A picture of a skunk caught her eye. Its front paw was lifted off the ground and its tail was curled and bristling.

'No, nothing really. Just little things. Cute girl trinkets . . . nothing too big or wild. No lions.' She attempted to laugh but felt stupid, so added, 'I find everything I need around the farm.'

How could she say such a dumb thing? What cute little

things? Like she walked around the farm and happened across dead mice that she felt compelled to stuff. God, she must sound mental.

'Cool,' said Ms Reed. 'I'd love to see what you've done. Bring one of your trinkets in and show me. It must be fascinating.'

'Mmm.'

'Fantastic. I've always been intrigued by the bird displays at the museum. I always wonder how they manage to get the various body parts in the right place. It must require a lot of measuring to get the eyes in the right place. So, don't forget to bring something in. I'd love to see what you've made.'

'Sure,' replied Chance. 'It might take a week or two . . .'

'No hurry,' said Ms Reed. 'Just whenever you're ready.'

WTF, thought Chance as she rode home. She looked around the school bus, searching the faces of her schoolmates, wondering which, if any, of them might have stuffed an animal before. Jasmine, a final-year girl, sat across the aisle, a gigantic pair of headphones perched on her head; she was looking straight ahead, her lips forming a wordless accompaniment to whatever she was playing. Chance had never talked to Jasmine before. She was known throughout the school by her nickname: General Jasmine. Chance wasn't certain why she went by the name but supposed it was on account of her being lesbian and a spokesperson for the school's LGBT group. She had once overheard Jack, a boy in her class, refer to Jasmine as a sergeant major in the lesbian army, but on another occasion he called her a babe, which kind of contradicted the other remark.

A couple of seats ahead of Jasmine were the Bergen brothers, or, the Burger Brothers as everyone called them. As far as Chance could tell that was a random name that had stuck. They would definitely know how to shoot an animal, but they were the type of boys who would get more of a buzz from seeing who could toss the dead possum or rabbit furthest than from making an effort to learn taxidermy. The boys at the front of the bus were still into computer games and probably never went outside at all. And the girls seated behind them were more interested in boys than animals — with the notable exception of horses and cats.

So that left two other girls: Amber and Hannah. Amber was a Year 9, and Chance didn't know her. She knew Amber's half-sister, Hannah, of course. Hannah was Michelle's number one groupie, and Chance didn't trust her. It was like Hannah didn't have a personality of her own, but copied other girls. She sucked up to Michelle and agreed with whatever Michelle said, even if it meant contradicting herself. Some of the girls in the group often tried to catch Hannah out, for the fun of watching her squirm. It was kind of like a game, though not one Chance found interesting enough to play. Despite her obvious flaws, Hannah was brainy. That was the surprising thing about her, that someone so dumb could be so smart. Once, during maths, Jack handed around a survey, asking everyone to name the one person in class most likely to go crazy on a shooting rampage. Hannah got the most votes: eight. Jack, himself, came in second with seven. If anyone on the bus knew how to skin and stuff an animal, it would be Hannah. But Chance was pretty certain she didn't want to find out how much Hannah knew. Just thinking about it made her feel uneasy. Luckily, it was pretty easy to avoid Hannah as she only travelled on the bus every other week, when she stayed at her father's.

No one was in the house when Chance arrived home. She walked into the kitchen and glanced at the list her mother had left on the table: 'washing, roast, water veggies, table'. From the kitchen window she could see the washing flapping in the breeze, her father's and brothers' underpants on the outermost line, slowly circling as the hoist spun on its axis. Her heart sank.

Outside, the sun was still hot, and as she took in the towels she pressed them against her cheek, enjoying the sensation of warmth. Her mother's top crackled as she half-rolled and folded it roughly into the washing basket, causing the blonde hairs along her forearm to stand upright. Her white school blouse also sparked. No matter how regularly it was washed, the cuffs remained a greyish white, and the fabric along the seams, particularly where her arms brushed her body, was pilled. Once in a while she made an effort to get rid of the small bobbles, using her brother's razor to shave the fabric, though never with much success. As usual, there were a large number of tea towels. They hadn't been shaken out properly before hanging and they had dried with stiff folds that she pulled free as she placed them neatly on top of the basket. All that was left were the underpants. With her foot, she nudged the basket closer to where she stood and spun the line once or twice, before catching it and pulling it to a stop as a pair of faded black underpants drew level with her face. She spun the line again, this time grabbing it when pairs of yellow pants came close. She sighed. Slowly raising her hand to the closest peg, she released it, allowing the coloured pants to fall. She had meant them to land in the basket but she had misjudged the position, and now they lay on the grass. She gave the basket a tap with her foot and spun the line again, released the peg on a pair of yellow boxers, and this time she was lucky.

Finally only her father's white underpants remained. She could barely bring herself to look at them. She turned the line slowly, lined up the basket and released the first pair, watching as they fell towards the basket before veering off-course at the last moment. She tried again with the second pair, but this time batted them with the back of her hand as they fell, knocking them into the basket. The third pair went straight in and the fourth missed. They sprawled across the grass by her feet. Chance looked at them, noticed the small holes along the inner seams, the baggy pouch at the front, and, unbidden, an image of Humbert Humbert filled her mind. She shook her head and tried to think of something else, anything to make him go away. He wouldn't budge but remained standing in front of her, hands on hips, his pale legs protruding from the loose-fitting pants. Under her breath she murmured, 'Get out of here, pervert,' and with the very tips of her fingers she stooped down and picked up the underpants and dropped them in the basket. Then, without thinking, she wiped the palms of her hands up and down her skirt, rubbing them repeatedly until they felt clean.

It took her only a few minutes to water the vegetables. It was a simple matter of making sure the sprinkler was in the correct place. She put the roast in the oven, and turned her attention to setting the table. As far as she was concerned, the whole exercise was pointless. Every evening she arranged the salt and pepper, placemats, plates, napkins, glasses, knives and forks on the table and every day her brothers spent minutes filling their plates before heading off to the living room to watch Sky Sport. Her father would begin his meal at the table, but after a couple of mouthfuls he would grow restless and start calling out to the boys, asking if anything good was on, and before long he would follow them out of the room. That would leave Chance and Trudy. The conversation was pretty much the same every night:

'How was school?'

'All right,' Chance would answer. 'How was your day?"

'Fine, thanks.'

Chance would nod, smile. 'Nice dinner. The roast is yummy.'

'Well, you cooked it.'

At this point the conversation would stall and Chance would have to work hard to renavigate her mother's mood. Over time, she'd learnt that it was important to alter the tone of her voice and to smile. This was something she'd first noticed some of the girls in Michelle's gang doing. They'd raise their voices, and change the direction of the conversation by pretending that an entirely new thought had entered their head. When they did this, they'd often start their sentences with the word 'Hey!' or 'Oh, yeah, I remembered . . .' Chance had seen it work numerous times with Michelle, so she had started trying it out on Trudy. If she were lucky, she'd find a topic that met with approval.

'Hey! We're doing this really cool thing in English at the moment.'

Trudy looked up from her plate and waited, her mouth chewing a stringy piece of lamb.

'Yeah, so. It's so cool.' Chance grinned and opened her eyes wider. 'We're doing a book and movie project where we read a book, then watch the movie of the book, and then compare the two.'

'Why?' asked Trudy.

Chance cleared her throat. She smiled once more as she desperately tried to remember the reasoning behind the project. 'It's about the different treatments, you know, straight prose and then the way it gets adapted, you know, into screenplays.' She stopped before adding the words 'and that'. She knew Trudy didn't like it. She'd once taunted Chance about it, in a jokey way, intoning, 'In the beginning God created heaven and earth, and that.'

'So, we're doing *The Great Gatsby*.'

Trudy set down her knife and fork. 'But we've already read that book, ages ago.'

'Yeah, I know. I told the English teacher that and she was totally impressed.' This was a lie. Chance rarely spoke to the teacher for fear of being noticed and forced to read aloud. 'I told her about all the books we've done.'

Trudy inhaled sharply and then stabbed at her food. 'The book is better than the film . . .'

'Oh, yeah,' interrupted Chance. 'I know. But the film was pretty cool and the music was great. We had big arguments over the music — the Amy Winehouse fans got stuck into the Beyoncé cover of "Back to Black".'

'You've lost me,' said Trudy.

'In the film. During one of the last parties . . .'

Trudy let out a long sigh. 'I don't know what you're talking about.'

'The film. *The Great Gatsby*?'

'Robert Redford, Mia Farrow . . . Yes.'

Now it was Chance's turn to look confused. She sensed her mother's growing impatience and her mind scrabbled to undo whatever it was that she had said to annoy her. Suddenly it clicked. 'Argh, sorry. Not that film, a different one. A new one, with Leo Caprio as Gatsby.'

'Leo Caprio?'

'Sorry. Sorry. I meant Leo DiCaprio. He was in—'

'I know who he is.'

Chance laughed nervously. 'Sorry. Yeah.'

They ate in silence. Suddenly Trudy said, 'I'm not that old, you know.'

Chance caught her mother's eye and a flood of relief went through her. Trudy laughed. 'I've not been living under a rock for the past ten years.'

Chance joined in with the laughter, but she noticed that in the fraction of the second between her last statements, Trudy's voice had hardened once more. Whatever light had glimmered briefly was extinguished. Chance coughed. 'I'll clear the table. If you've finished?'

'Mmm, thanks.'

'Oh, yeah, I forgot,' said Chance, as she arranged the plates in the dishwasher. 'I got the book back. *Lolita.* I was using a printout of my timetable as a bookmark and someone handed it in to my form teacher.'

Trudy listened, her mouth set in a tight smile. 'I've decided we're not doing that book any more. You're not mature enough to handle the themes so we're going to do something contemporary, something you can handle. Something *easy.*'

Chance glanced at her mother, then lowered her eyes. 'What?'

'Haven't decided yet. I'm still researching the options.'

Chance took a deep breath, began to speak and stopped. She looked down at her hands, then up, and began again. 'Maybe I could choose something.' She smiled, faintly. 'Just for a change.'

Trudy tilted her head as if she had heard a noise, something barely audible, a long way off. After a moment's silence, she slowly nodded her head. 'Yep. Why not?' A look of amusement crossed her face. 'Let me know when you've made your mind up. I'll look forward to seeing what you come up with.' She cleared her throat and smiled. 'Good. Can't wait.'

CHANCE DIDN'T HAVE THE FIRST IDEA about what book to choose. She understood that it wasn't enough to select a book that she might enjoy; she had to factor in her mother's response to the choice. So she had to make it look as if her decision was casual, a reflection of her personal interest, knowing there was no way she could pick up one of the books popular with her friends. Although the book had to look like it might be something Chance wanted to read, it was more important that it was worthy of being chosen, in her mother's eyes. It would be a lot easier, therefore, to let Trudy come up with the book in the first place.

———————

It was Friday evening, family night down at the track, and Bruce, the boys and Trudy had gone out straight after an early dinner, leaving Chance at home. Chance had no idea why Trudy had gone. Go-karting wasn't her mother's thing, although sometimes she tagged along for the sake of getting out of the house. When Trudy was in a good mood, she joked that her presence 'raised the tone' of the place, but when she was feeling mean she'd complain about the wives of the club members, referring to them as trashy or boring, or both. She would go on and on until Bruce would get angry and respond that at least all the other wives were friendly, to which Trudy would sneer, 'Yes. Lovely and friendly . . .' in a tone that suggested that being pleasant was some sort of crime.

On this particular Friday, Trudy was in a good mood, which was why Chance hadn't had to fight to be allowed to stay home. The reason for Trudy's high spirits was related to Higgs's success in recent events. For months he'd been placed in all his races and it looked like he might get the opportunity to travel to the Gold Coast for the champs. If he went, Bruce and Ishmael would go, too, leaving Trudy in charge of the farm. This wasn't what was making Trudy happy. What cheered her up was the knowledge that she would be able to insist on a holiday to Auckland or Melbourne, as compensation. It was kind of silly, really, because no one in the family would have stopped her from going away in any case. She could take off at any time, without an excuse. Nothing would make the rest of the family happier than a few days' relief from the tension that hung about them. But they would never suggest she go away. She wasn't a bad mother, after all, and no one wanted to risk hurting her feelings.

Chance had spent an hour on Amazon, scanning its best-seller lists, and now she was bored. She'd been able to dismiss the self-help books, the colouring books, the books about cats and the books they'd already studied, but that still left a lot to go through. They'd never read a thriller, but there was probably a good reason for that, although she didn't know what it was. They'd not read anything that might be described as a comedy, nor had they attempted any science fiction or fantasy. Historical novels were out — unless they were old books, written during the time in which they were set. Child narrators were out. Books about the upper class were out, unless they were written by a member of the lower class or, better still, a socialist. Sport was a definite no, as was anything to do with outer space or war. Books that were too popular were also forbidden — unless the author had been dead for more than a hundred years. As far as Chance could tell, that didn't leave a lot to choose from.

There was one person who might be able to help her decide on a book, and that was Ms Reed. It would be even better if she actually chose the book. That would be the ideal solution, as it would let Chance off the hook. But ever since the episode with the taxidermy book, Chance had been avoiding going to the library. She couldn't go back until she had an example of a stuffed animal to show Ms Reed. So she was in a tricky situation: should she select a book or stuff an animal? After a moment's thought she figured it would be simpler to stuff an animal. It couldn't be that difficult — and it wasn't as if she hadn't dealt with dead creatures before. During a class trip to the university she'd watched a guy dissect a rat, and it had looked pretty straightforward. All she needed was a knife, a pair of scissors, some pins and a pair of gloves. And a rat. That would be the hardest thing to find.

For a while they'd had rats in the shed. There was the time she'd gone to get some pellets for the goats and a big brown rat had been in the bin, looking up at her. If there was one rat, there were probably hundreds more lurking around, and it shouldn't be that impossible to find them. They were pretty ugly, though. And Ms Reed might not like rats. Maybe a bird would be a safer option — a starling or a seagull, perhaps. But what would she do about the wings? How could you stuff a wing? Maybe she should take a chicken. Make a joke of it. Stuff it with thyme and sage and laugh the whole thing off. Ms Reed had a good sense of humour, after all. A frozen chicken! That would be even better. Less messy. A pre-stuffed and seasoned frozen chicken bought straight from the supermarket. Perfect.

Well, not perfect, actually, said a voice in Chance's head. You have to try harder than that, Porsche.

So, chickens were out. Rats were a possibility, as a back-up. That left other birds, rabbits, hedgehogs and possums. Hedgehogs were probably not a good place to start. Birds, with the exceptions of the hens, were too difficult to catch. That left rabbits and possums. Rabbits posed a problem, unless she could persuade Ishmael to lend her his gun, and even then there was no guarantee she'd hit anything. That left possums. Shooting, roadkill or trap? Chance laughed. It sounded like some weird option at Subway: white, wheat or flat bread? Shot, squashed or snapped? Lettuce, tomato, cucumber? Sauce — ranch or barbecue?

Snapped. It would have to come from a trap. Problem: they had no traps because Ishmael got such a kick out of shooting things. There was a time, not that long ago, when he would sneak out at night and shoot road signs. And then there was the ancient dunny at the bottom of the paddock — he took hundreds of shots at it before Bruce told him to lay off. Finally, there was the time he went out every night with his gun, but no one knew where. He'd come home grinning from ear to ear, and make obscure remarks about having a licence to kill and saving the world for another day, until everyone, even Higgs, told him to shut up.

Maybe it would be easier if she chose a book. Any book. At random. She could go to the local library and select something from the middle stack, third shelf down, sixth book from the left. It wasn't like it mattered; Trudy would hate it anyway.

But that would be giving up. And she couldn't live with herself if she did that.

In the garage, leaning against the back wall, was Higgs's mountain bike. He hadn't used it since getting his driver's licence, and a fine cobweb filled the space between the brake cable and the handlebars. Surprisingly, the tyres were still inflated and nothing seemed to be wrong with the machine, apart from the fact that the seat was too high.

At this time of year it would be light until well after nine, and so, knowing that she had a few hours before nightfall, Chance took the bike and headed off down a rough track towards the bottom of the Stills' cow paddock, then cut across their property in the direction of the wetlands. Chance wasn't too familiar with her neighbours' farm, but even so she figured she'd be able skirt the lake and then head up to the poplars, where Riva had a couple of traps. Then, all going well, she could find an animal, skin it and be back home before her family returned from karting.

As she bounced along, the tune of a popular song filled her brain. As far as she knew, it was one of Michelle's favourites, a massive hit that everyone recognised but no one could sing along to because the only words anyone understood were 'sexy lady'. The first ten or twenty times Chance had watched it on YouTube she'd found it funny, but then, after a while, she'd grown out of it. It was still being played, despite being several years old, and she could easily visualise the crazy, horse-rider dance that, for reasons unknown to her, perfectly matched the movement of her body now as she hit each bump and rut, dried into the hard earth of the farm tracks. 'Gangnam style!' She called it out loud and laughed, and in response her feet came flying off the pedals and for a second she lost control of the bike, screaming as it skidded and veered across the ground, before she managed to regain her balance just as she reached the lower boundary with the Stills' land.

The lake was visible a short way off, so she dumped the bike in the bushes, clambered over the gate and went down towards a clump of flax and toetoe in the distance. There was a cry, a loud bellowing off to her right, and she stopped dead in her tracks. It was an awful, other-worldly sound, the kind of sound a person locked up in a basement might make. She heard the noise again, but this time the bellowing was followed by a series of braying noises and she realised it must be one of the old donkeys she had glimpsed on her way home from school. Again, it bellow-brayed and, as before, the sound carried with it a hint of strangeness and premonition, this time less madhouse than werewolf.

Chance hurried on through the brush, the ground giving way and her feet squelching as she got closer to the edge of the lake. She stopped for a second to take stock of her surroundings, and a plane, one of the last of the night, passed low above her. It was so close she could see its landing lights and wheels, talon-like, beneath the great hulk of its body. If she had money, she'd like to train to be a pilot. It wasn't going to happen, though. She suspected that she'd end up on the farm; or maybe, if she fared better at school, she might leave home and enrol in some kind of course. She didn't really know what she wanted to do. Unlike half the girls at school, she didn't feel passionate about anything. She hoped that would change, that something would happen and one day she would leap out of bed and have one of those eureka moments and announce for all to hear, 'I've got it! I'm going to sell sewing machines and craft supplies!' She prayed that she wouldn't go straight from school to marriage and motherhood, like her mother had done.

Chance's best friend from the year before had left school and moved away when her mother remarried, and now the only time Chance caught up with her news was when she went on Facebook, which wasn't very often. You couldn't really believe what you read on Facebook anyway. A girl who used to be in her class had posted some stuff about finding true love and it was all a load of rubbish. Michelle had posted something about being spotted by a plus-size modelling agent, but everybody knew she worked part-time out the back of the supermarket, where no one would see her. Hannah told lies, too. She reckoned she was going to move to France and Jack was going to join the army, though neither of them looked like doing either of those things in real life. Jack was too young, anyway. And Hannah had no money. The only thing Chance ever felt like posting was, 'Survived another day.' That about summed her life up, at the moment.

It was nice down by the lake. Chance didn't understand why she hadn't come down this way more often. It was peaceful, and it seemed such a long way from home. The ground and the bushes had a nice smell, like earth but nutty and sweet. That had to come from the gorse and willow growing all over the Stills' property. There was so much of it. Her dad wouldn't have allowed it to spread like that. He would have been out there with the spray, knocking it back, along with any thistle he came across. Spraying gave Bruce the same peace and satisfaction that other people got from gardening. He liked to 'clean up' and gain control of his surroundings. Typically he'd come back from an afternoon spraying gorse bushes and joke, 'They won't dare show their faces around here again.' His voice and manner would be kind of proud, and nine times out of ten he'd try and force Trudy out for a 'tour of the estate' so she could admire his handiwork. But she never went out with him. She never allowed him the opportunity to feel proud of his work. She'd wait a few days and then sneak down the paddock by herself. Later, at dinner maybe, she'd let them all know that she'd 'inspected' Bruce's work. She'd always start by saying he'd done a good job, but then she would insert a little barb. Always a question. 'You did a great job with the gorse, but I was wondering why you didn't bother doing the thistles along the fenceline, while you were down there?' It was like she felt obliged to say something to bring Bruce down.

If there was one question Chance would really like to ask her mother, it was this: 'Do you even like us?'

She was sure Ms Reed liked her family. Chance knew she had a son. Once, when going to one of the city shopping centres with her mother, she'd spotted Ms Reed in her car in the supermarket car park, her eyes fixed on the entrance. Suddenly, her face had broken into a huge smile. When Chance turned to see what the librarian was looking at, she noticed a kid lugging a guitar. The boy was dawdling towards the teacher's car and trying not to smile, but Chance could see it in his eyes, that he was glad to see his mother. But the librarian was even happier. She got out of the car and helped him with his case. She did something that Chance had only seen on television: she patted her son's head and then bent down and gave him a kiss.

Trudy had caught Chance staring and asked what was going on. 'That's my school librarian, Ms Reed,' she replied.

'Is she nice?' asked Trudy. 'She looks it.'

Without thinking, Chance replied, 'Yeah, she's really, really nice. I really like her.'

All she'd done was answer the question but somehow her answer appeared to offend her mother. They did their shopping in suffocating silence, and it wasn't until they were almost home that Trudy spoke up, asking, 'What was her name again?'

'Who?' asked Chance.

'That teacher,' said Trudy

Chance's heart began to judder and she felt sick. In a quiet voice, she pleaded, 'Please don't do anything.'

Her mother swung to face her, the car wheels skidding across the centre ridge of shingle. 'What do you mean?' she demanded.

'Nothing,' whispered Chance.

'No, tell me. What do you mean, "Please don't do anything"?'

'Nothing,' repeated Chance. 'She's kind, that's all.'

Trudy made a noise that seemed like a cross between a sigh and a small explosion. 'Why would you even say that?' she demanded. She fell quiet, fixed her attention on the road and changed down as they approached the tight corner before their farm. 'Why would you even say that?' she repeated as she swung onto the drive, the wheels battering over the cattle-stop.

'Sorry,' said Chance. 'Sorry.'

Another two questions, thought Chance: Why do I always say the wrong thing? Why do I never learn?

There was a narrow track meandering along the edge of the lake. It was barely wide enough for one foot, but it marked a route and was heading in the right direction so Chance followed it. She liked the way the track appeared as if drawn into the ground with a stick. Sometimes it disappeared, hidden beneath the reeds that grew either side of it, but then, just when Chance thought it had gone completely, it would show up once more and straggle on another fifty metres or so. Maybe fishermen had used the track, when they'd gone after trout. It was possible, though it didn't seem likely. The water was brown and muddy-looking, and shallow. She couldn't imagine fish coming in close to the shore, unless they floated up after they died, blown across the lake by the wind. Taxidermists stuffed fish. Maybe that was another option. A big trout on a wooden board. She could make it so its head and tail moved, and it could say something funny, like 'Sexy lady. Fishy style!'

The words 'fishy style' accompanied her along the track, over the fallen logs and through the trees that grew between her and what she guessed was the boundary with the wetlands. A small clearing opened up and Chance slowed down, enjoying the space and the smell of the mānuka. The ground beneath her feet was now dry and dusty. She sat down on a small log and allowed herself to look up, enjoying the sight of the treetops framing the sky and clouds. Sky light, she thought. It's beautiful.

As she looked about her, she noticed a large mound of branches piled into a shape like an igloo at the other side of the clearing. She'd go and check it out, in a minute. But for the moment she just wanted to look up at the sky and the way the branches were silhouetted against the light. The trees swayed in the breeze, slowly, gently, brushing back and forth, creaking softly, and the movement reminded Chance of a rocking chair, the kind an old lady might sit in when she stayed out on the porch, watching the dusk and the slow, warm creep of night.

'YOU WANT WHAT?' ASKED RIVA, even though she was pretty certain she had heard the first time.

'A dead animal,' repeated Chance, her ears burning as she thought about how stupid she must sound.

'Why?' asked Riva. 'Tell me again.'

Chance cleared her throat and began the long explanation again.

Riva laughed. 'Why don't you ask me what book you should read. It would save a load of trouble.'

Chance looked up, her eyes widening, 'Really? You'd tell me what to read?'

Riva rubbed the side of her nose, running her finger over a long red scratch that extended to her lower lid. She breathed out, her breath whistling between her teeth, and then beamed at Chance. 'Nah. Skin something. It will do you good.'

Chance could barely conceal her disappointment. 'But I don't know how to skin any animals.'

'Time you learnt then, isn't it?'

Chance shook her head. Even she had to laugh at how

out of control things were becoming. For an instant she felt sorry that Ms Reed hadn't caught her in the sewing section of the library. But it could have been worse. What if she'd been pretending to read a book about juggling or space rockets — or both? Could you even juggle in outer space?

'Okay,' said Riva, shouldering her bag. 'You come with me and we'll see what's on offer.'

As they walked, Chance began chatting about her attempt, the previous evening, to find a skin. 'It was like something out of *Hansel and Gretel*. I was in a little forest and it was like I suddenly felt kind of peaceful and it was all quiet, and the trees were black against the sky, and I lay down on the ground looking up, and I think I might have fallen asleep for a bit.'

'Sounds like you were bewitched.'

'Yeah, but then, when I woke up, I did a bit of exploring and noticed a weird shape, like a mound, made of branches. I thought it might be a pile of fallen trees or a mai-mai or something, but it turned out to be a kind of a den, with all kinds of stuff in it, like a table and a little bed. And the funniest thing . . .' She paused, rejigged the straps of her school bag and went on, 'The funny thing was . . .'

Riva didn't appear to be listening. She suddenly stopped by a strip of pink plastic tied to a branch and pointed towards the ground. 'There you go, take a look inside,' she said. Poking out of a tussock in front of them was a wooden trap.

Chance stood back, unwilling to bend down and take a look inside. Suddenly, the whole idea of skinning an animal grossed her out. It was one thing to think about it, but another to do it.

Sensing her unease, Riva asked, 'Do you want me to look?'

Chance nodded, 'Yes, please.'

'Not much of a wild woman, are you? You townie!'

She was teasing, but it was enough for Chance to feel

embarrassed about her squeamishness. 'I haven't done it before, that's all,' she explained.

In the time it took to say that, Riva had already inspected and reset the trap. It was empty. 'Right, let's go. Your turn next.'

Chance lagged behind as Riva went ahead. She pretended that her slowness was related to the fact that she was in her school gear and she didn't want to get muddy like the last time she was out with Riva, but really she was hoping that the older woman would take charge of the traps and save her from having to deal with any dead animals.

'So this den, I found . . .' Chance called out.

'Here we go, second time lucky. Take a look.'

Chance pulled a face, but took the screwdriver held out to her by Riva. She knelt down and unscrewed the lid on the trap, sliding it off when she was done. She glimpsed something furry and recoiled, unable to suppress a scream. 'It's a rat!' she cried, giggling nervously. She tried to stop herself from making so much noise but the high-pitched laughter kept bubbling out of her. 'Yuck, I'm not touching it.'

While Chance hopped nervously from one foot to the other, Riva stood motionless and waited, looking on, calmly. 'It's not a rat,' she said. 'Have another look.'

'No, I don't want to. It's all dead and horrible.'

Riva stood back, her hands by her side as she waited for Chance to move closer to the trap. 'You know what books I like?' she said, after several seconds had passed. 'I like books about eels. Now, if you think your mother is going to want to read books about eels, then fine, stay where you are. But,' and she gave Chance a slight nudge, 'if you think you need a better suggestion from your teacher . . .'

'Eels? You're joking, right?'

'No,' Riva scoffed. 'What makes you say that?'

Chance shook her head, 'That's what you read about? Really? Are they cook books?'

'Nope. They're a fish close to my heart, that's all.'

Chance wasn't sure if Riva was telling the truth or not. From the older woman's expression, it was impossible to tell.

By now Chance had edged closer to the trap and crouched down. She could clearly see a dark furry tail attached to a red-golden body. The creature's head was flattened against a metal plate, its body clamped down by a spring-loaded metal grid. Near its head was a hen's egg, untouched.

'Kind of gruesome, isn't it?' she said. In truth, she was stalling for time, hoping that Riva might step closer and clear the trap.

'It's a stoat,' said Riva. 'You'll have to take care when you skin it because they don't have a lot of loose skin. So, it can be difficult working the body free. And,' she added, her voice softening, 'they have scent glands. And if you puncture one of them with your knife, you'll know about it.'

'Thanks for warning me,' said Chance.

She hovered near the trap, then asked, 'Are there any other books you like?'

Riva didn't answer. She crouched down next to the trap and quickly released the stoat, resetting the trap immediately. The stoat hung limply in her hand and, before handing it to Chance, she ran her fingers over its fur, rolling it over, inspecting it. 'It's a male.' She reached in her pocket for a notebook and jotted something down, then measured the creature with a tape. 'It's a fair size, isn't it?'

Chance held her hand out but pulled it back at the last second, causing the stoat to fall onto the ground between them. 'Sorry,' she mumbled.

'It's okay. It's not like you're a midwife. Then we'd be in trouble.'

As Riva stood up, her knees gave out a loud crack.

'Are you okay?' asked Chance.

'Yep, good as gold.' She offered her hand to Chance and pulled her up. They stood facing each other and then, self-conscious, Chance bent down for her bag and opening it, placed the stoat inside. 'Thanks heaps,' she said as she began to walk away. After a few steps she hesitated, and turned back. 'Sorry if I was rude about your books.'

'No problem.'

'It's just,' continued Chance, 'it's really important that I choose something my mother likes. You know? I need her to like it. If I could make her like it . . .' Chance didn't finish. For some stupid reason she felt like she might cry, so she swung around and set off once more for home.

SHE'D READ THE CHAPTER on tanning a skin in Ishmael's copy of *The Dangerous Book for Boys*. At least, she'd read up to the part where the instructions became quite technical, and then she'd given up. She had the gist of it, anyway. In front of her, laid out on newspaper, was the stoat, a penknife, a pair of scissors and the salt pig. She would have liked to have had a pair of gloves but the washing up gloves were too long in the fingers to be much use.

The stoat, which had been quite floppy when she collected it, was growing stiff. There was something vaguely repulsive about it, though she wasn't sure what. Taking a deep breath, she placed the sharp point of her penknife against its chest and counted to three before pressing down. In her mind she pictured the stoat exploding, blood and guts spraying everywhere, so it was something of an anti-climax when nothing happened. From the small hole she had made, she began working the tip of the knife down towards the stoat's tail, stopping when she reached its penis.

She looked at the animal and felt sick. She didn't want to touch it.

Her classmates, she imagined, were probably out, wandering around town having fun, or ensconced in someone's bedroom, trying on make-up, and here she was with a dead stoat. If it ever got out that she'd spent her evening alone, skinning an animal, she'd be dead.

Now, with the blade, she began cutting the body away from its skin, working around from the chest to the spine. With her fingers she could feel the thin layer of flesh covering its ribs, and underneath the sharpness of bone. She tried to convince herself that what she was doing was no different from skinning and filleting a fish, but the addition of fur made the comparison difficult. She'd forgotten all about the salt, so quickly sprinkled a pinch over the inside of the exposed skin, and then did the same for the other half of the animal. Riva had been right about there not being much loose skin — she could barely squeeze her fingers around the body. With her knife she cut away a bit more, but managed only to stick the blade through the skin, creating a hole. Nevertheless she began tugging the skin off the stoat, as if pulling off a jacket, and despite making several more holes, almost succeeded in the task. She didn't know what to do about the legs, so cut them off. Now, only the head and tail region were still covered with fur. From where she sat, the whole thing looked like a super creepy Christmas cracker.

She didn't know what to do about the head either, so she

turned the stoat around and placed her knife into its skin, near its penis, and began slowly cutting towards the base of the tail. Without warning, a terrible stench rose up from the animal. The smell was so putrid that she began to gag. It was unlike anything she'd encountered before: a mixture of rotten eggs, poo and decaying flesh overlaid with a sweet, sickly scent, something that was putrid and vile. She ran to the window and flung it open but it was as if the smell in the room had bonded with her skin and impregnated the air. With her English folder she fanned the room, pumping her notes up and down in front of her in an attempt to move the stink, but all that seemed to achieve was a furious movement of air particles; the odour now swarmed around her head, stinging her eyes. With no option, she put her head out of the window and took one deep breath, then hurried from her room, slamming the door behind her.

In the living room were her parents and brothers, all eyes fixed on the screen, watching *Top Gear*. Even though Chance had washed her hands and splashed water on her face, she was aware of the lingering smell of the stoat; it seemed as strong as ever. She shuffled past her family and took a seat at the edge of the room, near the door to the kitchen. On the screen, a group of men were standing beside a racetrack, watching a helmeted driver roar around the circuit. The image cut to the driver of the car, a young woman, her head jiggling as she spoke into the camera. Chance remembered how boring she found car racing. It was noisy and frantic and seemingly pointless. Her father and brothers took the opposite view. They called out for the woman to ease up, or go faster, and laughed when, on the final bend, she lost control and spun off the track. As she climbed out of the car they sat back and talked about how they would have handled the track, interrupting one another and not listening. Suddenly, from out of nowhere, Higgs spoke up, more loudly than the others. 'Eurgh, Ish. Did you drop one?'

The room fell still, as if everyone was weighing up a suitable response.

'Wasn't me,' said Ishmael.

Trudy glanced from one son to the other. 'Have you got something on your shoe?'

Though they had all been sitting comfortably for an hour or more, they each raised a foot and inspected the soles of their shoes — all except Trudy, who was wearing slippers.

'Well, something's stinkin' up the place,' said Higgs. He raised his head and sniffed the air, like a dog at the kitchen counter. 'I reckon it's coming from near Chance.'

All eyes swung towards Chance, who slumped down into the chair.

'Don't be silly,' said Trudy, though she, too, was eyeing her daughter.

By now the second driver had taken the seat behind the wheel of the car and pulled out onto the track, the footage jolting along with him.

'I'm making a cup of tea,' announced Trudy. None of the men paid any attention as she stood up and walked towards the kitchen. As she drew closer to Chance she tilted her head, gesturing for her to follow.

Despite the warmth of the day, the kitchen was cool, and to Chance's relief the smell that had accompanied her into the living room seemed less strong now she was surrounded by the unwashed dishes and leftovers of that night's meal. Without giving it any thought, she began rinsing and stacking the plates into the dishwasher, scouring the saucepan in an attempt to loosen the grains of rice that had become glued to its base.

'Chance,' said Trudy, coming closer. 'Is there anything you want to talk about?'

Chance jerked, but kept her attention on the water gushing from the tap. 'No, why?'

'I'm not getting at you, or anything, but I've noticed recently that you haven't been spending as much time as you used to on your appearance.'

Chance stepped back from the sink. She had no idea what her mother was talking about.

'Personal hygiene . . .' continued Trudy.

'What?' Chance wasn't sure what she was listening to.

'Hygiene,' repeated Trudy. 'Sometimes people don't even realise that their bodies are emitting certain odours. It's nothing to be ashamed of. It's quite common. If you need some money for deodorant or, you know, women's products . . .'

'Women's products?' Chance wanted her mother to shut up and go away. She couldn't believe what she was hearing.

'Razors, for example. I recently read that body hair can trap bacteria if it's left to grow.' Trudy raised her eyebrows and sighed. 'Just saying.'

Chance shook her head. When she spoke she was embarrassed to hear her voice sound squeaky. 'It's all right. I take care of that kind of thing.'

Trudy didn't look convinced. 'How about in other areas?' Her eyes dropped, but Chance pretended not to notice and fixed her attention on rearranging the pots and plates in the dish rack.

Trudy took a breath. 'Discharges. That type of thing. Do you understand what I'm saying?'

The kettle began to boil. It bubbled ferociously but didn't shut off, the sound forming the backdrop to Trudy's insistent, 'You do understand what I mean by discharges, don't you?'

Her head still lowered, Chance nodded vigorously.

'I'm not saying that you're dirty . . . down there . . . but if you have something you're worried about.'

'I'm fine, thanks.'

The switch clicked and the boiling water felt quiet. 'You sure?' asked Trudy. 'Like I said, it's nothing to be ashamed of.'

'What's not to be ashamed of?' Without either of them noticing, Bruce had entered the kitchen and was standing by the door.

'Nothing,' said Chance turning to face him. 'Nothing. Go away!'

She saw Bruce exchange a questioning look with Trudy, who then said, 'I'm just telling her how both Ishmael and Higgs went through a musty pubescent phase and . . .'

'No, you weren't,' said Chance.

Bruce looked from one to the other and mumbled, 'Just wondering how the tea's coming along, but I'll leave you two girls to it.' He disappeared back to the living room, his voice echoing back as he told his sons, 'I wouldn't go in there if I was you.'

'Look what you've done,' said Chance, her cheeks burning with shame. 'You're always having a go at me and it's not fair.'

Trudy ignored her and added the boiling water to the pot. She swirled the contents around and then, without waiting for the tea to draw, poured it into four cups. 'I am *not* having a go at you. I am trying to help. It's not easy being a teenager and I'm trying to keep the lines of communication open.'

Chance knew her mother was lying. It was like Trudy was regurgitating something she'd read in a magazine or seen on television. She finished stacking the dishwasher and began to leave the kitchen. As she got to the door a fresh thought crossed her mind. 'How come you never ever pour me a cup of tea? You always make tea for the boys but never me. Why is that?'

For an instant a look of surprise crossed Trudy's face, but she quickly checked herself. 'Have mine,' she said, holding out her mug. 'Take this one.'

'No, I want my own,' said Chance.

'Don't be so childish. Just take mine.'

'No!'

Back in her room, Chance was upset to discover that the smell hadn't completely disappeared. Raising one arm, she sniffed at her armpit, angry to be doubting herself. She knew full well she wasn't smelly. In the big bathroom she found a can of meadow herbs air-freshener and brought it back to her room, spraying it around until the can felt light in her hand. After a few more minutes she approached her desk and took a look at the stoat. It seemed even more gruesome than before. Its teeth protruded from its jaw in a sickening grin and its black, beady eyes stared angrily at her, confronting her with an accusation of cruelty. She had the feeling that if it was alive it would jump up off the desk and bite her on her neck, hanging off her skin by its razor-sharp teeth until she sank to the floor dead.

With her hanky she covered the creature's face and tried to ease its tail from its skin. Try as she might, she couldn't free the fur from its tail. There was no space to get her fingers or knife into the space between the fur and flesh and by yanking hard all she managed to achieve was an ugly tear that ripped through the tail's black tip. The whole process was turning into a complete fiasco. Finally, unwilling to tackle the head, she left the hanky in place and cut through the animal's neck.

All that remained in front of her was the naked, skinless, headless stoat and a misshapen length of fur. Apart from the fact that it was fur, it looked nothing like an animal. It was bloody and fatty, with patches of white where she had sprinkled salt. In her mind she played out the scene of handing it to Ms Reed. In her mind, the librarian recoiled and screamed and dropped the mess, where it stuck, clinging to her shoe. It didn't take much imagination to speculate about what would happen next. She'd be called before the principal and her parents would be told. Somehow the story would change in the telling. What had begun innocently as an attempt to impress her teacher would transform into a myth of her capturing and torturing animals. The girls in Michelle's group would name and shame her on Facebook. She would become the psycho kitten killer. Someone would suggest that she had mental problems. A link would be made between torturing animals and serial killing. She'd be suspended. Her mother would never speak to her again. Strangers would picket their farm. In the end, she'd be forced to go into hiding.

Chance picked the skin up and inspected it. Maybe she should have asked Riva for the title of an eel book. Maybe that would have been the safer option.

CHANCE YAWNED. SHE'D BEEN UP ALL NIGHT trying to fix the stoat skin. After cleaning away all the bits she didn't need and dumping them in the offal pit, she'd sat up in her room, trying to figure out how to make the skin presentable. She'd gone back to the small toilet and reread the *Dangerous Book for Boys* chapters on skinning and tanning but, as before, she hadn't been able to focus on the instructions. She had a feeling that she hadn't used enough salt on the skin, and that there was a slight chance that it might rot. She also knew she should allow it to dry properly. But she didn't have the luxury of time. The most important thing was to get a book title from Ms Reed, and to do that she had to get the skin ready by the start of school. With luck, it wouldn't rot before lunchtime.

In the bathroom cupboard she'd found some cotton wool, gauze and foot powder and, with only the roughest plan in her head, she returned to her room and began sewing the stoat skin, working it into a shape that she hoped would resemble a rabbit's lucky foot. As she worked she began to feel happier, growing more and more optimistic as the desired result began to fix itself in her head. The foot would be about a couple of centimetres long, tubular with a plaited thread at one end so that it could be attached to a bag as an ornament. The fur was soft to the touch, and the skin, still slightly damp, was flexible, not too thick for her darning needle. She made small, neat stitches, working the skin inside out. When she had finished along the length of the animal, she turned it right side out and examined her handiwork. It was obvious, even to her, that what she had made didn't bear any resemblance to a rabbit foot. It was too long, and too narrow. If anything, it looked like a fat, elongated, hairy earthworm or, perhaps, a hairy condom. It didn't look at all lucky.

She trimmed the ends of the tube with scissors, trying to alter the proportions so that it was less weird. She didn't want to make it too short, however. She was worried it might end up looking like a furry tampon. She needed to strike the right balance — something between a condom and a tampon, something that didn't immediately gross out Ms Reed. She gave up on the idea of making something she could feel proud of. That was asking too much. It was enough to create an object that didn't cause offence.

With the gauze cut into strips and padded out with cotton wool dusted with foot powder, she began stuffing her lucky charm. For a moment, she tricked herself into thinking it might be all right, after all, that it wasn't a complete disaster, but the unevenness of the stuffing gave the charm a lumpy appearance. She couldn't help it: an image of goat or sheep poo entered her mind. But it was too late to start again so she kept packing more and more padding into the tube and then sewed up one end. Now all she had to do was try and make the charm look pretty. She plaited a short length of coloured wool, which she doubled and sewed into the opening. With the loop attached to one end, the charm looked slightly better. But it still wasn't good enough to present to Ms Reed. It needed more decoration. Something sparkly, perhaps. A quick search of her drawers turned up a few glow-in-the-dark stars and a small plastic charm, a daisy-shaped flower that she had found in the playground months before. From a pair of clean knickers she unpicked a tiny satin bow and quickly went about gluing all these things to her stoat charm. At last she was finished. She held the furry object in the palm of her hand and shuddered.

———————

When she got to the library at lunchtime the room was crowded with boys, most of them huddled over one computer, arguing good-naturedly over the pros and cons of a Fender amp. They'd been flicking through various reviews for ten minutes or so, ignoring the pleas of a younger boy who had a homework project to complete before the bell for afternoon class rang. 'I need the computer for one second,' he kept repeating. 'I have to check a date. It will just take a second, please.' There were no other computers free, and this was the only one being used by boys. Once or twice he'd move closer to the girls and hover but then lose his nerve and back away without speaking to them. It was quite sweet, really, thought Chance. If she'd been seated in front of a screen she would have let him have a go.

Plonked on a beanbag, she could feel the lucky charm in her pocket. Despite herself, she gave it a squeeze. Since the night before she had found it difficult to get the image of a hairy condom out of her brain and touching it filled her with distaste. She hoped Ms Reed would be too sophisticated to conjure up a similar image. In her best-case scenario, Chance prayed that Ms Reed might think of Scottish kilt pins, the type made from claws, which Chance had seen when searching images on Google. The very worst-case scenario would be an image of a wet dog turd covered in weird furry white mould.

Without her noticing, Michelle and Hannah had entered the library. They had joined the older boys around the computer monitor and appeared to be taking part in the discussion about amplifiers. Chance knew for a fact that Michelle didn't care about music. For her, all female performers fell into two camps: fat bitches and stupid sluts. There was one exception: Madonna. Madonna had a category all of her own: talentless scrub. Nothing made Michelle laugh harder than when Madonna had tripped and fallen off the stage during a recent performance. In a loud voice, she was reminding everyone of that incident now, but the boys weren't listening. Anyone could tell they weren't interested in Madonna. They were even less interested in Michelle's opinion of Madonna. Michelle began to grasp the fact that no one was listening to her so started to talk louder, shoving one or two of the smaller boys on the shoulder to make her point. Her behaviour irritated the bigger boys, who told her to piss off. As usual Michelle wouldn't back down. In one quick movement she pressed the power switch on the computer and the screen went dead. Immediately, a cry of 'What are you doing?' erupted from the group of boys. As one, they turned on Michelle, who laughed in response. 'Fuck you!' she taunted. She reached forward, grabbed one of the boys' bags and began to walk away, Hannah following close behind. A student hurried after her, calling, 'That's my bag. Give it back, you bitch!'

Chance could see Ms Reed heading over from the far end of the room. When she saw Michelle she seemed to hesitate. It was only a slight movement, but for a second Chance thought Ms Reed might turn and go back the way she had come. But she blocked Michelle and held out her hand to take the bag. 'I've warned you before, Michelle, about disrupting—'

'I didn't do anything,' said Michelle.

'Give me the bag.'

Michelle slung the bag to the floor, kicking it in the direction of its owner, who protested loudly: 'Did you see that? I could do you for damage.'

Michelle smirked.

'I want you to come with me,' said Ms Reed.

'No,' said Michelle.

It was clear to everyone that Michelle wasn't scared of Ms Reed. If anything, she seemed pleased to be the focus of the librarian's attention. She drew herself up and repeated, 'No.' Then, for good measure, added, 'You can't make me.'

Watching from her beanbag, Chance felt uneasy. Though she wasn't on Michelle's side, she had to conclude that it would be impossible to force her to do anything against her will. She was immovable.

Ms Reed took a step closer and reached out as if to take Michelle by the arm. The collective gasp from the students caused the librarian to stop. She glanced around, took in the faces of the onlookers and took a step backwards. Taking the librarian's hesitation as a sign, Michelle stepped closer to Ms Reed before remarking, 'What's your problem anyway?'

The students knew the question was a challenge. Chance hoped that Ms Reed would not crumple. She'd prefer her to spit in Michelle's face than show her fear. But Ms Reed didn't strike her as the spitting type.

'Okay, Michelle,' said Ms Reed. 'I think you've made your point.' To Chance's ears, Ms. Reed's voice was strangely quiet and flat. Rather than appearing flustered, she stood tall and faced Michelle. Inwardly, Chance cheered.

'Unfortunately, I'm—'

Before Ms Reed could finish, the oldest computer boy interrupted, calling out, 'Hey, Michelle, nobody likes you!'

Some of the boys started laughing, and another piped up, 'When are you and Hannah getting married?'

'She's not my girlfriend,' snapped Michelle.

'Yeah, right. We've seen you on the back courts!'

'That's not true. You're lying!' broke in Hannah. 'Michelle doesn't even like girls. Do you, Michelle?' Before she could say any more, Michelle shoved her hard and told her to shut up.

The room burst into jeering laughter. Only Ms Reed kept a straight face. To Chance's surprise, she spoke gently to Michelle and in a calm voice asked her once more to leave the library. She then turned on the boys and told them to show some respect. Her words were so unexpected that no one answered back. Instead, Michelle and Hannah shuffled off, the boys returned to their computer screen and Ms Reed went back to her shelving. Chance couldn't get it out of her head how cool and calm the librarian was. She was amazing.

The bell was about to ring for the start of afternoon classes when Chance finally plucked up the courage to approach Ms Reed. Since Michelle's departure, Chance had been waiting for an opportunity to talk but hadn't been able to catch the librarian's eye. She'd decided it would be weird to go up to Ms Reed's desk and present her with the stoat charm and yet she couldn't figure out a more natural or casual way to do it. In the end, she'd decided to ask about the book first, and then, as an aside, mention that she'd brought in an example of her taxidermy. If Ms Reed showed interest, Chance would hand it over, as a small token of appreciation. Going through Chance's mind were the words: 'Book first, stoat second.'

At the desk Ms Reed glanced up with a friendly smile. 'What can I do for you, Porsche?'

Chance cleared her throat. She could feel the charm in her pocket; it was soft and furry to the touch. Maybe it wasn't quite as badly made as she thought. Maybe Ms Reed really would be impressed. She drew it out of her pocket and then remembered, Book first, stoat second. But it was too late. A puzzled expression crossed Ms Reed's face. 'What have you got there?'

Chance didn't know what to say. From the tiny gaps between her neat stitches something white and oozy had begun to escape. She didn't think Ms Reed had noticed, but just in case she wiped the charm against her uniform and passed it across. 'It's a lucky charm. I made it for you, last night.'

Ms Reed looked confused but held her hand out to take the stoat from Chance. 'It's soft, isn't it? What is it?'

'Stoat,' said Chance. As she spoke she could see a faint trace of the white ooze reappear. Ms Reed must be squeezing the charm. 'It's a sample from my latest collection. I've got other designs I'm going to make . . . You know, things like . . .' She searched for the right words or, at least, some idea of what she could make. Suddenly she remembered the book Ms Reed had handed her a while back, the book about body adornment from the Pacific, and she cleared her throat. 'Body adornment. You know, Pacific body adornment-type things, adornments . . .' Her voice trailed away and she glanced nervously at the charm to see if it was still seeping.

'Lovely,' said Ms Reed.

Chance cleared her throat. 'Maybe I should give you one of my more finished pieces? I mean, that's a practice piece really. An experiment.'

Ms Reed turned the charm in her hands and a frown crossed her face as the white paste came into contact with her fingers. 'It's quite fresh, isn't it?'

Chance nodded, 'I think it's the salt and foot powder, but . . .' She was going to explain how she'd made it, but the memory of the stench of the punctured scent glands entered her mind and she stopped. 'I'll bring you something else. You don't have to keep it.'

Ms Reed looked like she might laugh. 'No, I like it. Thank you. Thanks very much.'

Chance didn't believe that the librarian liked it. It was not the kind of thing that you could like. 'It might smell a bit,' she began, 'I'm not sure I gave it enough time to dry.'

'That's okay,' said Ms Reed. 'It's the thought that counts. And I'd love to see the rest of your collection . . . when you have time.'

'Oh yes, sure! I'll show you a neckpiece I've just started. It's based on a Hawaiian tribal . . .' Chance didn't know why she was saying that. There was no neckpiece — not yet, anyway. She had no idea what she was doing. It was like her voice had taken over her brain and was rambling on by itself.

'Good,' said Ms Reed.

Chance watched as the librarian tucked the charm into her desk drawer. She wanted to run away, but she couldn't, not until she got the name of a book for her mother.

'Um,' she began.

'You said stoat, didn't you?' interrupted Ms Reed.

'Yes.'

'Where did you get a stoat skin?'

For the first time since talking to Ms Reed, Chance relaxed. 'From a trap. My house is near a wetlands and the woman who looks after it gave it to me. She traps rats and all kind of things. I think it's her job.'

Ms Reed looked like she was about to say something but then thought better of it. Her fingers rested lightly on her desk. Smiling, she said, 'I'm glad you didn't use a rat. I'm a bit scared of rats . . .'

Her voice faded away and she gazed at Chance, who shifted uneasily, moving her weight from one foot to the other.

'I hate rats,' said Chance. 'We get them in our goat shed sometimes. Great big ones.' She stopped, held her hands far apart to indicate the size of the rodents, then cleared her throat, and started again, 'Um . . . my mum says I can choose the next book we read.'

Ms Reed's expression brightened. 'You finished *Lolita*?'

'No. I stopped reading it. I didn't like it. I thought I said that last time we talked, but maybe not.' She could feel her skin redden. How could she not remember what she'd told Ms Reed? It wasn't like she'd talked about so many things that everything had become a blur. 'Um . . . so my mum says I can choose a book, and I was hoping I could take you up on your previous offer? I want it to be a really, really good novel so I was wondering if you could help me?'

'Love to,' said the librarian. 'Do you have any preferences?'

Chance shook her head.

'Maybe something by a woman?' asked Ms Reed. 'I'm doing a bit of a push on women writers at the moment. Harper Lee, Sylvia Plath—'

'Done both of them,' interrupted Chance. 'Sorry. Thank you, but we've done them.' She looked embarrassed and added, 'And Toni Morrison, Alice Munro and Doris Lessing — all the Nobel winners.'

Ms Reed raised her eyebrows, and laughed. 'It's going to be a challenge. Good. I like it. Come back tomorrow and I'll have something for you.'

Chance couldn't believe her luck. It was like Ms Reed was the nicest person in the world. Not only did she not call the dead stoat disgusting but she asked to keep it. And then, on top of that, she went out of her way to find a good book, and *give* it to her, from her own personal collection. Chance had it in her hands now, as the bus jolted along the road towards the wetlands. It looked like such a good book, too, one that her mother might like. In fact, it looked like the perfect book for Trudy. It was foreign, for a start, written in Swedish and translated into English. That was a good sign. The author had won lots of awards, so that was good, too. There was a long foreword, written by an expert, giving information about the book and why it was so important. So that was lucky. There were some nice photos, but not too many. It wasn't a picture book but a proper adult book, and yet it was nice and short. Best of all, it had a good title. A nice simple title, one that perfectly fitted the recent hot weather. *The Summer Book* by Tove Jansson. *The Summer Book*, repeated Chance to herself. Ms Reed had made the perfect choice. Chance turned it over in her fingers. Everything was working out well, after all. Her mother would be impressed. It was perfect.

'HOW DID YOU GET ON with your skin?' asked Riva. 'Did you get your book?'

It had taken Chance more than an hour to locate Riva. She'd followed the usual tracks skirting the waterways, expecting to find Riva near the traps, but in the end had found her in the shed. Riva grinned when she saw Chance. Her first words were, 'Oh good, you're here,' and for that simple greeting Chance felt grateful. 'You can give me a hand with all these,' added Riva, indicating the newspaper-wrapped seedlings arranged on the benchtop. 'You have time, don't you? And you can tell me how you got on with your teacher.'

It was warm in the shed. The late afternoon sun eased through the Perspex wall, casting the room in a pale greenish glow. The task, which consisted of separating out and potting each spindly plant, was repetitive, and this, in combination with the heat, made Chance feel drowsy. Her movements were slow and careful, and she took pleasure in the close work. As she moved about, she described what had happened at school that day, often pausing and interrupting herself to ask Riva the name of whatever native she was potting. Riva would reply, giving each specimen one, two or three names, much to Chance's astonishment. 'How do you remember all that?' she asked. 'All those Māori and Latin words. Did someone teach you?'

Riva stopped what she was doing, and looked up. 'I suppose so.'

'At university?'

Riva shook her head. 'No. I dropped out of university.' She took off the cap she was wearing and rubbed her fingers through her hair, before replacing it. 'My sister was a florist and a gardener, so I learnt from her. She worked in town, here.' She removed her cap again and held it in her hand, tracing her finger over the word 'Whitehorse', which was embroidered across its front.

'So she learnt all those Māori names?' pressed Chance.

'Yep, sure did. She was interested in natural medicines. The leaves and gum from that pittosporum you're holding, kōhūhū, was used for everything from perfume to chewing gum to treating eczema.'

'Really?' asked Chance, looking at the tiny plant.

'Well, I think so, but don't quote me on that. I could be wrong.'

'Was your sister Māori?' It was a dumb question and Chance regretted it straight away.

To her relief, Riva didn't laugh. 'No. No. As a matter of fact she wasn't.'

Chance waited, trusting Riva would supply more information, but the older woman seemed content to let the subject fall.

'Where were you born?' pushed Chance, hoping at least to get some explanation for Riva's accent.

'Me?'

Chance stopped herself from rolling her eyes, but nodded impatiently. 'Yes. You.'

'I've moved around a lot,' responded Riva. 'My father was a mining engineer and worked all over the place: New Zealand, Australia, the Pacific, Asia, South America . . . But I was born here. First-generation Kiwi. My mother was part-Norwegian, but spent more than thirty years here. And my younger sister, Irene, was also born here. It's complicated.'

'I thought you were American,' said Chance.

'Well, I spent a lot of time in the States. I married an American and lived in a place called Carson City, in Nevada, for many years, until we split up. Then I went to Canada, the Yukon, to see my father, and then over to Europe to nurse my mother. And then, after she died, I came back to New Zealand to be with my sister. I like travelling, but this is my home, for now.'

'Do you think you'll leave again?' Chance couldn't disguise the note of disappointment in her voice.

'Yes, I think so,' said Riva. 'Probably. Sometime. If I can find someone to take over my work here.' She patted down the earth around a small rimu sapling and sighed. 'Maybe.' She smiled to herself and then glanced across at Chance. 'So, are you going to tell me about the skin? I'm guessing it went okay?'

It was past six by the time Chance left Riva. After finishing up in the potting shed, they walked together, taking a track that meandered through mānuka and kānuka bushes, heading towards the lake. They were caught in a brief shower of rain, and sheltered beneath an old macrocarpa, standing in silence as they watched the drops bounce off the hard earth, splashing around their feet. When the shower passed, the ground steamed and the smell of dust and resin and kānuka rose from the earth, surrounding them in a veil of perfume. They breathed deeply, and stood still, unwilling to let go of the scent. 'Irene,' said Riva, 'spent a long time trying to capture that smell. It was what she loved most about this place. She could describe it — you know, break it down to its base elements, but she never managed to replicate it.' Riva took off her cap and shook the drops of water from its peak, before replacing it on her head. 'Personally, I didn't see the point of perfume. Not when you have the real thing all around you. Why not breathe the air?'

Listening to Riva, Chance was suddenly reminded of the trouble she had had getting rid of the stench of the stoat. 'I forgot to tell you, I accidentally punctured the scent glands and—'

Riva laughed. 'Ugh. I warned you.'

'I know,' said Chance. And then she told Riva about her mother's response and how their conversation had spiralled out of control. 'It's always like that between me and my mother. It's so stupid, but that's how it's always been, forever.'

Riva listened quietly, then took another deep breath and held the air in her lungs, before slowly breathing out. 'I used to argue with my mother, all the time. We didn't speak for years and years.'

'What did you argue about?'

'Oh, most things. My childhood. Money. Dropping out of 'varsity. My marriage. Divorce. The way I dress. Irene. Not taking life seriously enough — me, not her. She took life very seriously. To say she was critical would be an understatement. She was toxic.'

She inhaled again, allowing her shoulders to relax, before exhaling.

'But you got on okay, in the end?' asked Chance.

'Well, once I got older I let go of my feelings of shame and found it easier to detach myself emotionally from her outbursts. I also realised that my crappy childhood was nothing compared to hers and that she was a deeply troubled person, and so I was able to make sense of certain things.'

'And you're okay now?'

'Now? Course I am.'

A look of relief crossed Chance's face. 'That's good, eh? That things got better.'

Riva let Chance's comment hang in the air before answering, 'Yeah, once she kicked the bucket.'

They continued on their way, Chance trailing a little behind Riva, who was faster over the rough ground. Once in a while Riva would stop and take a photo of the lake. Eventually they reached the shore and Riva stopped. She skirted the edge of the lake, taking more photos of the bank and the raupō. After a short while she returned to where Chance waited and sat down, retying the lace on her left boot before speaking. 'I heard a bittern here, the other day, around dawn. It was funny because I'd thought I'd heard one a few days earlier when I'd been mooching about, over by those trees. I haven't seen it, though. Maybe that could be my summer project, like reading *The Summer Book* is yours. I could track down a bittern. What do you think?'

Chance didn't know what a bittern was but nodded anyway and said, 'Good idea.'

A few minutes passed in silence and then they continued on, following a narrow track around the lake edge.

'How come you work here?' asked Chance.

'I just like nature.'

'Did you always do nature stuff? Is that why you had no money?'

Riva stopped, and turned around. 'Oh, did I say that I was poor? Sorry. No, I had a lot of money. Back in the States I owned an outdoor clothing company.'

'So, what happened?'

'Oh, you know . . .'

Chance shook her head.

'Well, after many years of working around the clock I decided to sell up and move back to New Zealand. My husband took half in the divorce settlement. Irene needed backing for her floristry business. I bought this land and created a wetlands sanctuary, invested in several businesses, became a mentor for women starting up in business, created a trust for environmental projects and land restoration—'

'So you actually own Tinker Wetlands? This is all yours? I thought you were a volunteer. Tinker's your name?'

'Yes, to the first and second. No, to the third. I named this place after Tinker, my old cat. But I named her after a book, you'll be pleased to know. *Pilgrim at Tinker Creek.*'

'Oh my God, so you're the crazy old cat lady my dad talks about. That's you!'

Chance wished she'd kept her mouth shut but the words had slipped out automatically, without her even thinking. She'd seen the pained expression flicker across Riva's face and felt ashamed of herself. However, she made things worse, if anything, by adding, 'There's nothing wrong with liking cats. We used to have one, a wild one, but then it ran off and we never saw it again.'

Riva smiled, but then looked at her watch and said something about needing to get back, that she had a call to make. It was horrible watching her walk away. Chance couldn't put her finger on it but it was as if Riva had suddenly grown older, or more tired. She didn't swing her arms when she walked, and her head was lowered, as if she was deep in thought or looking for something on the ground.

Chance didn't feel like going home. Just thinking about her parents was enough to make her sad, and she decided to put off her return as long as possible. Without planning to, she lingered by the lake, taking her time as she meandered slowly through the bush, skirting the flax and cabbage trees as she headed towards the mānuka forest. From time to time, her thoughts were interrupted by a volley of gunshots. It must be club night at the range. She'd been there once with her brothers and father but hadn't enjoyed it. It was kind of blokey and the constant banging of guns was annoying. She'd noticed, too, the way all the birds were constantly spooked by the noise. They'd be settled in the paddocks, doing their own thing, and then the sound would startle them and they'd all rise up in the air in flocks, circle around a bit and land. The seagulls would take the longest to settle down. There was one that circled, squawking and crying for ages, and she'd wanted to be able to take it aside and explain to it that it was all right, that no one was actually aiming at it. She'd watched as it went around and around and finally landed in a paddock, only to be scared up into the sky once more. It was just a seagull, she'd told herself, but she'd found its distress upsetting.

Her father and brothers didn't even notice. They stood around joking with the other men, listening avidly as the younger guys skited about all the animals they'd shot, the long list of creatures ranging from wapiti and goats to rabbits and ducks. One of the men reckoned he knew someone who had shot a kererū. Another mentioned that a friend of a friend had shot a grizzly bear from his truck. Higgs had thought that was pretty sick, but Ishmael loved the idea of killing game animals and had gone on and on about man pitting his strength against nature. Listening to him had reminded Chance of one of the first books her mother had made her read, a short novel about an old guy who caught a big fish for no reason.

Chance was surprised to find herself inside the den. It was just as she remembered, except the flowers had changed. The kānuka from her previous visit had been replaced with buttercups. The place needed a good cleaning. It felt unloved, despite the presence of the flowers. More than unloved: vacated, as if the owner had deserted the place. With a bit of work, though, it could look good again. She could fix it up a bit and then, maybe, she could spend more time out here. It could be her sewing room, the place where she created her accessories. She wouldn't have to do much. All she needed was her basic sewing kit and a few other bits and pieces, objects she could incorporate into her creations. James Bond could be her fitting model. She could imagine him in one of her works. A tribal neckpiece might be a nice contrast to his tuxedo.

Best of all, no one would disturb her out here. It would be hers, and she could do what she wanted.

Riva never forgot the moment the doctor informed her sister, Irene, that she needed a mastectomy. The doctor's voice was calm and sympathetic, but Riva had experienced the horror and panic of finding herself lost. It was a feeling she'd experienced only once before in her entire life — the morning she had looked up from a rail of party dresses in a central-city department store and realised her mother was nowhere to be seen. Riva had been around four at the time. Irene, two years younger, was still in a pushchair. She wasn't expected to walk everywhere. Her slowness would have frustrated their mother, who preferred to get on with things as quickly as possible, counting off all daily pleasures as if they were chores. Mother was always on the move and everyone was expected to keep up.

Riva had been keeping up. She'd spent the morning trotting alongside her mother, her short legs moving so fast that she resembled a dachshund. Mother had even praised her for doing so well. She hinted that there might be a hot chocolate, later, if she continued to behave. Riva hoped that Irene wouldn't start wailing and spoil everything, and to her joy the little girl remained placid, and fell asleep somewhere between the florist and the chemist shop.

After arriving at the department store, the largest building in their small town, they had gone straight to the children's area. This had been a treat in itself. There was one dress that captured Riva's attention. A blue and white sailor dress, with a red appliquéd anchor on each of its patch pockets. She lingered over the dress, hoping that her lack of movement would capture her mother's attention and draw the older woman to her. Riva didn't dare look up because she knew that if she caught her mother's eye she would have to leave the dress and hurry along.

As she waited, her inspection of the garment became more and more exaggerated. She tugged at each of the four buttons, twisting them to ensure they were fastened correctly. She then checked the hem, as she had seen her mother do, for the possibility of lengthening the dress.

After a few minutes, when there was still no sign of her mother, Riva started her inspection again, repeating every gesture with greater emphasis, a large theatrical smile of satisfaction emphasising her features. When her mother still didn't appear, Riva sneaked a look, expecting to see her mother's pale blue hat above the other racks. There was no sign of her in the immediate vicinity so Riva lifted her head and looked more closely, this time scanning the shop floor quite openly. Still her mother was nowhere to be seen. A surge of panic registered in Riva's stomach and she swung around, looking from side to side. Hoping her mother wasn't far away, she clutched hold of the dress and began walking through the racks, each step matched by increasing fear. Her mother had gone.

She wanted to call out but knew that if her mother heard she would be scolded for her ridiculous performance. So she remained quiet. She wanted to run, dash between the aisles of shelves, but knew that this, too, would be unacceptable in her mother's eyes. So she hurried as fast as she could without breaking into a jog, and as she hurried she became more and more frantic, her heart beating hard. No matter where she searched, her mother remained out of sight. She'd vanished. Simply abandoned Riva and gone off on her own. Eventually, it became apparent that her mother would never reappear and that Riva had no way of finding her way back home. She would never see her family again. Distraught, and unable to contain her emotions, she let go and sobbed.

Riva heard the doctor repeat, 'I know it's a bit of a shock,' and tried to keep calm. Then her shoulders shuddered and her entire body heaved, engulfed by the keening sound that rose from her lips. Tightly woven into the physical mess she had become was an even larger sense of shame. How could she behave this way? How could her body and emotions let her down like this? But she couldn't stop.

'Oh, lovey, it's all right. Come here.' She felt strong arms enfold her and her sister's voice returned. 'Don't cry. Don't cry. You know I never liked my tits anyway. It's going to be okay.' Irene squeezed her tightly, 'Come on, let's not do all that sad stuff. We knew this might happen, so we'll handle it, okay? It's just a bit of a shock.'

The doctor had looked on quietly, her face impassive as she watched the ill younger woman comfort her healthy sister. Two thoughts attached themselves in her head. The first was that the women would handle it. She could tell, despite the older sister's tears, that they were strong and that they loved each other. The second thought was less optimistic. Both Irene's mother and her grandmother had died from ovarian cancer and it was unlikely Irene would beat the disease.

As they left the surgery, Riva promised Irene that she would look after her. Irene responded by saying she didn't need looking after. She wasn't an invalid and she could look after herself. In other circumstances they might have argued the point, but on this occasion they decided to follow a different route. They went to the closest dairy and ordered double scoops of strawberry ice cream and stood on the corner licking them, until nothing was left but the tips of the soggy cones. They glanced at each other and then went back and ordered two more ice creams, double chocolate, laughing out loud when the dairy owner expressed wonder at their appetite. Back on the corner they ran their tongues over the rich, sweet creaminess and did all they could to finish their cones. Teenagers passed by and pulled expressions of disgust. Men and women of their own age averted their eyes. An older woman, who had been in the neighbouring wool shop, came out and spoke to them, commenting on how happy and alike they looked. 'I could tell you were sisters,' she said without even asking if they were. 'It's so obvious.' She looked as if she might walk away and then added, 'Do you mind if I join you? I haven't eaten ice cream for years and never while standing out on a street.'

'Be my guest,' said Irene.

The woman came back with a dainty, single scoop of vanilla. Her tongue poked between her frosted pink lips as she took a tentative lick, then stopped and looked around, as if embarrassed.

'Good, isn't it?' said Irene.

The woman blushed. 'Yes, it is rather good. I don't know

why more women don't do this.' Emboldened, she took another lick, running her tongue around the ice cream and drawing it back into her mouth. A smile of contentment touched her lips. 'Mmm. This is fun, isn't it? I could see myself making a habit of this.'

The night before being admitted to hospital for surgery Irene complained that it was all pretty unfair. When Riva sympathised, Irene just laughed at her. 'Listen, tomorrow will be the first time in years that anyone has fondled my breasts, and I won't even be awake. That's what's not fair, idiot.' Riva couldn't bring herself to smile. Sooner or later, she reasoned, Irene would crack. The façade would drop and she'd better be there when it did. She sat on a chair in the waiting area, her eyes fixed on her feet, willing herself to believe that everything would be all right. After several hours a shaft of light that had begun as a squashed oblong by the window lengthened and stretched across the linoleum, cutting a line across her toes.

Less than three weeks after the operation Irene insisted on going out. 'You can stay at home and mope, but I'm going to the movies. And if you won't come I'll ask Valerie. I'm pretty certain she'll keep me company. She's kind, like that. Not that you're not kind, but she's one of those nurturing, kind people. Plus, she's lonely.'

They went to see a film about a man whose arm became trapped beneath a rock. Five days after becoming stuck, he was forced to cut his lower arm off below the elbow. Irene made scoffing sounds throughout the movie. In a whisper loud enough for the audience in front of her to hear, she remarked that the protagonist was lucky it was a boulder and not a mammogram machine. 'I'd like to see him spend a hundred and twenty-seven hours with his tits stuck in one of those.' Some of the women nearby sniggered, but Riva shushed her sister and warned her to behave. But Irene became more and more fidgety. As the actor portraying the hero began cutting through his arm with a pocketknife, she exclaimed, 'This is ridiculous. Why the hell are they making a film about a man who cuts off a bit of his arm? What about all the women who get their breasts sawn off? Why aren't they making movies about them?'

Embarrassed, Riva hissed at Irene to be quiet. Softly, she said, 'Well, he had no choice. He'd die if he didn't cut his arm off.'

'And I wouldn't die?' snapped Irene. 'You reckon I had a choice? Chances are they'll rip out my ovaries before too long. Will they make a movie about that?' She gestured towards the screen. 'He's all right. I bet he's making a fortune on the lecture circuit. What's so brave about him? What about us!'

This time a man in front of them turned in his seat and demanded Irene be quiet. But she wouldn't back down. 'This is typical male bullshit. This isn't inspirational. It's not even interesting.' She lurched to her feet and began edging along the row, heading for the exit. 'You want to know what's brave? Go to a fucking cancer ward, you idiot!' She was talking to the screen, not the audience, but by then she had lost all sympathy. Riva hurried after her, apologising as she squeezed past. Once in the foyer, Irene burst into laughter. 'Jesus, sorry. I don't know what came over me. I got so irritated. I'm really sorry, Riva. We can go back in if you want. I promise I'll be quiet.'

Riva shook her head. 'No way am I going back in there after all that.'

She could see, though, that Irene felt bad about what had happened, and she didn't blame her for losing patience with the film.

Irene reached out and hugged Riva. 'I'll nip to the loo then let's go and get an ice cream. A proper cone, from the dairy. You wait for me outside, I'll be a minute.'

It was cold on the street. A sharp wind cut between the buildings, stirring up pieces of cardboard and paper that had been put out for the next day's recycling. As Riva waited, her eyes settled on a man not much older than herself who was standing on the other side of the road, in the doorway to a bar, smoking a cigarette. With a shock, she realised that he was watching her, too. There was nothing at all threatening about him but after years of feeling almost invisible, it was disconcerting to find herself the object of someone's attention. She wished Irene would hurry up so they could leave, but her sister was taking her time, probably mucking about trying to reapply the bright red lipstick she'd taken to wearing since beginning cancer treatment. Irene wasn't a natural when it came to putting on make-up. She usually ended up with lipstick on her teeth, and had to wipe them with her fingertip before she was ready to leave the bathroom.

To pass the time, Riva started making a mental list of all the flavours of ice cream at the dairy. She had counted nine, when Irene came bursting out of the cinema, a large cutout figure hoisted under her arm. 'Come on, quick. Let's go,' she said as she hurried past Riva.

'What the hell is that?' asked Riva as she tried to keep up.

'It's Bond. James Bond. It was propped up against the wall in the disabled toilets so I took it.'

'You can't do that, it's stealing.'

Irene didn't reply. She was having trouble maintaining her grip on the figure as the wind whipped around, twisting it one way and another. Irene started giggling, quietly at first but then louder and louder the more she struggled with the action hero. 'God, Riva. Tell me, am I going mad? What am I doing?' She stopped, breathless, and fell against her sister, who took her by the elbow. 'What would Mother say, if she could see us?'

'You,' corrected Riva. 'You're the one who's going to jail, not me.'

'Honestly. I think I'm going mad,' giggled Irene. She took a deep breath and looked at Riva. 'Promise me you'll be all right. Promise you'll be happy, all right? Try and have some fun, for a change. Promise?'

Riva felt the tears prick at her eyes. She couldn't promise to be happy. 'Do you remember when we were kids?' she asked, taking the James Bond figure from her sister and leading her up the road towards the car. 'Do you remember how Father always promised to make you a tree house, and how he never did, and how you used to whine and sulk about it?'

Irene nodded.

'Well, the other day when I was in the specialist's waiting room I picked up a kids' book, a kind of boys' annual full of dangerous things, and there was a chapter on building tree houses and it made me think of you. It suddenly dawned on me that we spent most of our childhood living in apartment blocks or in compounds for international families, so it was no wonder we never had a tree house. We never had any trees!'

They had reached the car and Riva felt in her pockets for her keys, before adding, 'Father must have known that he couldn't build a tree house, so why did he always promise?'

'Because he was sweet and didn't want to disappoint us?'

Riva opened the rear door and manoeuvred James Bond inside. 'Yeah, that's what I think, too. Although there's a possibility that Mother might have prevented him from building one for us. But, anyway, I was thinking that we have trees now, so we could give it a go, eh? I know a perfect spot by the lake, at the edge of the sanctuary. It's fully sheltered and accessible by boat so you don't have to worry about walking if you can't manage it. What do you think?'

Irene pulled open the passenger door, looked across to Riva and nodded. 'Yep, sounds good.'

Riva was thrown by the speed and ease with which Irene accepted the suggestion. She had expected her to raise some opposition to the idea and had even worked out a response should persuasion become necessary. Arguments supporting the project began to form, automatically, in her mind. 'We can take a sleeping bag and a bed so you can rest if it gets too much—'

'I said all right,' interrupted Irene.

'We can take a stove and drink cups of tea.'

'Yes, I've already agreed. Why are you going on about it?'

'It doesn't even have to be a tree house. A den might be easier.'

'Tree house. Den. Igloo. Teepee. Yurt. Burrow. Whatever you want. It's fine by me.'

'Are you sure?' asked Riva.

'Yes,' said Irene. 'Yes. Yes.'

Riva pulled out of the parking space and headed through the central city, en route to the dairy. Irene sat in silence beside her. There was something reassuringly normal about their lack of conversation. In recent weeks, Riva had become increasingly aware of the number of times she used conversation to blanket what she was thinking. In the cancer clinic's waiting area, sitting with Irene before an appointment, she would often do strange things like draw her sister's attention to a vase of artificial flowers. She had no interest in the display and yet she would talk about how life-like the flowers were and then attempt to draw on a distant memory, of a motel room, say, or a wedding reception, and remind Irene of the grim location or occasion.

199

Sometimes Irene would listen quietly and smile weakly when the long, drawn-out anecdote reached its anticlimax. At other times she would sigh or roll her eyes, or simply shut her eyes. Once or twice she would laugh at Riva, and then shift the conversation around to whatever she was thinking about. There was the time Irene loudly posed the question of what had become of her removed nipples, imagining various scenarios in which they might have found a new lease of life — as decorations on top of iced cupcakes, as replacements for malfunctioning earbuds on a teenager's iPod, warts for the bad witch in a secondary school production of *The Wizard of Oz*, doorbells at massage parlours. The brief, horrified silence that met Irene's suggestions gave way to an embarrassed but lively conversation among the other women in the waiting room, some of whom offered suggestions of their own. One woman pictured her nipple set in rose gold and surrounded by rubies and diamonds, dangling from a fine chain around her neck. Another suggested hers would make a fine lightswitch in the All Blacks changing room. One woman, who, like Irene, had had a double mastectomy, joked that she would thread them onto a cord and use them as worry beads. A young woman near the door broke down and cried, her whole body shaking, as she tried to apologise for being silly. Within seconds she was enfolded in the arms of her neighbour, her hair patted and soothed, oblivious to the fact that at least half the women in the room were fighting back tears. Irene looked sheepish, fumbled an apology, then muttered, 'What's wrong with me?' and some of the women smiled in sympathy.

When they were standing outside the dairy with their ice creams, Riva reminded Irene of the nipple incident. A smile crept over Irene's face. 'Do you think I push it a bit far, sometimes? Like back then in the waiting room, or in the movie tonight?'

Riva guffawed. 'What do you think? Let's just say that I think your idea of funny is pretty warped.'

Irene smirked and poked her ice cream with the tip of her tongue, easing out a small yellow wine gum, which she displayed on her tongue before swallowing it. 'It's so tiring. I'm so sick of being a cancer patient. I haven't changed, you know. Not inside. But now I'm expected to be this bland cancer victim-slash-survivor and that's not me. I'm still the same person as before.'

Riva bit into her cone, shards of which sprayed down her jersey. 'You know, I was actually enjoying that film tonight. I wouldn't have minded watching to the end.'

Irene didn't respond but continued to run her tongue in slow circles around her ice cream.

'So, is this what we're going to do now, is it?' asked Riva. 'Stand on street corners and eat double cones?'

Irene nodded. 'And the den, I want to do that. On top of eating ice cream.'

'Okay,' said Riva. 'And we'll ignore the whole cancer thing?'

'No,' said Irene. 'Not ignore it.' She hesitated while she tried to summon the words she needed. 'Not ignore it,' she repeated.

A band of twenty-something boys pushed past them and entered the dairy. Irene watched as they walked, en masse, to the pie-warmer and began emptying it of its contents. A voice rose above the others, complaining loudly that he'd been left with bacon and egg, and asking if anyone would swap. Someone offered a potato-topped vegetable pie and he shook his head, answering, 'Nah, you're right.' One or two of the boys finished their pies before reaching the counter to be served; others barged ahead and ordered ice creams. One by one they filtered back onto the street and formed a small bunch near where Irene and Riva stood.

At first the boys ignored the older women, but then one caught Irene's glance and nodded his head in greeting. 'All right?'

'Awesome,' replied Irene, laughing at her ability to slip into teenage-speak so rapidly.

'Dinner?' asked the boy.

'Are you asking me out?' said Irene.

The boy blushed deeply. 'Nah, I meant is that your dinner?'

Irene nodded. 'Yep, but this is just the main course. We'll be moving on to dessert in a minute.'

The boy nodded, then gesturing towards Irene's beanie, said, 'Cool hat.'

Instinctively, Irene put her hand up and tugged at the edge of the beanie so that it slipped from her head, revealing her pink scalp.

The boy's look of surprise gave way to embarrassment. Irene registered his discomfort but ran her fingers over her scalp and sighed, 'It's like a Brazilian wax, only better.'

The boy coughed, choked and looked away. His lips, however, began to curl into a smile, and he turned back to face Irene. 'Pretty rad — for a lady.'

'You're beginning to make me nervous,' observed Riva, once they were away from the boys, 'every time you open your mouth. Is this just your way of masking your fear and desperation? Because I could understand that. In fact it would strike me as less crazy, to be honest.'

Irene ignored her. Her attention was already focused elsewhere, on a display of 1950s knitting patterns and a knitting machine in the neighbouring shop. 'Didn't Mother have a machine like that?' she asked, using her cone to indicate the contraption.

Riva nodded, then tilted her head from left to right, not entirely certain.

'She was so uptight, wasn't she?' said Irene, more to herself than to Riva.

'She was strong, though,' replied Riva. 'When she got sick, she drew on all her strength and decided to go into battle against the disease.'

Irene appeared not to have heard. She had bent forward and tried to decipher the name of the knitting machine. 'Prazisa,' she said. 'That the same as hers?'

'Yeah, maybe.'

'But Mother lost, didn't she?' murmured Irene. 'Really, she might have been better off befriending her cancer.'

'She wasn't much into friends, though, was she?' answered Riva.

Irene leant against her sister, resting her head on Riva's shoulder while she finished her ice cream. 'Can you imagine what Mother would say if I told her I planned to befriend my cancer.'

'She'd call you contrary and possibly cruel and spiteful, too.'

'And stupid,' added Irene.

'And insane.'

Giggling occasionally, they walked back to the car, hand in hand.

IT WAS A GOLDEN MORNING. The sun was beginning to catch the far shore as Riva stood on the bank watching a small group of kayakers make their way towards her. Though they were still some distance away, she could make out the sound of their paddles dipping and pulling into the water, the splash catching in the air like fish rising. Dragonflies flicked among the reeds close by. Some, bonded, head to tail, moved awkwardly, their exaggerated length making them appear cumbersome beside their slim, more agile neighbours. The sky, still yellowish in the early morning light, brightened, becoming blue. A plane rose into the sky, its fuselage dazzling, mirror-like, as the aircraft turned to the north.

There were nine people, all from the polytechnic canoe club. They'd been coming out to the wetlands for the past three years, spending a day exploring the shoreline, pulling out willow and gorse from areas that couldn't be reached from the land. Today, Riva would ask them to inspect the smaller islands along the northern boundary of the sanctuary. She hadn't managed to maintain all the pockets of land herself during the previous year, but, now that she was more organised and had more time, she intended to lay down traps on as many of the islands as she could.

It had been almost four years since she'd planted a grove of forty-four native trees on a small island where the stream entered the lake. When she'd first visited the hillock it had been thick with gorse and bracken, and she'd had to fight to reach its low summit. Over a period of months she had cleared the land, creating a trodden path as she dragged and hauled the bushes into piles that she eventually burned, one by one, during the winter. In the space of those almost four years, the trees had flourished. Not one of them had died, and several now stood as high as her waist. Eventually they would reach up to twenty metres high and be visible from a good distance.

Soon, on the fourth anniversary of Irene's death, she would

attempt to fulfil the promise she had made to her sister. The number of passing years was significant because it had come as the result of a hard bargain. Somewhat perversely, Irene had later insisted on putting the conversation 'on record' as proof of the terms of settlement, so that Riva would not be able to worm out of the agreement once time was up. Riva hadn't replayed the recording — it was too painful to hear Irene's voice — but she recalled the discussion nevertheless.

It had begun, as always, with Irene catching Riva off-guard. On this occasion they'd been killing time in the supermarket while waiting for the car to get its warrant. They were wandering the aisles, moving slowly, when Irene announced, in a voice loud enough for the woman next to them to hear, 'I don't want you to waste your time moping around after I'm dead.'

The stranger's hand, Riva noticed, stopped mid-air between the shelf of tinned tomatoes and her trolley. Her head flicked around to see who had spoken, and catching sight of Irene she took a small step backwards, before regaining her composure and continuing along her way.

'You're not to blub too much. And I definitely don't want a funeral.'

Riva was used to Irene's outbursts, but even so she asked her sister to be quiet, suggesting they might postpone this particular conversation until they were somewhere more private. But Irene shook her head. 'I'll be finished in a minute. There's not much to say.'

She walked ahead, every now and again lifting something from the shelf, before examining it and replacing it, willy-nilly, as she moved forward. Riva followed, reshelving the goods as she passed by. 'I've already told Valerie I'm not having a funeral, but I'm not sure she understood. She got quite upset and told me not to talk about it.'

Riva almost laughed. She could imagine what happened. Valerie was most likely putting together a bouquet for a customer and wasn't prepared for her boss's bombshell. It was even possible that the customer was hovering in the background, waiting for the flowers and forced to eavesdrop on the conversation. No wonder Valerie had got upset.

'Were you alone with Valerie when you sprang the topic on her?'

'Kind of.'

'Kind of?'

'Well, she was putting together an arrangement for a customer . . .'

'So there was a customer in the shop?'

Irene sighed impatiently. 'The customer started it. She wanted flowers for a colleague whose mother had died.'

'So, you took advantage of the situation to talk about your own funeral . . .'

'Well, no . . . yes . . . It was because of the flowers. She wanted an all-white arrangement and it struck me as so blah — but I didn't say that. I only said that I'd like something with a bit of guts when I die, something unlovely like gorse or broom, which smells delicious by the way — not that I can smell anything since having chemo — or even proteas, because I know Valerie likes them. So, in a way, I was being kind to Valerie. I told her I didn't want a funeral but, if she felt compelled to do something, she could chuck together a bunch of proteas and stick them in a jar, and put it somewhere nice and peaceful, preferably with an outlook over a river or lake, and that would do me.'

'Goodness, Irene. How could you do that to Valerie?'

'You've never even met Valerie. Every time I try and invite her along you make some excuse not to meet her.'

'I've spoken to her, though,' replied Riva. 'She phoned every day when you were having treatment. She cares about you. She sounds like a lovely person.'

'Well, of course she's lovely. I employed her, didn't I?'

They walked on, skipping the household cleaners and pet food aisle, going straight to the biscuit shelves. 'I'm not eating gluten,' said Irene, 'so don't buy biscuits for me.'

'What are you on about? You've been eating ice cream in a cone for the past year.'

'That's not gluten.'

"Course it is. What do you think a cone is made of?'

Irene threw a packet of chocolate biscuits into the trolley, then another. 'That's probably what's killing me. I knew it.'

With another half-hour to wait before collecting the car, they headed to the nearby gardens and sat on a bench, their bags of groceries flapping by their feet. Seagulls landed nearby, scuttling around, chasing one another, in anticipation of being fed. Irene reached into one of the bags, ripped a hole in the top of a packet containing wholemeal buns and threw crumbs into the air. The gulls jumped up, then flapped back to the ground before scurrying after the morsels.

'As I was trying to say before,' said Irene, 'you're not to go all mopey when I die.'

By now Riva knew better than to contradict Irene. Not so long ago, she would have said 'if' you die, not 'when', but now she didn't bother.

'You're allowed two years maximum, and then I expect you to pull yourself together and start doing things.'

'What things?' asked Riva.

'Oh, stop being awkward. You're worse than a teenager. Seriously, Riva. Two years. And that's it!'

'Ten years,' said Riva.

'Two years.'

'Eight. But I'm still allowed to lose it on your birthday,' countered Riva.

Irene threw a large crust at a duck, which it caught and swallowed so quickly that the outline of the snack was clearly visible in its crop.

'Two years,' replied Irene.

'Six,' said Riva. 'Final offer.'

'Three years.'

'Five years. That's a good round number.'

'Three years,' repeated Irene.

'I'm sick of this.' Riva stood up.

'Okay, okay. Four years. I'll give you four years, but on the condition that when the time is up you do two things.'

'What?'

'One: on the anniversary of my death I want you to do something absolutely spectacular—'

Riva snorted, blowing air through her lips as she laughed.

'—and two,' continued Irene, not to be put off, 'I want you to have made a new friend. I do not want to see you holed up in that caretaker's cottage on your own. You are to have found a friend.'

'Why don't you make it a spectacular friend and save me a bit of trouble?' grumbled Riva. 'This is ridiculous. You know I don't do friends.'

Irene pushed herself to her feet and passed Riva the shopping bags, one by one.

'You are going to make a new friend, and I'm not talking about another dopey cat or Facebook. I mean a proper human friend. A talking companion.'

'I am not getting married again.'

'I know that, you idiot,' laughed Irene. 'I'm not asking for a miracle. It's not like I'm asking you to walk on water!'

The kayakers were close to shore now. Riva raised her hand in greeting and they waved back, putting on a final spurt to reach the bank. The fastest paddler, a young man, glanced back over his shoulder, checking that he had beaten the others. Further back three women maintained their distance, watching and waiting while Gerry, the leader of the group and a student already known to Riva, did the talking.

When Riva had finished giving her instructions, the team set off, paddling steadily towards a distant bank. As before, the men led the group, an unexpressed competitiveness between them as they started racing to be first. And, as before, the three younger women lagged behind. At one point, drawing close to a flock of swans, the women drew up their paddles and drifted silently, their single canoes gently butting against one another as they formed a makeshift raft, and watched the large birds float by. Once the birds had passed, they resumed their paddling, arriving on the lakeshore several minutes after Gerry and the rest of the boys. They located the tools Riva had dropped off the day before, and immediately went to work, and before long the sound of chopping, sawing and digging could be heard echoing across the water. With the kayakers fully employed, Riva stepped into her own canoe and started paddling slowly in the direction of a low promontory overlooking the lake, intending to retrieve the crates of flax cuttings she had hidden away the previous day in the trees by the old den, before rejoining the group and getting down to work.

For some time now, she'd been having trouble sleeping, worrying more and more about having to do something spectacular in time for the anniversary of Irene's death. Some nights, when she was unable to sleep, she propped herself up in bed, Googled the words 'spectacular' and 'anniversary' and watched footage of explosions, variously associated with spacecraft, zeppelins, Formula One cars and fireworks. Though many of the events were undeniably spectacular, none was simple to replicate — even if she'd wanted to. Musical stage shows and circus performances were also prominently featured, as were fashion shows. These spectacles held Riva's attention, but she didn't plan to emulate them. She felt constrained by reality: she had no contacts in the entertainment business and no desire to face an audience herself. She scrolled through the pages of 'spectacles', occasionally stopped by sightings of more appealing words: plumage, butterflies, courtship, volcanoes, icebergs, waterfalls.

Reading the entries awakened a hidden desire to get away, to travel and see the world. Her day-to-day work at the wetlands which, only the week before, had filled her with satisfaction, now left her frustrated. Sometimes, there seemed little point in what she was doing. Without widespread cooperation, the wetlands would continue to silt up, and would grow more and more polluted, eventually becoming uninhabitable for native fish species. In the past she had celebrated each small success, but recently she could see only the never-ending list of tasks and chores still waiting for her attention. She knew there would never come a time when she could stand back and look at the wetlands and announce, 'All done. Finished.'

Her sister had been the one to offer support and encouragement when Riva needed it. During the last eighteen months of Irene's life, they'd spent a lot of time together, the happiest of which was spent first building and later relaxing in the den by the lake. Neither of them had a clue about construction.

They didn't bother with plans, but for inspiration relied on their vague memory of the tree house chapter Riva had seen in the kids' book. None of the details relating to the actual construction process stayed with Riva but she recalled a phrase that had appeared at the start of the chapter — something like 'Better ask Dad!', which they ended up repeating ad nauseam, whenever something went wrong.

Because they didn't know what they were doing, they enjoyed total freedom every step of the way. The first thing they did, once they'd agreed on the site, was attach a bottle of sugar water to a nearby tree so that they might enjoy the calls of tūī and bellbirds while they worked. Once music was taken care of, they set about making the site comfortable: ferrying a tarpaulin, a camp bed, sleeping bags, fold-out chairs, cooking equipment and food across the lake. The cutout figure of James Bond joined them on their third visit, and on the fourth they carried an ornate vase in which Irene arranged flax flowers. Next came books and photographs, candles, a silver-plated candelabra and an old typewriter. At this point, it became clear to Riva that Irene had lost sight of the original den idea and had entered a fantasy world that called to mind something resembling Karen von Blixen's *Out of Africa*.

Though the interior was more or less taken care of, the den's exterior was still a work in progress. In conversation, Riva frequently reminded Irene that a 'den' was synonymous with lair, hidey-hole, hideout, burrow.

'The look we're going for is makeshift, feral — a bivouac. You need to channel your inner child, the one Mother tried to squash.' Irene brought *World of Interiors* magazines and sat around reading and sipping tea, swooning over images of barn conversions and log cabins. Riva worked the chainsaw and dragged branches into the clearing, stacking and arranging them against the partially fallen pine tree that formed the den's central beam. Irene threw crumbs for the sparrows and entertained Riva with reimagined fairytales, from *Hansel and Gretel* to *Goldilocks and the Three Bears* to *Little Red Riding Hood*, all with the purpose of creating the proper context for her sister's work.

'Why don't you help?' asked Riva one afternoon. 'Couldn't you draw on your Amazonian powers and give us a hand with this branch?'

Irene laughed. 'I see myself more as an experience designer than a hired hand. I bring vision to this grand project.'

'Muscle would be more useful at this stage,' grimaced Riva. 'How about a cup of tea?'

They sat together in the shade of the mānuka and looked out over the lake, taking pleasure in the way the sun caught the water, or from the occasional sightings of heron or pūkekō. For dinner they fried bacon, inhaling the scent and waiting impatiently for the fat to become crisp and curl. They each took two rashers, laying them on fresh white bread and then adding tomato and avocado. It was only when they began to eat that Riva noticed the difference between them. Whereas her hunger was intense, causing her to bite quickly into her sandwich, Irene picked at her food, sliding out the bacon and snapping each rasher in her fingers before nibbling gingerly at the meat. Riva watched her sister's slow progress.

'Are you okay?' she asked.

'Mmm, fine,' replied Irene.

'Not hungry?'

'Not really,' said Irene.

'Are you in pain?'

Irene glanced at her plate, broke away a crust and fed it into her mouth. 'Just the same,' she said. She held her plate up, offering the sandwich to Riva. 'Take it. I'm really not hungry.'

Although in the space of a few minutes Riva had lost her appetite, she took the plate from Irene and took a small bite. She chewed slowly, ashamed of her health.

'I can take you home, if you like.'

'No, I like it better here. It's peaceful. I'll be all right in a minute.'

They sat in silence. Riva didn't trust herself to talk. She listened intently to Irene's quiet sounds of discomfort. A faint gasp followed by a slow exhalation had Riva on her feet, and in one quick stride she was beside Irene, where she stayed, rooted to the ground, helpless, as she watched her sister's face contort with each grimace of pain.

During the night they lay side by side on camp beds. Riva rested her hand on her sister's sleeping bag, drawing comfort from the sensation of warmth beneath her fingers. She fell asleep, waking only once or twice, and awoke in the morning feeling guilty that she had passed the night so easily. To her relief, Irene was chatty, full of plans for stage two of the development.

'I was thinking that we should get a solar shower. What do you think?' Irene asked.

'If you want.'

'It would be quite handy,' continued Irene.

Riva imagined standing under a thin drizzle of lukewarm water. 'Or we could nip back to my place and have a bath there,' she replied.

A grin spread across Irene's face. 'Yes!' she said. 'That's what we want. An outdoor bath. You could arrange that, couldn't you?'

Riva groaned.

Undeterred, Irene went on. 'With your skills you could easily whip up one of those outdoor bath things with a fire and a chimney.'

'What skills?' laughed Riva.

'Plumbing skills,' said Irene.

'Plumbing skills? We've got a twenty-litre plastic bucket and a toilet seat. That's not much to skite about.'

'It works. It's a good system. The lid hasn't come off when we take it home to empty it. You should have more faith in yourself.'

As Riva watched, Irene began pacing out the ground around the den, marking out areas in the dirt with a long stick. Locating a spot for the bath, she sat down on the hard earth and pretended to scrub herself while taking in the view of the lake. Irene had always loved deep, hot baths. They used to share the water as kids, and for some reason Irene always managed to bags the first bath; Riva made do with the soapy second.

'You know you need water for a bath,' said Riva as she continued to watch her sister's performance.

Irene ignored her, and pretended to wash her hair.

'All the raw sewage from the settlement over there is pumped straight into the lake. And then there's all the run-off from the surrounding farms . . .'

Irene turned on Riva and pretended to splash her, and then held her nose and ducked down. A feeling of hopelessness gripped Riva. There were two things she really cared about in the world — her sister, and the wetlands — and they were both facing death.

It took a long time for the den to be completed. It amazed Riva that it stood its ground and didn't disintegrate during the first northwest gale. They held a christening ceremony, and Irene created a sign to hang above the entrance: 'The Debacle. Keep Out — Ladies Only.' She located native plants, clematis, kākā beak and rātā, and created a small reserve to one side of the den, a garden that would outlive her and bring birds to the area.

It was the destruction of these plants, more than the gradual theft of the chairs, the typewriter and the candelabra, or the bullet holes in James Bond, that destroyed Riva's fragile peace. The discovery of the clematis broken and trampled into the ground and her sister's 'Debacle' plaque floating in the water was all that it took to dissuade Riva from returning to the den. For over three years she kept her distance, afraid of what she might discover. But during the past year, with the anniversary niggling away at her, she returned, making fleeting visits in the vague hope of finding inspiration, or a solution to the problem of doing something spectacular.

On the first visit after her long absence, she had been surprised to find the den itself in reasonably good condition. It had withstood the wind, floods and snow of previous years and appeared to be bearing up well, despite the loss of some of its exterior features. Inside she had been even more surprised to discover several items dating back to Irene's time. One camp bed remained, as did the table and shelves. Articles of bedding and one or two crates containing cooking equipment had been upended, their contents littered about the floor, but although it was clear they had been tampered with, it seemed, on first glance, that nothing had been taken. Tree stumps were arranged in one corner and there was a pile of empty cans, mostly of high-energy drinks and mixers, by the entrance. Most remarkable of all was the presence of the old ornate vase and the figure of James Bond. The vase appeared undamaged, even though it had been tossed outside, and was lying in the soft dirt where the kākā beak had once grown. Bond had fared less well. Not only was his chest pockmarked with holes but his lips had been painted pink. The presence of a beauty mark added to his odd appearance, putting Riva in mind of a sex toy, or some tarted-up vaudeville star.

It took Riva more than an hour to sort through the rubbish and tidy up the mess. Her final touch, before leaving, was to place a bunch of kānuka in the vase. She returned once more, not long afterwards, half expecting the place to have been trashed in her absence. To her relief, nothing more had been damaged, though it seemed to her that one or two things might have been moved. She wasn't certain, however, and so paid little attention to her gut feeling, instead replacing the spent kānuka with a fresh bunch, picked from the stand of trees beside the Stills' boundary fence.

The next time she visited, she knew at once that she had been right to suspect someone else was visiting the den. The kānuka was gone. In its place was a bunch of buttercups. The flowers, yellow against the green leaves, were still fresh, round and waxy, as if polished. For a full half-hour she sat on the camp bed staring at the flowers. They were too small for the vase; the blooms barely poked above the opening, giving the impression of treading water, of struggling to keep from drowning. Despite their fragility they were beautiful and exactly the kind of flowers Irene would have picked. In fact, she had, once.

During their last trip together, Riva had left Irene alone for an hour or two and gone to work, skirting the bank, knocking back thistles and blackberry, attacking the weeds with a sense of urgency, all the time anxious about her sister, who was outside the den, on a bed. She knew, as she worked, that this would be Irene's last night in the Debacle and that she would not be returning to the wetlands. In fact, both of them knew, but they had chosen not to speak about it, instead pretending that everything was fine, that summer was still ahead of them and that with the days becoming warmer and longer they would spend even more time outside, relaxing, chatting and sleeping under the stars.

Sleeping under the stars was something they had never done as kids. Their mother had always worried about night creatures and insects and, in any case, hated to be uncomfortable. Their father, to be kind, occasionally took them to the rooftop of their apartment block and stayed out with them, talking above the sound of traffic, motorbikes and the shrill warning screech of sirens and horns. He entertained them with stories of the jungle, tales of spiders bigger than his hand and snakes longer than his leg, and comforted them when the sound of rats scuttling nearby frightened them.

Irene maintained a lifelong fear of rats, something Riva was reminded of during their last night by the lake.

'Did you hear that?' asked Irene long after they had turned in for the night.

Riva listened, but said nothing.

'Are you awake?' persisted Irene.

'Mmm.' Riva's eyes were shut, her body caught midway between a spell of deep sleep and a growing awareness of needing to wake.

'There's a rat,' said Irene. 'I can hear it ... Listen.'

Riva rolled onto her side. She heard the lapping of water, the breeze in the trees and a distant call, a braying sound. 'It's probably a possum,' she replied. 'There was a lot of fresh poo on the ground beneath the lancewood.'

'It's a rat,' repeated Irene. 'Aargh, something just ran across my feet!' A light snapped on, its beam scanning crazily across the air between their beds, before lowering to the ground. 'Save me!' Irene started laughing but there was a hysterical edge to the sound. 'Come on, Ruthie, you're my older sister. Protect me!'

Riva groaned. Her sleeping bag was warm and she had no desire to struggle up and hunt for a rat she'd never find.

'Ruthie, please, please. Come on, get up,' pleaded Irene.

'Stop calling me Ruthie.'

Riva knew she had lost the battle. If she didn't get up, Irene would continue to plead, calling 'Ruthie' in the same irritating tone she had used long ago, when Riva was Ruth.

'You're a baby,' grumbled Riva. She felt for her boots, pulling them on over her bare feet.

'And you're mean!'

'I tell you what,' said Riva. 'I'll set a trap under your bed and sit up with you until you fall asleep. How does that sound?'

'Thank you,' said Irene.

Riva sat on the edge of Irene's bed, the hard ridge of its metal frame digging into the backs of her thighs. It was colder now that she was no longer under the protection of her sleeping bag but she couldn't be bothered moving. She stretched and yawned and tried to get comfortable, but was scared that the bed might collapse if she shifted around too much. Besides, she didn't want to disturb her sister, who seemed to be asleep.

Close by, the rat ran over the hard ground, beating a path that seemed to take it back and forth between the two beds, close to Riva's feet. Every so often a sound, halfway between a squeak and a chatter, would reach Riva's ears and she would draw her legs up in anticipation of feeling the rat brush by. It wasn't that she was scared of rats — she didn't share her sister's horror of their long, bald tails — but she didn't like them. She wouldn't mourn if they disappeared from the world.

She had the sensation that the rat was nearby, that something had captured its attention, and she was about to switch on her torch when she heard a sharp thwack, the sound of the trap beneath the bed going off. To her surprise, she felt jubilant and was unable to prevent herself from exclaiming 'Yes!' in a loud voice. Irene stirred beside her, turned in her bed and mumbled, 'What?'

'The rat,' said Riva. 'I've caught it.'

Irene didn't respond. She drew the sleeping bag around her neck and appeared to fall asleep again but a moment later roused herself, asking, 'What are you going to do with it?'

'Nothing, go back to sleep.'

Irene pushed herself up onto her elbows. 'You can't leave it under my bed. That's creepy.'

'It's dead,' said Riva.

'I know. That's why it's creepy. Who wants to sleep with a dead rat beneath their bed?'

Suddenly, Irene was sitting upright, swinging her feet off the bed, wriggling her way out of the sleeping bag. 'I want to see it.'

'It's late, Irene. Wait till the morning.'

'No, come on, let's have an adventure.'

'It's the middle of the night,' protested Riva.

But it was too late. Irene was already standing, dragging on Riva's arm, shoving her in the direction of the trap, insisting, 'I want an adventure. Hurry up . . . I won't get another chance. Just think of it as a last request!'

The lightness with which the last remark was uttered didn't fool Riva. She couldn't turn down her sister, and so she got down on her knees and pulled the trap towards her. The dead rat was big and healthy-looking. Its fur was lush and its body still warm to the touch. She held it up by its tail and, gingerly, Irene reached out and poked its back leg with a finger, before recoiling.

'What do you want to do now?' asked Riva, placing the creature on the ground.

Irene thought for a minute. 'Let's feed it to the eels.'

'What eels?'

But her sister was already leading the way towards the bank, calling back, 'Come on. This will be fun.'

For an hour they sat in the Canadian canoe, close to the shore, the rat submerged just below the surface of the water. 'Jiggle it,' instructed Irene. 'Jiggle it like a tea bag.'

Riva did as she was told, jiggling the rat up and down in the water, hoping its scent would attract an eel. Every time her fingers started to cramp and her arm tire, Irene would prompt her, repeating, 'Jiggle it,' and like an automaton Riva would jerk back into action. Eventually, however, her arm gave way, the rat's tail slipped from her fingers and the animal sank from view.

'Sorry,' said Riva.

Irene shrugged. 'It's okay. It was fun enough watching you.'

They drifted in the breeze, neither of them in any hurry to return to shore. At one point the bow bumped against the bank and Irene reached out and picked a clump of buttercups, their petals all the more vivid under the beam of the torch. She held the flowers tight in her hand and then, spotting something a short distance away, pulled the boat further along the bank, reaching out for a small white flower that Riva did not recognise.

'What is it? An orchid?'

'A violet,' said Irene. 'A native. *Viola lyallii*, I think.'

'Show-off.'

Irene handed the fragile flower to Riva. 'Pretty, isn't it?'

'Yeah, it's nice. I like how wonky it is. The stem doesn't seem strong enough for the flowerhead. Can I keep it?'

Irene nodded and then leant back against the bow of the canoe, allowing her fingers to trail in the water. She hummed a tune in a low voice, and then, without pausing, said, 'Funny how neither of us had kids. Did you never want one?'

Riva stopped paddling. She held the paddle above the water,

watching the drops form and fall into the lake. 'I guess not.'

'Do you think you might have done, if our own childhood had been happier?'

'Don't know. Probably not. How about you?' asked Riva.

Irene pushed herself up into a sitting position and took the paddle from Riva's hands, dipping it into the lake, making small forward strokes. 'I feel bad about leaving you alone, sometimes.'

'Don't feel bad.'

The wake made scrolls in the calm water. The canoe turned one way and then the other, barely making progress towards shore. Irene had a look of concentration on her face; the tip of her tongue poked between her teeth as she tried to correct and then modify her steering. Riva watched and waited and tried not to grow impatient. Eventually she reached for the paddle: 'It's a job for dads.'

Irene laughed. 'Well, it's not a job for our mother, is it? She wouldn't have wanted to get her gloves wet.'

'I like being alone,' said Riva after a while. 'I'll be okay, I promise. Being alone doesn't scare me.'

She meant it and she knew that Irene understood, because ultimately she, too, liked being alone.

As they skirted the shore, they could see headlights from the first commuter traffic across the lake. These were the people who didn't have offices to go to but worked on farms, in factories, hospitals or on building sites. It would be another hour, at least, before the rest of the workforce began making its way towards the city.

Irene broke the silence. 'Valerie will be at the flower market. She's done such an amazing job since I've been away. I can't persuade her to stay on and take over the business, though. She reckons it would make her sad, being in the shop without me. You know, you should meet her sometime. I keep saying that, I know, but you should.'

Riva turned the canoe in the direction of an island, one of several low humps that rose from the lake. As she neared the island she stowed the paddle and allowed the canoe to drift, bumping against the shallow bottom and coming to a rest several metres from dry land. She twisted in her seat, and pointed to the dark outline. 'This is my next project. I'm going to clear it and plant natives. What do you think?'

'Cabbage trees,' said Irene.

'Yes, I know you like cabbage trees but I was thinking of kōwhai and tōtara, maybe some rātā. There's a beautiful view from the top. There's a little scoop near the summit and it's completely sheltered, and you can sit up there and read a book, or watch the sky and clouds, or the planes . . . or whatever. You would like it. I'll take you up there.'

'Can you buy ice cream up there?'

Riva grinned. 'No.'

Irene sat in silence, her face turned towards the hill. After a while she spoke, quietly — barely loud enough for Riva to hear. 'I'm not going if there's no ice cream. I'm sorry but that's how it is. I refuse to go and you can't make me.'

'But . . .' began Riva, and then she too fell quiet. She felt her shoulders begin to shudder and she gripped the paddle tightly, pulling on it with all her strength as she tried to free the boat from the ground beneath. The sound of splashing and scraping filled the air, and then, finally, they were free, travelling away from the island as fast as Riva could paddle.

For twenty minutes neither of them spoke. Riva focused all her attention on trying to keep a straight line. Irene slumped back in her seat, once more leaning her head against the bow, as if relaxing in a hot bath. Now and then, the call of a bird reached them. The song of a blackbird filled the air, only to be replaced by the clear ring of a tūī and the distant boom of a bittern. A splash caught their attention. Both turned to face the sound but they were too slow to see what had made it.

The sky began to lighten, the blackness fading to slate, and then the first pink streaks of dawn appeared to the north. 'I'm hungry,' said Irene.

'That's because you didn't eat dinner.'

'Yes, Mother.'

Riva smiled at her sister. 'What do you want for breakfast?' she asked as they drew up to their campsite.

'Depends what's on the menu.'

'Well, we have bread and honey, or bacon and bread. Or any combination of those elements.'

'Like bread and bread?'

'Yep.'

'Mmm, tasty,' said Irene.

The canoe bumped against the bank. Riva clambered out and then went to the bow, holding out her hand for her sister to take. Despite the warm air that had enfolded them, Irene's fingers were cold to the touch, and her hand felt skeletal. Riva noticed the way Irene's legs buckled as she took the weight of her sister's body, supporting her as she tried to step out of the boat. On the second attempt, Irene managed to get one foot onto the bank, but needed a firm tug to get the other leg across the gap, and even then ended up doing a slight skip in her attempt to regain her balance. Despite herself, Riva laughed. 'Steady there.'

Irene draped her arm around Riva and hugged her, allowing her weight to fall against her sister. 'Come on, old girl. Get me some bread and bread before I die.'

Together they walked to the den and it was only as the

223

domed shape came into view that Irene pulled Riva to a stop and whispered to her, 'Cabbage trees. Don't forget. Cabbage trees and ice cream.'

EVERY MUSCLE IN RIVA'S BODY ached from her day with the students. She made an 'oomph' sound as she pushed herself up into a sitting position. Swinging her legs to the side of the bed, she hauled herself up, took a ginger step but could not straighten up. She walked, hunched over, down the hall towards the kitchen, and then rested, palms on the bench, while she summoned the strength to fill the kettle. Her left hip throbbed, her calf muscles felt tighter and shorter than they had the day before, and even the soles of her feet were tender from spade work. Blisters formed a neat row along her palms. The skin on her face felt taunt and burnt, from too many hours spent in the sun and wind.

The morning before she had told Gerry and his team that she intended to pull her weight and now she was doing just that. She lifted the boiling water and filled the coffee plunger before shuffling slowly, painfully, towards the table by the window.

Outside the sun was shining; it was already well past eleven and she was still in her pyjamas. At two she was due to speak at Caroline Freeman High and, as usual in these situations, she had little idea what she would say. The invitation had come from an Environmental Studies staff member, a teacher named Paul Park, who had contacted Riva via email, asking her to address a group of students undertaking a project on freshwater fishes. The email was respectful and flattering in equal part. It acknowledged the work she had done at the Tinker Wetlands and expressed a hope that she would share some of her knowledge and stories with his class. He added, for good measure, that they were a good bunch of kids who had already spent most of the term working on various environmental projects. She should expect informed and lively questioning.

In a burst of enthusiasm she responded immediately, confirming one of the dates and times put forward by Mr Park. She felt sure she would remember the event but made a note of it anyway, on a scrap of paper that she left on her table. In time, the paper fragment got covered by other papers and cleared away for recycling. She forgot all about the presentation and had Paul Park not phoned the previous afternoon and left a message explaining he had been called away, and that a relief teacher would be filling in, she would have missed the appointment. Park's message ended with an apology and an instruction. Riva would be met in the reception area by a staff member, Loretta Reed, who would escort her to class, introduce her to the relief teacher and remain to provide technical assistance.

As she sipped her coffee, Riva glanced around the room, hoping against hope that something would capture her attention and provide inspiration for the talk. She had spoken to school groups many times, but always from the safety of her familiar environment — the shed where she worked, or out and about in the wetlands. When words failed her, she had been able to distract the kids with worksheets. Talking to a group in a classroom environment was something else entirely. She didn't have a 'presentation' as such, had no idea how to use technical aids or PowerPoint and wasn't interested in learning now. With no time left to do more than scribble a few headings, she decided to wing it. She would rely on her knowledge and enthusiasm. She would present herself as a slightly eccentric expert — the wetland equivalent of classicist Mary Beard.

Riva's red and black cowboy boots gleamed with polish. Earlier, when she fished them out of the cupboard, they were covered in a dusting of dull green mould, but, looking at them now, no one would ever know. Putting together the rest of her outfit was not so easy. Her one dress no longer fitted, but hung like a sack from her shoulders. Her faithful skirt, the one she wore to meetings with her lawyer, trustees and the council, looked frumpy and worn. Her good pair of trousers were muddy at the hems from wearing them around the sanctuary. Fortunately she had a pair of black jeans that looked presentable.

Deciding to go with a younger vibe, she pulled out her T-shirts. The first to capture her attention was one screen-printed with the earliest design of her outdoor clothing company, BRA(IN)STORM. In the early days of her business, she had been struggling to find the courage to launch her company and the words gave her strength. She'd latched onto the slogan and printed two hundred T-shirts, all yellow with red lettering. A signwriter friend was employed to create a storefront sign that she mounted on the façade of her first Carson City retail outlet. She sewed thirty Irene jackets and placed her first orders for outdoor equipment, boots and trail provisions and, with barely enough stock to fill the shelves, opened the doors and began trading. Within a month she knew she was not going to be able to make ends meet. She was in debt and needed an investor. Ivan, her landlord and a successful lawyer, came to her rescue. They began dating, got married.

It was Ivan who first noticed that customers had started to

complain about having to write BRA(IN)STORM on cheques. 'It confuses them. They're always asking if it's "Brainstorm" or "Bra in Storm" and what does it mean? We're losing customers — plus, I'm worried about the whole women's thing. We need to rebrand. Make it simpler, snappier.'

Riva protested but gave in. For weeks she searched books for an alternative name, reading and rereading the work of Emily Dickinson, Elizabeth Bishop, Maya Angelou, Judy Grahn, Mary Oliver, Rachel Carson and Annie Dillard in the vain hope of finding the perfect word to encompass her brand. Meanwhile Ivan came up with a solution: Mountain Street Depot. 'It's perfect,' he said. 'On one level it's our address and on the other it encapsulates our customer base.' The name stuck and Mountain Street Depot went on to become a huge success, but Riva mourned the loss of BRA(IN)STORM all the same.

Riva unfolded the BRA(IN)STORM T-shirt and pulled it over her head. She hadn't noticed but there was a hole in the armpit where the fabric had worn through. Reluctantly she took it off and put it on her bed. Aware that she was running out of time, she quickly pulled out a second pile of T-shirts: a lime-green 'Save our Wetlands' top, a black Sea Shepherd shirt and a white T-shirt with an image of a steaming cow pat and the words 'Stop Dirty Dairying' underneath. A third bundle revealed a 'Save the Arctic' shirt, a brand-new and unworn 'I (heart) Carson City' top, and two more T-shirts: 'Eat More Ice Cream' and 'Greenham Common Women's Peace Camp'. These were Irene's and Riva hadn't worn either of them for fear of erasing the lingering scent of her sister's favourite jasmine perfume oil with her own body odour.

It was almost time to leave and Riva still couldn't make her mind up. Finally, growing impatient, she pulled out a bright orange T-shirt she had recently uncovered, much to her delight and surprise, in a record shop. Printed across it in bold capitals was the word 'EELS'. She pulled it over her head and looked at her reflection, turning her body this way and that, before nodding her head in approval. Not too bad for an old lady. All she needed now was Irene's beanie for luck and her silver earrings and she'd be good to go.

Despite her best intentions she was late. As she explained to an anxious-looking Loretta Reed, who was waiting by the visitor car park, she had been distracted by a honey stall on the side of the road and had got into conversation with the apiarist, who happened to be restocking the shelves. 'I've been thinking about getting hives, myself, you see,' she explained as she followed Loretta down a series of corridors, across a courtyard and towards a block of dark blue prefabs near the playing fields. 'I've read about beekeeping but I don't really know where to start. I'm hoping I can persuade Otto — that's the beekeeper — to put some hives on my land. That would be great, don't you think?'

Without slowing, or turning to face her, Loretta answered, 'I've always fancied bees, too. But I'm not sure if we've got enough food in our garden. Not like you, with all that mānuka down by the lake.'

Riva missed a step, skipped to keep up. 'You've been to the wetlands?'

'Yep,' said Loretta. 'Many times.'

Riva suddenly felt happy, and the nerves that had been building since she left home abated.

They had reached the classroom. Outside, hanging from the branches of a kōwhai tree, were a variety of bird-feeders, some containing sugar water but also some with grains visible through a clear plastic tube. Silver-eyes and sparrows darted up into the branches as the women approached.

'I hope you don't mind,' said Loretta, 'but I'd like to sit in on your talk, if that's all right with you?'

'No, that's fine by me,' said Riva. 'You don't have a class?'

'No. Sorry, didn't Paul explain that I'm the librarian? I'm not the actual teacher for this class.'

'No . . . yeah,' said Riva. 'Oh, I'm sure he did mention it but I'm a bit slow sometimes with names and things.'

Loretta stood to one side, allowing Riva to enter the classroom first. As Riva walked past, it finally dawned on her who Loretta was: Chance's librarian. The stoat-skin woman. It was too late to say anything, however, as the relief teacher was already approaching, hand outstretched, welcoming her to the session.

There were about fifteen students, teenagers — more like adults really. She could tell from the way some of the girls looked at her that they found her appearance slightly amusing. It was the cowboy boots, or the beanie, maybe, that captured their attention. Or maybe it was the T-shirt. It was as though they couldn't place her, and recognising that gave Riva even more confidence.

'The truth is,' said Riva, 'that until last night, I'd forgotten all about coming here today so I haven't prepared a talk.' She paused, smiled in the direction of the teacher and then turned back to the class. 'So I'm going to talk to you about some of my personal experiences, about how I first got interested in wetlands, about what I do and why I think long-fin eels are cool.' She gestured towards her T-shirt and made a little curtsey and a couple of the kids laughed. In her head a voice went, 'Whoops!', but she didn't really care. It wasn't her job to try and impress the class. She just had to talk honestly and enthusiastically, and she could tell by looking at their faces that most of the kids were prepared to listen.

'How many of you read the newspaper or follow news sites on the internet?'

A smattering of hands went into the air. 'Okay, good. So what headlines can you remember from the front pages, recently?'

A few voices rose up from the class: Aging rocker to give free concert. All Black cousin on glamour list. Politician refuses to apologise. Search for missing local woman called off.

Riva listened, nodded and said, 'I have to admit that unlike you guys, I don't follow the news or read the papers any more. I used to, until about five years ago, but then I realised I was cluttering my poor old brain with too much worthless information. I had to rid myself of all that white noise. On top of that, many of the stories I regarded as newsworthy weren't being told. So, that was depressing. Here's an example of what I think should be in the news.' She cleared her throat and took a deep breath. '"Ninety per cent of all New Zealand wetlands vanish during last one hundred and fifty years".' She paused, looked around the room to check if anyone was still listening, and added, 'In other words, only ten per cent of our original wetlands are left.' She drew back her shoulders and continued, 'In the case of the Tinker sanctuary, we know that a hundred and fifty years ago the wetland area was seven times bigger than it is now.' Once again she stopped talking and glanced around the room. 'Another headline: "Three-quarters of our native freshwater fish, mussel and crayfish species are listed as threatened with extinction".' The room was silent, so she went on. '"Two-thirds of New Zealand's monitored rivers are too polluted to swim in". I could go on and give you more and more newsworthy stories but I reckon you probably know most of these facts already.' She smiled and waited to see if anyone would ask a question, or challenge her.

'But your news is heaps more depressing than ours,' called out a girl. 'I mean, hello? "*MasterChef* blamed for chocolate shortage" versus "Holidaymakers swim in raw sewage"!' The class clapped and Riva breathed a sigh of relief. It was going to be okay. They were on her side.

She talked for thirty minutes, pausing frequently to allow the students to chime in with their own stories or questions. At one point, two kids entered into a heated discussion about marine reserves and Riva let them go for it, even though it had nothing to do with her own presentation. Just as she thought she had run out of things to say, the teacher wound up the session, asking, 'Are there any last questions? Before we finish up? John?'

'I was wondering where you got your T-shirt?' asked a scrawny boy at the back of the room.

'Sure. From Funk City. Here in town. Why?' said Riva.

John looked a bit embarrassed but replied, 'Because it's the name of a band.'

'What is?' asked Riva.

'Eels,' said John. 'It's an American band.'

Riva glanced once more at her T-shirt and then up at the class. She caught Loretta's eye and shook her head. A couple of students giggled. 'I thought there was something weird about it being in a record shop,' said Riva. 'I even said as much to the guy behind the counter. No wonder he gave me a strange look. He must have thought I was some crazy old lady.'

'No, it looks good,' piped up a girl in the front row. 'It's cool. Better than any of my nana's outfits.'

A smile crept across Riva's face and glancing across to Loretta she raised her eyebrows. The relieving teacher cleared her throat. 'Any more questions?'

The room fell silent. 'In that case,' said the teacher, 'I'd like to thank Riva for coming along today and, as a token of our appreciation, we'd like to present you with some kākā beak and kōwhai seedlings from our nursery.' At her nod, John walked to the back of the room where he picked up a banana box full of plants that he carried back and presented to Riva.

'Thanks very much,' she said. 'Wow. Kākā beak. That's clever of you. What a wonderful gift. Thank you.'

Clutching the box against her body, she followed Loretta out of the class and back across the school grounds. The students' response to her talk had been so positive that she was on a high, barely able to contain her excitement as she repeated snippets of the discussion in her head. The teenagers were so much more interested in environmental issues than she had been at their age. They'd asked a wide range of intelligent questions from Māori consultation, the problem of high nutrient levels, through to seeking her thoughts on imposing a moratorium on whitebaiting and commercial eeling.

'What amazing kids,' she said to Loretta as they neared the office. 'That was the best group.'

'But you were good, too,' said Loretta. 'You're so enthusiastic and honest. The kids found you inspirational.'

Riva brushed Loretta's remark aside. She didn't want to divert attention away from the class. 'They even knew the meaning of "eutrophic". Half the university students I talk to don't even understand what that means.'

By now they were standing in the small waiting area, but Riva couldn't bring herself to leave. She didn't want to get back in her car and go home. 'I should offer a prize . . . no, a scholarship. Something long term that would foster research into—'

'Yes,' interrupted Loretta. 'Even if you targeted the school to help the wetlands with a specific project, like trapping, or something.'

Riva was only half-listening. Her thoughts were far ahead. 'A mentorship. No . . . they don't need me.'

'What about an environmental think-tank,' offered Loretta.

For the first time since meeting her, Riva took a good long look at the librarian and something clicked inside. A thought took hold in her mind. It was so simple and yet so startling that she could barely contain it. The voice inside said, I like you. If she teased the thought out further it would have included: You are a good person, you are smart and you get me. I can talk to you.

But, really, all that was necessary was, 'I like you.'

Riva took a breath and her lungs filled with fresh air. She smiled at Loretta and in that moment felt self-conscious. She opened her mouth to speak, but then changed her mind. 'Well,' she said eventually, 'I shouldn't hold you up any longer.' Then, as she was about to turn away, she remembered their connection. 'You know Chance, don't you? She visits me sometimes and talks about you. I get the impression you're very important to her, and I can see why.'

Loretta's face reddened. 'She's a neat wee kid. So sweet. I think things have been a bit tough for her recently . . .' She stopped.

'From what I've heard, her mother's got a thing about books,' said Riva. 'I don't understand where she's coming from with that. Do you?'

'No,' said Loretta, then murmured, almost to herself, 'I don't think there's any physical abuse going on.'

'Well, there's definitely a case for literature abuse,' said Riva. 'It's ridiculous, forcing novels onto your daughter and then cross-examining her.'

Loretta exhaled slowly. 'I met her mother, Trudy, just last term. At first she was very charming, but then she quickly became quite patronising, and began to lecture me about the importance of books. I don't think it ever occurred to her that she was preaching to the converted.' She shifted uneasily. 'I shouldn't really be saying that.'

'Yeah, well. Doesn't surprise me.' Riva coughed, and quickly added, 'About Trudy, I mean.'

'I suppose Chance could leave home, if it all gets too much. I'm guessing she's old enough.'

'I think she's only just turned fifteen,' answered Loretta, 'so leaving might be a bit drastic.'

'At least she has you,' said Riva. 'She clearly appreciates all that you've done.' She caught Loretta's eye and saw that her words had taken the librarian by surprise.

'I haven't done anything special,' stammered Loretta.

'Well, she thinks you have.' Riva paused and readjusted the box in her arms. 'I never really found out what she made with the skin.'

'You know about that?'

Riva nodded.

'It was nice, in a slightly ghoulish way. A lucky charm made from a stoat.' Loretta chuckled, then stopped herself. 'Unfortunately, it went off and began to stink. I wasn't sure what to do with it so I popped it into the freezer until I work out how to fix it.'

'It took her all night to make it,' said Riva. 'She was up till dawn.'

'Really?' Loretta looked shocked.

'And you found her a good book,' said Riva.

Loretta nodded.

'You think her mother will like it?'

Loretta grinned. 'I think Chance will like it.'

Riva looked at Loretta and knew for certain that she liked this woman.

It was raining by the time Riva left the school car park. Through the foggy windscreen she could see the first of the students walking through the gates, some in clumps of two or three, others alone, heading towards the buses lined up on the street. Despite the wet weather, few had coats. Many of the boys wore short-sleeved shirts, seemingly oblivious to the change in temperature. A group of girls crossed her path, running across the road without looking for traffic. Riva tooted her horn and one girl turned back, scowled and gave her the finger, mouthing something that could have been 'Fuck you' before catching up her friends.

Riva was about to pull onto the road when she spotted Chance waiting by the bus stop. She raised her hand, hoping to catch the girl's attention, then beeped her horn once more. When Chance failed to notice, she turned into the bus lane and eased her car towards the front of the queue, waving as she passed. This time Chance saw her and came running up to the passenger door and climbed in beside Riva, who quickly lurched forward, moving the car out of the way of a bus that was trying to get around her.

'Want a ride?' Riva asked.

Chance jerked at the seat-belt strap. 'Yes please.'

As they passed the 'fuck you' girl Riva pointed and asked, 'Who's that charmer?'

'Michelle,' said Chance.

'Do you know her?'

'Unfortunately. That's my brother Higgs, with her. They both work part-time at the supermarket, but Michelle is going around telling everyone he's a champion racing-car driver, and that he's asked her to move to Australia with him.' She glanced back over her shoulder before adding, 'I don't think Higgs knows that that's the plan. He's never mentioned her, anyway.'

'What about those boys over there?' Riva pointed to a group of teenagers, dressed in the senior uniform. 'Are they your friends?'

'Nah,' said Chance. 'I'm not really into boys. Some are okay, I guess. But then I think, What if they turn out to be idiots, like my brothers? And that kind of freaks me out.'

'There must be some nice guys,' said Riva, remembering the students in the environment class.

'Probably,' said Chance. 'I don't know. It's me, I guess. I find them all a bit icky.' She fell silent, pulled out her phone and checked the screen. 'No messages.' She smiled. 'That's good. Means I'm not needed.' She tapped out a message, pressed the return button and waited. A moment later there was a beep, and she studied the screen, her face relaxing. 'Mum's out and Dad says I don't have to be home till six. Cool, eh?'

The rain was coming down in thick sheets, forming streams down either side of the road. There was a roar and a clatter and suddenly the rain turned to hail. Stones the size of polystyrene beads bounced off the bonnet and windscreen of the car. The wipers cut arcs across the glass, forcing the balls of hail to pile up along the channel between bonnet and windscreen. Then it was raining once more, thick drops streaking along the driver's and passenger windows. A minute later the sun was shining and, with one departing crack of thunder, the rain passed.

'Do you believe in global warming?' asked Chance, indicating the steam rising up from the asphalt. Before Riva could answer, the girl continued, 'My father reckons it's all rubbish. He says the planet goes through hot and cold cycles and that climate change has nothing to do with farmers. It's another thing my parents argue about. Mum says he's stupid and that it won't be long now before all the petrol runs out and that he and his go-karting mates will realise what colossal idiots they are.'

She cleared her throat and wiped the palm of her hand over the windscreen, clearing a window in the fog. 'She also says that we might as well kill ourselves now as the world isn't going to be worth living in by the time I reach forty.'

'I'm sure she doesn't mean it,' said Riva.

Chance gave a bleak laugh and cleared the windscreen once more. 'Have you ever met my mother?'

Riva shook her head.

'Funny. I thought you might have done.'

'I've brushed shoulders with a couple of local farmers, people like the Stills and your dad. When I bought the wetlands I organised meetings with the locals. I let them know what my plans were and tried to get them interested in addressing issues with drainage and pollution.'

'But they weren't interested?' asked Chance.

'Some were. Some weren't.'

Chance sniffed, wiped her nose with the back of her hand. 'I bet my dad didn't get involved. He's only interested in two things: goats and racing. He has names for some of his favourite does. Makes of cars, mostly, like Audrey Audi, and Holly Holden. Sometimes when I'm in the shed I'll hear him talking to them, saying stuff like, "You're my pretty girl". It's kind of funny cause he'd never say anything like that to us. We're just "bloody kids"!'

They were on the outskirts of the city, heading towards the outer suburbs. The clouds had all but cleared and the sky was a bright pale blue, the colour of starling eggs. It seemed a shame to rush home, especially when there was no need to. As they travelled along the motorway, advertisements for an antique and bric-à-brac fair at the local memorial hall began to pop up, attached to lampposts or hanging as banners from overbridges. Chance became excited, wishing aloud that her mother might take her along.

'It would be great if we could go today, before all the good bargains go. If Trudy's not too tired, we could go before tea. Maybe?' As she spoke her voice became softer, more uncertain, and after a moment she let out a long sigh and said, 'It's not going to happen.'

She fell silent, her attention fixed on the road ahead, no longer turning to look at or read the posters as they drove past. Riva had no interest in the fair but she felt sorry for Chance, and as they neared their exit she pulled across to the left-hand lane, following the main street towards the shopping precinct rather than taking the more direct route to the wetlands. If Chance noticed, she barely registered the change in direction and maintained her silence until Riva slowed down and turned into a car park.

'You're not in a hurry, are you?' said Riva.

Chance shook her head.

'Good, let's go then.'

Riva led the way across the tarmac in the direction of the memorial hall. 'Hope we find something good,' she said, before noticing that Chance was no longer beside her, but had stopped to talk with an attractive woman in her early forties. From the proximity of their bodies it appeared they knew each other well and as Riva watched their interaction she noticed similarities in the way they held their bodies and in their gestures. Just as she concluded that this must be Chance's mother, the older woman gave Chance a slight shove and the two began walking towards Riva.

'This is my mum,' said Chance as she came up to Riva.

'Trudy Chance,' said the woman, not quite frowning.

'Riva. Nice to meet you.'

Trudy gave a tight smile. 'There was really no need for you to go out of your way. I hope Chance wasn't pestering you . . .'

'Not at all,' answered Riva. 'It was my idea.'

The woman tried smiling again, but the flicker of her lips gave her face a brittle edge. 'Anyway, it's nice to meet you.'

'You, too,' said Riva.

As they spoke they began to move out of the way of a car reversing from its parking space. Trudy's shoulder knocked against Riva's and she took a step backwards, losing her balance. 'I'm fine,' she snapped, brushing away Chance's steadying hand.

'Are you going in?' asked Riva, indicating the hall.

Trudy nodded and the three of them slowly walked towards the entrance, Chance staying several steps behind her mother.

'I've only got a few minutes,' said Trudy. 'I'll need to get back soon.'

'Must be busy,' answered Riva. From behind her, she heard the sound of coughing but ignored it.

'It's *always* busy,' said Trudy.

A middle-aged woman sat by a desk at the entrance to the hall, collecting an entry donation from visitors. Because she had been talking, Riva failed to notice where the money was headed, but nevertheless reached into her pocket and pulled out a $10 note. 'For the three of us,' she said, posting the folded note through a slot on a cardboard shoe-box.

Trudy ignored her, and fed two gold coins into the box. 'That's for my daughter and me.'

The collector looked flustered, her eyes darting from one woman to the other as if she was expecting Riva to ask for a refund. When Riva showed no response, she became even more rattled and blurted, 'It's for a lovely cause. We're sending our Glowing Nana winner to Wales. It's the first time a New Zealand contestant has made it through to the finals and we're so proud. Thank you so much.'

'Glowing Nana?' asked Riva. 'Is it a beauty pageant?'

'No, not really.' The woman reached forward and flicked open a brochure that was lying next to the collection box. Pointing to a heading, she paraphrased: 'It's a celebration of wisdom.' She slid the paper closer. 'With a focus on raising self-esteem through beauty in the over-sixties.'

'And how do they judge that?' asked Riva. 'The wisdom bit.'

'Well ...' the woman hesitated. She picked up the brochure and scanned the page, then turned it in her hands. 'It doesn't really say.'

Riva began to move away, but then thought better of it and took a step back to the desk. 'I don't mean to go on about it,' she said, 'but it seems to me that society only ever *talks* about wise old women. Nine times out of ten I'm treated in the most patronising fashion, as if I'm some kind of sixty-year-old imbecile. Do you know what I mean?'

The woman's eyes opened wide and she glanced about before responding, 'Sorry. Do you want your money back?'

'No,' said Riva, 'it's fine. Keep it. Give it to the glowing nana.' She smiled at the woman and said, 'Don't mind me. I'm just more of a glowering granny type.'

The woman laughed nervously.

Trudy and Chance were shifting through boxes of books laid out on the nearest trestle table. Riva watched as Trudy passed a small stack of paperbacks to Chance, telling her to hold onto them while she continued looking. Her fingers passed over the spines, as if flicking through files, and as each new book caught her attention she handed it to her daughter, who took it without speaking. Riva moved closer and gestured towards Chance, taking some of the books from the girl's pile. She glanced at the titles but recognised few of them. They were all novels, and all by male writers. Apart from that the selection appeared random.

'It's ten for $5,' said Chance, as if guessing what Riva was thinking.

'A bargain,' said Riva.

At the sound of Riva's voice, Trudy swung around. 'It's not about the price. It's about the work.'

'Of course,' said Riva. She scanned the covers of the top three books, reading out the names of the authors: Saul Bellow, Hermann Hesse, Vladimir Nabokov. She looked up, and addressing Trudy's back, observed, 'You're keen on Nabokov, aren't you?'

Trudy's palm settled on the books in front of her, and, without turning, she answered, 'Yes. Of course.'

Riva passed the books back to Chance and took another bundle, once more reading out the authors' names in a loud voice. Speaking to Trudy, she began, 'And you like male writers?'

Trudy cleared her throat and began searching through the books again. 'Yes. Why not?'

Riva shrugged, 'Nothing. Just something I was thinking about the other day ... after Chance's last visit.'

'What?' asked Chance.

'Well . . .' began Riva, 'I was daydreaming and thinking about books when I came up with something I call the compass theory of literature. I don't know if it's original. It was a bit of fun, you know.'

From the corner of her eye she could see that Trudy was listening. She'd been searching through the rows at a steady pace, but now she took her time, lifting one book after another from the table.

'So, my theory is that the literary establishment — males — consider all books by men as north on the compass. And, in their world, readers are represented by the compass needle. And as you know, the needle bobs around a bit but nevertheless always points north. In other words, it always swings towards the male point of view.' Riva paused and smiled. 'So, in order to upset the status quo you need a bloody big magnet and it's only by sending the whole compass completely haywire that anyone other than Western men get a look-in.' She stifled a laugh but grinned at Chance, who, in return, stared at her unblinkingly.

Trudy scoffed, put down her book and turned on Riva. 'What kind of rubbish is that? Are you trying to tell me that I shouldn't be reading books by men?'

Riva shook her head, 'No, I'm not telling you anything.'

'So you don't like male writers, is that it?'

'No,' smiled Riva. 'I don't like men, full stop.' She laughed once more, as if expecting Trudy to join in.

Chance took a step back, putting more distance between herself and the two women.

'You don't like men?' Trudy's voice was harsh, with an ugly tone.

'Well, I was married once and there are exceptions, of course, but as a general rule I can take 'em or leave 'em.'

Now Trudy's eyelids fluttered and she glanced from Riva to Chance and slowly back to Riva. 'So you'd rather hang out with pubescent school girls, is that it?'

Riva was aware of her body becoming very still, her mind very quiet, alert, as if caught midway between flight and fight. She hesitated and slowly constructed an image of herself as a tree, a tall and straight matai, with roots that held fast. She counted the seconds until she felt in full control and then, when she was ready, looked Trudy square in the face. 'I've met many kind and intelligent young women in the past, women who have been the magnet to my own fixed way of thinking, and I feel very grateful for that.' She took a deep breath and a shudder travelled through her body. She shifted her attention from Trudy to Chance and relaxed.

A moment later, a man's voice broke in, asking, 'Are you wanting to pay for those?' It was the stallholder and in his hand was a supermarket plastic bag. As he reached forward to take the books from Chance, he hiccupped. 'Sorry, bit of heartburn.' He tapped his chest with his fist and then, holding up the full bag with one hand, presented his palm while Trudy slowly counted out her change. The books paid for, she passed the bag to Chance, who took it without a word.

While Trudy made her way towards a vintage clothing stall, Riva and Chance began searching the tables that displayed what could loosely be labelled craft. They skipped the displays of wheat bags and quilted oven cloths, but paused long enough to witness the final moments of a demonstration of scented-candle making and the start of one for soap. At a table loaded with quartz, crystals and semi-precious stones, Chance stopped and read out the labels describing the healing powers of each coloured rock. 'Agate — good for stress.' She held up a sliver of brown- and golden-layered quartz for Riva to admire and then replaced it gently in its tray, adding, 'My dad should have that one.' Quietly she worked through the stones, laughing as she read about the properties of a piece of icy-blue celestite. 'This one helps with public speaking. I could use that. Here's one for you, look, it's green like the wetlands.' She read the label, nephrite, and looked more closely at the stone. 'I like the depth of the colour, how it's almost black and then more speckled around the edges. It's beautiful.' She lifted the stone above her, trying to line it up with the neon tube light that hung overhead. 'Strength and love,' she murmured, then put the stone back.

Riva cleared her throat and, keeping her voice low, so only Chance would hear her, said, 'My sister once gave me a beautiful pounamu ring almost the same dark green as that piece of nephrite you were looking at. I loved it so much that I wore it all the time, which was stupid because it broke one day, when I was out digging.'

'But you still have it?' asked Chance.

'Yeah, I made a little pouch for it and wear it around my neck.' She felt under the neck of her T-shirt and pulled out a cord that was tightly bound around a small piece of leather.

'That's nice,' said Chance, stepping closer to look. 'That's really cool. And I bet the ring prefers being snuggled up in there to being dipped in water and mud all day.'

Riva felt a wave of gratitude. She gave the pouch a gentle squeeze and slipped it back.

'What's this?' asked Chance, pointing to a black stone.

'Obsidian,' said Riva. 'It's volcanic. I found some a long time ago, when I was travelling around the east coast of the North Island. It's like glass.'

Chance listened patiently, then asked, 'No, I meant this . . .' pointing to a word inked in silver on a black piece of card. 'Scrying?'

'Scrying?'

'Yeah, it says it's useful for scrying. What's that?'

Riva hesitated, trolling her memory for the word. 'It's when you gaze into a shiny object . . . you know, like the way you kids are mesmerised by the screens on your phones and iPads. It's for fortune-telling, really. I thought it was related to using a crystal ball, but I guess any shiny surface will do. Not that I've tried it.'

'I'm impressed,' said Chance.

'I don't think it's very reliable, as a tool.'

Chance bumped her gently on the arm. 'Don't tell me you're a scryer denier.'

244

'Just call me a sceptic,' said Riva.

Finally, they made their way towards the largest stall, a squared bay of tables covered with a wide variety of objects, from small appliances to electronics to ceramics and jewellery. Few of the pieces were antique or old and most would have been equally at home at a school fair. But there were lots of items and this fact alone seemed to instil an air of urgency among the other browsers, who only just managed to refrain from pushing or shouldering their perceived competition.

Riva wasn't interested in the sale. Although she could still recall the pleasure she had once felt on uncovering a bargain, she now tended to feel appalled when presented with so many goods. The sight of a table weighed down with discarded juicers, coffee machines, massage foot-baths and hair-straighteners caused a corresponding heaviness in her own body, which grew as she watched shoppers gather and buy armfuls of rubbish to take home. She felt disconnected from the people around her, and, as one woman edged past, a still-boxed, possibly unused popcorn-maker held tightly against her chest, Riva had to fight back the urge to call out, 'Stop. Enough. You don't need it. It won't save you!' Instead, she held her tongue and made her way towards Chance, who was kneeling beside the trestle, looking at a bright red, hard plastic case that sat on the floor.

'It's a sewing machine,' said Chance as Riva drew near. 'An 830. It's the exact model I've been saving for.' She leant closer, carefully unfastening the two metal clips that held the case together and uncovering the machine. Oblivious to the people milling nearby, she lifted the machine free and slowly examined it, checking the components for any broken or missing parts. When she was satisfied that it was intact, she turned her attention to the case, checking the foot pedal and box of accessories, checking over every bobbin and foot attachment with the care and attention of a child selecting a chocolate from a box. Finally, she took out the manual and flicked through its pages, pausing once in a while to read or take in an instruction or diagram. Only when she was fully satisfied did she replace the machine in its case and look up at Riva. 'It's all there,' she said. She glanced around then, searching for the stallholder. 'I wonder how much they want for it?'

By now Trudy had joined them and stood above Chance, looking down on her daughter.

'It's the sewing machine I've been saving for,' said Chance, smiling nervously up at her mother.

'How much is it?' asked Trudy. Then, without waiting for Chance to reply, she called the stallholder over, and indicating the machine asked, 'How much?'

The woman looked from Trudy to the machine. 'Is there a price on it? There should be.'

When Chance shook her head the woman told them to wait, and shuffled to the far end of the stall, searching out her sidekick, who was busy wrapping plates in newspaper. After a short discussion the woman took over the task of wrapping crockery and the man returned to where Trudy waited, asking how he could help.

'That sewing machine,' said Trudy, 'how much do you want for it?'

Sensing a sale, the man began a spiel that included the words 'favourite with collectors', while ranking the machine as the most sought-after model produced by the Swiss company. 'It's in immaculate order,' he concluded before giving the price, $375.

Riva saw Chance's whole body slump. She watched as the teenager slowly rose, and her heart lurched. 'It's a good price,' mumbled Chance. 'I've seen them go for more than $500 on the online auction sites.'

Trudy scowled at her daughter, then turned to the stallholder. 'The handle on the case is clearly worn so you'd have to come down. Also, I'm not convinced it's in good working order. When was it last serviced?'

The man didn't know. He was selling the machine on behalf of a friend.

'Well, I don't think it's worth more than $340,' said Trudy.

The faintest glimmer of hope began to shine in Chance's eyes. She half turned to her mother, began to say something and then thought better of it. Whereas minutes before her body had begun to cave in on itself, she was now tense, like a dog anticipating a scrap, all her attention focused on the conversation taking place between the stallholder and her mother. The negotiations continued, the price dropped to $360 and then $350. Turning to Chance, Trudy demanded, 'And that's the machine you want? You've researched it, haven't you?'

Still unable to trust her voice, Chance nodded and Trudy turned back to the man, saying, '$350.'

He nodded.

A smile broke on Chance's face and she thanked her mother.

It was only then that Trudy asked, 'How much have you got saved?'

The smile faltered but remained as Chance answered, 'I have $290.'

Trudy covered her mouth with her hand and ran her fingers up and down, across her lips as if trying to solve a mathematical problem.

'It's all at home,' added Chance. 'I can give it to you as soon as we get back.'

'Mmm,' said Trudy.

'And if you pay me at the end of the month, I'll have another $50, so I'll only be short by $10.'

Trudy's eyes narrowed. 'So you're telling me you don't actually have $350.'

Riva felt anger rise up in her and she took a step forward to intervene, only to be held off by Trudy, who spoke to her daughter. 'You've just watched me bargain this man down.' Her voice was low and thin. 'But you don't have the money?'

'Not yet.' Chance's voice began to crack, and in a last effort to make herself understood, she said, 'But if you advance me my wages, and lend me $10 that I'll pay back. I can do extra jobs …'

The movement and sound that had filled the hall seemed to evaporate, leaving only an echoing silence and stillness that closed around the small group. A second passed, followed by another and then, as if fuelled by a tiny glowing ember, Trudy turned to the man still waiting behind the table. 'I'm sorry. It seems I've been wasting your time. As you've heard, my daughter doesn't have the money.'

ALMOST TWO DAYS HAD PASSED since the fair, and Riva still couldn't get her head around what had happened. The way Trudy had put an end to the sale had taken them all by surprise. Chance was the first to react. She flinched and jerked her head to the side, as if reeling from a slap. Her face immediately reddened and then, as Riva watched, all colour seeped from her skin, leaving it a dreadful, ghostly grey. She hugged her arms across her body and in a faint voice apologised to the stallholder before hurrying out of the hall. As she slipped from view, both Riva and the salesman came out of their daze and began talking, their words jostling in an attempt to be heard:

'She can have it for $320,' offered the salesman. 'I'm happy to let it go for that.'

'I'll cover the difference,' said Riva. 'It's only fair after all the work she's put in at the sanctuary. I've been meaning to pay her—'

Trudy listened, her movements mannered, as if she were finding pleasure in being the centre of attention. Her expression mimicked concern or sympathy, but her face was mask-like and the emotionless tone of her voice lent her words a politician's insincerity: 'I know Chance will be disappointed and I doubt she'll understand—'

Repulsed, Riva interrupted. 'Well, I'm confused . . .'

The stallholder nodded in agreement but his attention was elsewhere, drawn to a customer who was signalling from the far end of the table.

Trudy addressed Riva in a low tone. 'It's not my intention to hurt her. It's really not. You're not a parent?'

Riva shook her head, 'No.'

'Well, if you had a daughter you'd want her to be resilient, wouldn't you?'

Riva felt the muscles around her mouth tighten and she fixed Trudy with a stare.

Unperturbed, the other woman said, 'If nothing else, I want her to learn that life doesn't always go to plan. She must be able to face bitter disappointment, and get over it.'

Now the sewing machine sat on the floor beside Riva's desk. She had bought it on impulse, in an attempt to erase the nasty residue left after Trudy's departure. But she felt no sense of victory, just a deepening sadness as she tried and failed to see

Trudy's words in a better light. There was a terrible logic to them, yet they failed to acknowledge the cruelty with which she had set up and humiliated Chance. It was the woman's lack of self-awareness and empathy that preyed on Riva's mind. Trudy clearly believed she had done her daughter a favour.

At times like this, Riva missed Irene. She wished her sister had been with her at the fair, or at least were here now. She knew Irene would reject Trudy's explanation. Of all people, Irene would be the one who wasn't scared of offending Trudy. She'd come right out and say, 'What a load of rubbish! You humiliated your daughter in public. You're no better than a bully!' Later, when they were alone together, Irene would work herself into a state of indignation, saying, 'We'll have to kill her. It's that simple.' Irene, who never hurt anyone, would come up with a plan to zigzag or buttonhole Trudy to death. She would make a joke of it, but her sense of justice would propel her into some kind of action. If Riva held back, she'd cajole her, saying, 'What was the original name of your company again? "We Are Wet Blankets"? Come on Riva, make it right.'

'I will,' murmured Riva. 'I was going to, even before you started bossing me around.'

She looked at her watch; it was past nine but the sky was still light, the sun not yet set. From the kitchen door she could see down to the lake, a finger of brownish water shimmering in the distance. The flax shelterbelt behind the washing line clattered in the breeze, and a tūī that had been feeding from its flowers took to the air, its wings thrumming as it flew away. The flax specimens near the house looked healthy, but elsewhere in the sanctuary the number of yellow and dying bushes had increased. She'd ripped out and burnt the affected plants in the hope of stopping the spread of the bacterium that was killing them, but wasn't certain how effective she'd been.

It was too late in the year to risk a fire now. Besides, she'd be unlikely to get a permit this far into the season. Only a few days before, a fire had taken hold fifteen kilometres away in the hills above the dam, and although now under control it had managed to destroy a long strip of native forest. The cause of the blaze was unknown but rumours had already spread around the community that it had been deliberately lit. The thought there might be an arsonist in the area was disconcerting. Riva wasn't scared for her own safety but she was worried about the damage a fire would do to her land. For the next week or two she planned to carry out night checks on the property. It might not do any good but at least it would make her feel stronger and more in control of the situation.

From a young age she had always believed it was better to confront a problem than passively accept the situation. She hated the idea of huddling in a corner, dreading the worst. In practice there had been so many times when she wasn't brave, and on those occasions she was aware of the gulf between who she was and who she wanted to be. She was never as courageous as Irene, whose strength had been formidable but reckless, too. More than once, Riva had been left thinking that Irene didn't care enough about life. That is, her own life. When Irene decided, early on, to discontinue treatment for her cancer, Riva had been heartbroken. She'd felt a kind of gut-wrenching horror and helplessness that made her gasp with pain. Irene, by contrast, had been not only calm but relieved.

'Life's too short to spend in hospital,' she had said, on more than one occasion.

'The reason your life is too short is *because* you refuse to go to hospital,' argued Riva.

Surely, Riva hoped, some survival instinct would kick

in and Irene would change her mind. But Irene remained fearless and, as she had threatened, befriended her illness and followed it to the grave.

Riva yawned and stretched. It was the lingering hour: too early for bed but too late for work. Between time. She suddenly remembered that Chance's school bag was still in her car. The girl had left it when she rushed out of the fair and went home with her mother, and Riva hadn't seen her since. Was it too late to return it? Probably. But Chance might need it and it wasn't yet dark, so there was no reason why she couldn't quickly pop over and drop it off.

It had been years since Riva had made her only visit to the Chance property with the intention of introducing herself to her neighbours. She hadn't found anyone in the house, so had done a quick search of the sheds in the hope of locating someone. It had struck her as a well-organised place, with every machine, every implement stored and locked away in its rightful place. The large shed, which housed the goats when they weren't out in the paddocks, was clean. She'd never been inside the house, but guessed it would be the same as the rest of the place. She imagined that Trudy was not fond of dirt.

It was only a short drive down the road and it took less than ten minutes before Riva pulled up to the house. She wasn't out of the car before Bruce appeared from around the corner, wiping his hands on a rag that he tucked into the pocket of his blue overalls as he approached. She was surprised by how much older he looked than the last time she had seen him. It was as though he had aged in dog years; from the way he walked it was clear his knees were stiff, unwilling to bend unless necessary. Riva waved and to her relief he returned her greeting. She recalled then, that during her one or two exchanges with Bruce, she had always got on okay with him. They didn't agree about many things but their face-to-face conversations were at least civil, which was more than she could say for some of the other neighbours, who clearly resented her 'meddling' in their business when she was trying to establish the wetlands. She recalled, too, that after a series of break-ins a few years back, Bruce had dropped by her house to check up on her and offer reassurance, saying that if she needed help she was to call and he and the boys would be there straight away, before the cops. She'd forgotten he'd done that. She hoped she'd thanked him.

'Everything all right?' Bruce asked, by way of greeting.

'Yes, thanks.'

They stood facing each other, and then Bruce pointed to something behind Riva's shoulder and added, 'Out late?' Riva turned and caught a glimpse of a kingfisher perched on the powerline just before it took to the air. 'Me or the bird?' she asked.

'Both. What can I do for you?'

'Just returning Chance's school bag. She left it in my car.'

'She's not here,' said Bruce. 'Haven't seen much of her since Friday, but I caught sight of her a couple of hours ago, heading off towards your place. She had a bag full of stuff. I thought she must be running away.'

Riva started. 'Really?'

'Nah. But something's going on. I saw her poking around in the workshop, going through the bins. A box of borax is missing and a handful of eartags. No idea what's she's up to.'

'That's a relief. I thought . . .' Riva fell quiet.

'Funny kid,' answered Bruce. 'We don't get to spend a lot of time together because Trudy thinks . . . I don't know . . . I'm a bad influence . . .' He hesitated, and glanced away, towards the house, before continuing, 'so I don't really understand what makes her tick. But a couple of weeks ago she started questioning me about goatskins and Higgs reckons he caught her standing in the middle of the road, staring at a dead hare yesterday evening. I can't make sense of it.'

Bruce eyed Riva suspiciously, as if trying to figure out her involvement. Seeing her smile, he relaxed and pointed to the bag, 'Leave it with me. I'll give it to her. Unless you want to go in — Trudy's home. She's in the middle of a book, though, so best not to disturb her. I caught her smiling before I came out. Bit of a worry.' He glanced at the house and shook his head, adding, 'Suppose you like books, too? Don't really understood the attraction myself. Never had much luck with Shakespeare, but I guess Porsche's probably filled you in on that debacle.'

He looked at the ground and murmured, 'Bloody hell, what a stellar performance.' Then he looked up and smiled. 'You okay? Not worried about the fires? Offer still stands . . . if you're ever in trouble.' He shifted uncomfortably and gestured back in the direction he had come from. 'Better get back. I'm giving the boys a hand with their shopping carts. I reckon they must be assembled by monkeys . . . heaps of junk, most of them. Bloody monkeys all right.' With that he raised his fingers in a friendly salute and turned away, laughing quietly as he repeated 'monkeys' to himself.

Riva started the engine, making sure the tyres created as little noise as possible as she eased the car around on the soft shingle and headed back to the drive. As she gathered speed, she checked the rear-view mirror, half-expecting to see Trudy waving her back. She crossed the cattle-stop at the end of the drive and breathed out slowly. It was when she felt her shoulders relax that she realised how tense she had been. She checked the mirror once more and pulled out onto the road, humming to herself, 'Made it.'

A short distance ahead of her, in the left wheel rut, was a

hare. She lifted her foot off the accelerator and braked gently. She'd been so intent on getting to the Chance house that she hadn't noticed it on the way over, but now she steered the car towards the verge and shut off the engine. For years she'd been in the habit of dragging away roadkill. It was still a bit early in the season, but soon the young harriers would appear and begin feeding off the animals killed by cars. These juvenile birds were slow to learn that roads were dangerous places and often fell prey, themselves, to passing traffic. During the summer months she'd see their corpses along the highways, their wings rising and falling, mimicking flight, as trucks roared by.

It was a big hare, an adult male. No doubt he had been on his way to her sanctuary, intending to join his mates and eat the tops off her young trees. The thought of all those juicy, green tips must have distracted him and — thump — dead. She crouched down and grabbed the hare by its ears, lifting it slightly as she began dragging it to the verge. Its fur was matted and part of its belly was missing, as if something had already had a go at it. The strangest thing, the thing she should have noticed straight away but had somehow failed to observe, was that all four legs had been neatly cut off at the joint. With a swing of her arm, Riva hefted it over the fence, watching as it landed on a tussock before slumping to the ground. She wiped her hands on her jeans and then returned to her car.

It could only be Chance. No one else would track down roadkill. All the farmers had guns, and if they wanted to spend an evening making lucky charms they'd simply go outside and shoot a rabbit. It had to be Chance. It delighted Riva to think that the girl could be that hard-case. She admired the fact that the first foray into skinning hadn't dampened her creativity. She'd like to know, however, what Chance was planning. Her thoughts wandered as she imagined Chance perched behind a trestle table at a craft fair, a neat pile of lucky charms on display in front of her. If she were smart, she'd give the charms some kind of spiritual property. Rabbits for luck, of course, but what about the other pests? Why not stoats for determination, rats for tenacity, hedgehogs for strategic thinking and goats for curiosity? Chance could fashion beautiful pendants or fur-and-crystal combinations. In truth, it wasn't such a crazy idea. No crazier than the ideas she had dreamed up for her own company.

Back in the 1970s, it had been all about designing women-specific outdoor clothing. She was one of the first to design jackets for women with busts. Every other women's jacket on the market was created with a flat-chested model in mind, which meant most women had to buy clothes two sizes up just so they could fasten their coats. Finding good rain- and winter-wear was extremely frustrating. She could remember the time she got into a vicious argument with a sales assistant over the way the cloth pulled and the zip strained on every single jacket she tried. 'What's the problem with these clothes?' she demanded.

Cupping her breasts in her hands she gave them a little jiggle, before launching into a detailed analysis of everything that was wrong with women's gear. 'Do you think we enjoy having our tits squashed flat? Do you not think the world would be a better place if we could do up our jackets *and* breathe at the same time?' The assistant had steered her towards the men's section and Riva went through the whole performance once more, this time focusing on the way the shoulders were too wide and the hem too tight around her hips. 'I'm not a wrestler,' she heard herself say. 'I'm just a woman. A small woman with two decent-sized boobs and a pair of hips. I'm not asking for anything fancy. I don't need a thermal codpiece. I simply want a jacket that's comfortable and doesn't force my tits up into my armpits. Do you get it?'

She spoke slowly, drawing out every word. She was so angry, she wasn't able to see the funny side of the situation — if there even was one. Suddenly she wasn't fighting for the right to buy a proper-fitting jacket, she was fighting for women everywhere. Women who had been squashed, pushed, flattened, bound — every one of them.

It had been one of the most invigorating rages of her life. She left the store intent on setting the garment world to rights. If no one else would make beautiful busty clothing, then she would. She went to the pawn shop and bought the first sewing machine she saw, an ancient green Husqvarna Viking, and then went home and searched out her old mummy-shaped sleeping bag with the broken zip and got to work. She'd never sewed before, but she was on a mission and nothing was going to get in her way. Within minutes of her starting, the floor of her two-room apartment was clouded with feathers. Every time she tried to gather them up and stuff them into a pillowcase, they would puff out of reach and float around the room as if inside some large-scale, conceptual snow-dome. She didn't have a pattern, and so contented herself with placing a white fake-fur coat that she was fond of on top of the hollowed-out sleeping bag and tracing around its outline. The only scissors she owned were the ones she used for trimming the fat off bacon, but she put them to good use, cutting and slicing through the layers of nylon until something that roughly suggested a jacket shape appeared.

She knew that her jacket was flawed, that it was the type of design that might possibly be adequate for a scarecrow but not a human. She only had two pieces: a front with sleeves, and a back with sleeves. In normal circumstances, she would have chosen this moment to reconsider going into the clothing business, but she was still angry enough that she wanted to continue, to prove her point. Without further thought, she ran the scissors down the centre of the front, planning to attach the zip from the sleeping bag later. Then she sat back on her heels and tried to figure out how to introduce some kind of three-dimensional element into her garment.

It was long before the internet or Madonna had come onto the scene, and the thought of adding frontal cones to the jacket didn't enter her mind. Instead, she searched her memory for images from nature that might solve her problem. The first to pop into her head was a kangaroo. A kind of breast pouch: looser at the front, becoming more tailored at the waist, then flaring at the hips. It was worth keeping in mind but she continued to search. She thought of cows, gorillas, pelicans and then, finally, three images entered her thoughts and she paused. A frog. A frigate bird. A monkey. Not any monkey but one with a large throat pouch. In a second her problem was solved. It was the fabric that was wrong. She needed to find a strong, waterproof, stretch fabric. That was all. All those nylon down jackets and nylon raincoats were bound to fail because they had no stretch. It was 1974 and she was on her way.

It took more than a year before she opened the door of BRA(IN)STORM. A year made up of research, optimism, panic, failure, success, travel and constant work. Sourcing the material for the Irene jacket had been the first problem, but in the end she'd found a medical supplier who was able to put her in touch with a manufacturer who, in turn, was able to supply a bandage-like strong, woven, waterproof product. At the same time as tracking down fabric, Riva had been hard at work on the design of the jacket. Her pattern-cutting skills were non-existent and so she'd searched the local community for someone with dressmaking experience. She'd located a German-Mexican woman by the name of Jutta, who made her living sewing communion dresses for a large Texan clothing chain. Jutta was sixty-nine, a bottle blonde and a chain-smoker. Her workroom and everything she made carried the scent of cigarettes and violets, the result of her liberal, and frequent, use of Guerlain's Après L'Ondée. Stick-thin and never married, Jutta joked that she had no need for food. 'You know, Ruth, I get all I need to survive from air, smoke and perfume. The only time I almost died was in 1942. For two weeks I had a cold and a blocked nose and I thought it would be the end of me.' Jutta cackled when she spoke, and when she cackled she coughed, spitting discreetly into a lace handkerchief she kept tucked up her sleeve. Apart from being a formidable seamstress, Jutta was able to hold more pins in her lips than any other person Riva had seen. She held pins the way puffins carried fish: twenty to forty at a time. She claimed to have swallowed a whole pin-cushion's worth, saying that she sometimes drifted off while working and inhaled, mistaking a pin for a cigarette.

'I am crazy to do your work,' she would mutter every time Riva visited with a new idea or design needing attention. 'You think my people need your stupid jackets?' She'd shake her head and tug dismissively at the seams on the samples Riva had made. 'You are stupid to make work for yourself. And you are wasting my time.'

Jutta's tough streak extended to the pack of half-wild cats she kept. At any one time, several adults and numerous kittens would be wandering in and out of her porch, drinking from fly-speckled saucers of milk that was yellow and rimmed around the edge of the bowl. Once, sitting with Jutta, waiting for her to finish her cigarette, Riva noticed a tiny, scabby kitten lurking in a dusty corner of the room. When she pointed it out, Jutta scoffed, 'God has plans for that one.' It was clear to Riva that the kitten needed medical attention and so, when she left, she took it with her. Two weeks later, during her next visit, Jutta questioned her about it, asking if it had died. 'No,' said Riva. 'She's filling out.' Riva was too afraid to admit that it took $400 in vet fees to get Tinker back to health. She knew Jutta would never approve of such sentimentality. She used to joke that she wished she had been a laboratory dog for a cigarette company. 'Have you seen the photos?' she used to ask. 'They spend their days smoking, for free! Me? I have to pay fifty cents a packet. It's outrageous.'

It was Jutta who got Riva through her early days at BRA(IN)STORM. Although she thought the brand name was ridiculous, and grumbled every time she handled each garment's label, she took pride in her work and, over the space of ten years, created the patterns for the best-selling Irene jacket, the Fanny salopettes, the Junko vest, the Freda windbreaker and the Arlene workpant. The one thing Jutta never grew tired of hearing was the backstory for the names of each garment. 'Irene is your sister. So, Fanny is your mother?'

'No, Fanny Bullock Workman was a mountain climber back in the late 1800s. She was one of the first women to climb mountains above 6000 metres in the Himalaya. She used to do incredible bicycle trips, too. But she was wealthy so she always travelled with lots of porters.'

'And what or who is this Junko?' pressed Jutta.

'She was the first woman to climb Mount Everest. Not very long ago, in 1975. She's Japanese: Junko Tabei.'

Jutta dismissed the idea of mountain climbing. She believed there was 'too much fresh air' in the mountains and that if she ever went to the Himalaya she would die because her lungs wouldn't know how to cope.

'Freda?'

'Freda du Faur. She was Australian and became the first

woman to climb New Zealand's highest mountain, Mount Cook,' answered Riva.

Jutta shook her head and softly clicked her tongue in disapproval.

'She wore trousers when she climbed,' said Riva.

'Ha, like you,' answered Jutta. 'A man-hater.'

'I'm the one who's married!' said Riva.

Jutta took a long drag on her cigarette, and wagged her finger at Riva. 'You don't fool me. I recognise you . . .'

Riva laughed.

'Arlene?' Jutta asked, while working on a new design for a pair of women's trousers.

'Arlene Blum. She led a team of women-only mountaineers up a mountain called Annapurna in the Himalaya in 1978.'

'Phew, what a mess. Can you imagine? Tell me, do women still bleed up there on the mountains when there is no air?"

'I expect so.'

'Tut, tut, tut,' went Jutta. 'What a mess.'

Jutta's greatest scorn was reserved for Riva's husband, Ivan. At least once during every visit she would lean back in her chair, place her burning cigarette carefully on the lip of the ashtray-cum-pin-container next to her machine and ask, 'And how is Comrade Ivan today?' She'd got it into her head that the spectacle-wearing Ivan was the spitting image of Trotsky, despite the fact that Ivan, typically, wore an off-duty uniform of denim jacket and jeans and fancied himself as a kind of Robert Redford character. 'I know his kind,' she'd warn as she inspected the garments made by one of the fifteen machinists Riva employed. 'He'll bleed you dry.' Riva always protested that Ivan was a good, generous man, but Jutta would roll her eyes and mutter, 'Ivan the Terrible. Mark my words. A lawyer in cowboy boots is not to be trusted.'

Jutta died long before her prophecy came true. Riva discovered her one morning looking drawn and pale, her hand shaking uncontrollably as she raised a cigarette to her lips. When Jutta stood up, her legs gave way and she had to be helped to the sofa, where Riva left her briefly in order to phone the doctor. When she returned a few minutes later, Jutta was lifeless, her still-burning cigarette smouldering on the carpet where it had fallen.

Every once in a while, Riva smoked a cigarette in memory of Jutta. Standing in the back garden under a maze of stars, the flax clacking in the night breeze, she exhaled the smoke into the night and imagined Jutta's response to her move to New Zealand and, more specifically, this wetland. She held only a distant memory of Jutta's voice, but even so she could conjure the tone of incredulity and bafflement of her reaction, a reply that could be summed up in one word: 'Why?' In the imagined exchange that took place, Riva always came off second-best. The more she reasoned with Jutta, the less convincing she sounded:

'Because I want to be closer to my sister.'

'Ach. If your sister is so keen to see you, why doesn't she come here?'

'It's not that easy for her to leave her job.'

'It's as easy as you make it,' insisted Jutta's ghost voice.

Riva took a low, slow draw on her cigarette and allowed her thoughts to drift.

'I want a change of lifestyle.'

'So you run away, like a school girl.'

'Well, you left your home.'

'I had my reasons.'

'Well, I have my reasons . . .'

'You think living in a swamp is going to help? You will be eaten by alligators . . . for breakfast.'

Riva was in full song as she picked her way down the track, intending to do a small circuit of the property before turning in for the night. She had a non-singing voice: it could be quiet or loud but nothing in between. As was usually the case, she fumbled her way through the verse of each song and then launched into power-mode when the chorus came into view. Tonight's music was courtesy of a band she had listened to back in the States, and heard nothing from since. It had been so long since she had played any of Social Distortion's CDs that she couldn't be sure of the words, but was happy to settle for an approximation, breaking out with the few random words she could be sure of: stand-up, strong, pain. As the lyrics of 'When the Angels Sing' faded from her memory, she threaded in words and tunes from numerous other sources, regardless of genre. Thus, in the space of a few minutes she managed to sample snatches of blues, country, disco and jazz.

But of all the tunes, the one she loved the most, and almost managed to capture in its entirety, was a song she had seen performed live back in the late 1970s, when she had first travelled to Britain with the hope of finding stockists for her clothing. Joan Armatrading's 'Love and Affection' held a special place in her heart. The words of the song reminded her of the days she had spent travelling through the rain, Irene samples in her backpack, as she tried and ultimately succeeded in introducing her products to laconic managers in wood-panelled mountain equipment stores throughout the north and in Wales.

Riva was onto her third cycle of songs, having added a couple more Armatrading tracks to the mix, when she noticed a bright light ahead of her, slightly below the main track, in the vicinity of the poplar-tree crossing. She guessed straight away that it must be Chance, as no potential arsonist would choose an area of boggy land to start a fire. She quickened her step and half-walked, half-trotted the length of the straight, hoping to reach the girl before she moved away. She was puffing and out of breath by the time she came to the spot where she had seen the light and, to her disappointment, Chance was not there. She was about to call out, when a sound, a splash, caught her attention and peering into the gloom, she spotted a light fifty metres or so further on.

She called out and the beam shot up towards the sky, before circling and falling in a line to Riva's left.

'Chance,' she called again.

The light dipped and rose, growing brighter as Chance drew nearer. 'Gosh, you gave me such a fright,' she said.

Dressed in a large hoodie, leggings and gumboots, Chance looked smaller and younger than she had at the fair. But, seeing Riva, her face broke out in a smile and she held up a possum by its tail. 'It was in one of your traps. Is it okay if I take it?'

'Yeah, of course.'

As Riva watched, Chance lowered the possum head-first into a plastic bag and stuffed it into her bag. 'I've been making stuff,' she said, by way of explanation. 'A proper collection, but I'm still a bit slow. I've managed to skin quite a few animals, though, and I think I'm getting better. I even succeeded in emptying one of your stoat traps without chopping off my fingers. Hang on a mo . . .'

She rummaged in her bag and pulled out a scrap of paper, passing it to Riva. 'I took note of the traps so you can keep track of what's been going on. I figured that would be helpful.'

'Are you okay?' asked Riva. 'I've been thinking about you.'

Chance gave a shrug and without answering looked up at the sky, saying, 'It's nice out here, eh? The other night the sky was an amazing colour, all green and purple, like the tourmaline stones we saw at the fair. Have you ever seen it light up like that?'

Riva nodded. Although it wasn't uncommon to see an aurora this far south, it had been a while since she'd been fortunate enough to witness one. She was usually in bed by nine, and so missed most displays. Nevertheless, she remembered the feeling of wonder a shimmering, rainbow-saturated night created. One day she would travel back to Tromsø to see the Northern Lights and spend time exploring the home of her mother's ancestors. The only other time she had been to Norway was during late summer, when her mother was dying. She had been ill prepared for the emotional battle her mother was determined to win, the days of painful silence broken only by outbursts of bitter and hysterical recriminations that left Riva shattered. Back then her head had throbbed from lack of sleep, and she had sought solace in the dull limbo-light of early morning, making her way past the university and up the hill to the towering ski-jump structures that loomed over the town. She could never look at the slides without feeling overwhelmed by vertigo. She didn't dare climb to the top; it was enough to look up from the grass below. On stormy nights, the wind would create a low, humming sound as it swirled between the towers, giving the place an abandoned, haunted atmosphere. She would remain on the hillside for an hour, staring upwards, trying to persuade herself that she was not afraid while all the time imagining the hurtling speed of falling.

'My mother's hometown, in Norway, is above the Arctic Circle and it's an area famous for the Northern Lights. It's not unusual for the whole sky to be lit up by an aurora. So beautiful.' She paused, and smiled at Chance, who was busy looking up at the sky, unaware of being watched.

Chance spoke without shifting her gaze from the stars.

265

'I'd like to go to Finland. That's where the book I'm reading is set.'

'Is it good?' asked Riva.

'I love it.'

Riva thought of Loretta and felt a soft wave of warmth wash over her. 'Did your mother like it?'

Chance's head went down. 'We're doing it together this coming weekend sometime. I'm going to spend the week on background research and make some notes. This time I want to be totally prepared, but I think it will go well. All the characters seem so real, if you know what I mean. They're different from the ones in the books my mum chose. Mine are kind of normal, if that makes sense? They go out and do things instead of being self-absorbed and acting weird all the time.'

As Riva listened her heart missed a beat. 'It sounds like a book I would like.'

Chance laughed. 'There aren't any eels in it.'

'There never are,' said Riva. 'It's a shame, really. Most books would be the better for an eel.'

'You remind me a bit of the grandmother in the story,' said Chance. 'She'd like eels.'

'What about the mother? In the book?'

Chance looked back towards the stars, shifting her weight so as not to lose her balance as she tilted her head. 'There isn't one,' she said. 'She's dead.'

Again, Riva's heart heaved, and she had to fight an urge to protect Chance or warn her that all might not go well with Trudy. But Chance appeared so focused and optimistic that it would be mean, Riva thought, to sow doubt in her mind. Instead, she brought the conversation back to Chance's skin project. 'I found a hare on the road. A strange thing, though — it had no legs.'

Chance turned to face at her. 'You must think I'm gross.'

She paused and added, 'I'm not really. It's not like I'm cutting up animals for the sake of it. It's more of a hobby, you know. And the funny thing is, I really enjoy mucking around with skins. Maybe I could sell my pieces one day and then get some money for a sewing machine and—'

Riva reached forward and touched Chance lightly on the arm but the girl pretended not to notice.

'I'd better get home,' she said. 'But I'll come and find you next weekend, and we can celebrate.' Her face opened into a smile. 'The last book of the year, what a relief!'

Riva took a step back. She felt cold, all of a sudden, and wrapped her arms, about her waist. 'It would be good to see you,' she said. She began walking slowly back towards the house, Chance beside her. After a minute she said, 'Saturday marks a significant day for me, an anniversary, and I was thinking I should do something special.' She paused, and looked back down the track, towards the tall shadows of the poplars. 'There's a place down by the lake, a kind of a den—'

Chance's phone sounded, a loud jingly burst that shattered the night air. 'It's Mum,' she said, looking at the screen. 'Sorry, what were you saying?'

'I'll be down by the lake—'

'Sorry,' interrupted Chance. 'I have to—'

Chance began to walk away, heading down the track, away from Riva. As she lifted the phone to her ear, she called out, 'I'll find you, okay? Wish me luck with my mum.'

And then she was gone, swallowed into the shadow, leaving Riva alone once more.

The quiet spectac

acular

L oretta clambered through the tangled twigs and leaves from a fallen tree and then stopped to catch her breath. Since her last visit to the den a storm had blown through the region, snapping branches and downing some of the older pines near the lake. In some ways, she was surprised the damage wasn't more apparent. The winds, according to the forecasters, had reached 140 kilometres an hour at the airport, and the papers had been full of stories of toppled powerlines, wind-tossed trampolines and lifted roofs. Here, in the wetlands, sticks and leaves torn from poplars and willows littered the walkways while, along the water's edge, debris from the surrounding properties and paddocks lined the shore. A long length of ghostly green plastic, from a hay bale, was caught around the trunk of a cabbage tree, and further afield peach-coloured sleeves used to protect seedlings from predators lay scattered about.

Despite being in a hurry, she made several small detours to collect and retrieve as many seedling protectors as possible, weighing them down as best she could with stones and branches so they could be gathered and reused. For the first time since visiting the wetland she gave some thought to what Shannon had noticed during their one and only joint visit. Whereas Loretta had always overlooked the vegetation, assuming it had always been a permanent feature of the wetlands, Shannon recognised the effort that had gone into restoring the landscape. Knowing now, that someone — Riva — had created the sanctuary from bare land gave Loretta a new appreciation of the woman's hard work. More than that, it gave her an appreciation of Riva's humility. At the talk Riva had barely mentioned the hours she put in, instead focusing on her gratitude for being allowed to spend so much time in nature. How wonderful that one woman, acting alone, could achieve so much with so little fanfare.

It was nearing dusk by the time Loretta reached the den. Even before stepping inside the shelter she was aware of an unfamiliar smell, something feral, meaty, quite unlike the earthy scent she recalled from her previous visits. During her absence someone had taken over the space, creating what appeared to be a kind of makeshift workshop. Covering the floor were strips of faded material and battered cardboard boxes and on top of these were various animal skins. Arranged by size, the skins ranged from what looked like rabbit feet and tails, through to stoat and possum skins. Bags of salt took up space either side of the vase and the bunch of proteas left from her last visit, and on the bed were smaller bags that, upon inspection, contained all sorts of odds and ends: bones, snippets of coloured wire and plastic. More surprising still were the broken badminton racket, a punctured bright yellow

Swiss ball and an old computer keyboard, all of which bore the stamp, 'Property of Caroline Freeman High'.

James Bond took up the centre of the space. His embellished breastplate had increased in size and now included two more rows of trinkets. His face was partially obscured by an ornamental headdress that sat low across his eyebrows. Less MI6 spy than exotic totem pole. His lipstick-coloured mouth smiled grotesquely, suggesting that he was rather smitten with his new makeover.

The smell inside the den was no longer overpowering. If anything, it began to lend a homely feel to the place, more like a farm kitchen just as the plates from a Sunday roast were being cleared from the table. Taking her time, Loretta examined the elaborate fur decorations more closely and when she came to the James Bond neckpiece she noticed a coloured cardboard tag in the shape of a sitting rabbit attached to the ribbons holding the adornment in place. Printed in neat capitals were the words: 'NATURAL ORGANIC PEST. Sourced from Neighbourhood Roadsides and Traps.' On the flip side of the label was another brief description: 'All products 100% by Chance.'

Loretta burst out laughing. She turned the label over in her fingers, rereading the description and shaking her head in delight. Suddenly the skins took on a new meaning for her and she circled the den once more, picking up and stroking each piece with the tender appreciation she had shown for her own children's handcrafts and art works. She returned to James Bond, and this time carefully lifted the headdress and placed it on her own head. It fitted, crown-like and, to her surprise, was remarkably stable. She shook her head gently from side to side and made a little skip but the headpiece remained fixed. With her back straight, she did a little twirl and took five steps, commanding, 'I am Loretta. Queen of the Wild Pests!' She did a curtsey and was about to do another twirl when a voice interrupted, 'And I'm Riva. Lady of the Bog.'

Loretta started, and the crown, which up to that point hadn't budged, slipped to the front, covering both her eyes.

Riva laughed. 'Whoops. Allow me, Your Majesty.'

Fingers brushed Loretta's cheek and a moment later she was standing bare-headed facing Riva who, with a bow, presented the headdress to her. 'Your crown, Your Majesty.'

Loretta blushed, mumbled her thanks and quickly turned, replacing the headdress on James Bond.

'Quite a castle you've got here,' said Riva, scanning the space. 'I like what you've done with the floor — got a nice Aspen Skid Row vibe going there.'

Loretta followed Riva's gaze. Resting her fingers on her chin, she appraised the floor. 'Not too *House and Garden* for you?'

'No,' answered Riva. 'It's got exactly the right amount of edginess. I particularly like the locally sourced Fisher and Paykel box, and it's so great that you even found room for your gym equipment.'

'Yes,' said Loretta, prodding the Swiss ball with her toe. 'It really adds value. That and the home office . . .' She suddenly felt awkward and lowered her eyes.

When she looked up again Riva was smiling at her, an expression of warmth lighting her face. 'I was going to ask if you come here often,' said Riva, 'but I don't want to sound sleazy . . . or nosy.'

'I'm not trespassing, am I?'

Riva shook her head, 'No. It's fine.' She walked across to the table and absent-mindedly lifted the vase, then replaced it within its circle of dust.

'The candle and buttercups?' she asked, 'Yours?'

Loretta nodded, and replied, 'The kānuka?'

'Yep,' said Riva. 'That's me.' As Loretta watched in silence she picked up the proteas and ran her fingers over their pointed petals. 'My sister used to work with a woman whose favourite flowers were proteas. Funny what you remember — nothing very important, usually, in my case.' She placed the flowers back on the table, lifted the scented candle and inhaled. Satisfied that she had found the source of the scent, she returned it and said, 'I'm glad this place has found a new lease of life. I got out of the habit of visiting.'

For a second her lips seemed to tremble and then she smiled, gestured towards the fur. 'I'm guessing that all this belongs to Chance. Do you two visit together?'

Loretta shook her head, 'No. I haven't seen any of this — well most of this — before.'

Riva crouched down next to the cardboard flooring and took a skin in her hands, turning it over to inspect the back. 'You know she's doing her book this weekend?'

Loretta didn't know. For the past ten days she'd been sending out reminder notices to students, asking them to return all library books before the end of the year. She'd seen Porsche's name on the list but had forgotten almost immediately, despite making a mental note to quiz her about the novel. Now she felt guilty for not having paid more attention.

'How did she seem when you saw her?' asked Loretta.

'She seemed to be putting on a show of confidence. She's so desperate to please her mother, poor kid. I keep wanting to tell her to leave the evil witch and come and live with me . . .'

'But you haven't, of course,' said Loretta.

'No, it's a pretty small community and I've already experienced one remark that gave me pause to think. Something about an older, single woman befriending a young school girl.'

'So you've been painted as some kind of Humbert Humbert . . .' Loretta trailed off, suddenly aware that her comment might be hurtful. 'Sorry, I didn't mean . . .'

Riva looked at Loretta, holding her gaze.

Without saying anything, the two women moved towards James Bond, standing next to each other as they took in the fur-themed breastplate.

'One hundred per cent by Chance,' murmured Riva, smiling. She examined the adornment more closely, running her hands over its soft background, checking the stitching and fastenings with a keen eye and pulling on the seams. When she was satisfied, she stepped back for a final appraisal. 'It's pretty good, isn't it?' she said after a moment. 'In terms of its design and manufacture. It's not too bad at all. I bet we could find a market for it.'

Loretta made her own inspection and nodded in agreement. 'You need to open a shop out here in the sanctuary,' she said. 'Organic pest products.'

Riva checked the neckpiece once more. 'Brainstorm by Chance,' she replied, and then shook her head, laughing. Facing Loretta, she explained, 'I used to have a shop. Actually, three hundred and forty-seven shops to be exact.' She paused, walked towards the den's entrance and stood looking out over the lake. 'I have to admit, I kind of miss being in business. It was nerve-wracking and exciting and I was good at it. I learnt a lot about myself, stuff I didn't expect. For instance, I have a bit of a cold streak and I really enjoyed the feeling of power. Strange, because I was a hippy at heart. Guess, maybe, it was more a sense of determination and ambition than anything. I felt quite . . . deranged at times because the ruthless "what I was" didn't fit neatly with the laid-back "who I was" — if you get my meaning.'

'I think I'm the opposite,' said Loretta. 'At school I feel intimidated by some of the teenage girls — really intimidated — and I cover up by presenting a hard exterior. It's the same with my husband, only different. I'm terrified he'll leave his job and lead us towards a life of eternal poverty, but, instead of telling him I'm afraid, I egg him on, saying, "Do it!" And now, on top of everything else, I keep thinking about my son Kit and how little time I have left with him. In a year or two I won't be able to hug him any more without seeming like some needy, middle-aged mother.' She paused and took a deep breath. 'I had a friend who used to lecture me about parents becoming dependent on their children.' She tried to smile and said, 'It's so true.' She swallowed hard and then sucked in her cheeks, softly biting the fleshy pads in her mouth. 'And yet everything's fine,' she said. 'Honestly, there's nothing wrong with my life. It's perfect, by most people's standards.' Already she felt ashamed for being so pathetic. That wasn't who she was, at all.

'I wish you'd met my sister,' said Riva. 'I think you would have liked her. She was wonderful — one of the warmest, kindest, funniest, strongest women I knew. It's the anniversary of her death — that's why I'm here. We built this hovel together. It used to have a garden but vandals destroyed it and, because of that, I haven't been back very often. It's almost like someone kicked over her grave . . . I don't know. I really miss her. She was so funny, so full of bravado, and so young.' Suddenly Riva made a heaving sob and her shoulders began to shake. Within seconds she was crying uncontrollably, too grief-stricken to manage even an embarrassed smile and then, just as abruptly, she stopped. She remained where she was, panting slightly, staring into the distance.

'How long has she been dead?' asked Loretta.

'Just four years,' said Riva. 'I'm not allowed to mourn after today. My time's up.' Her lips began to quiver and she gave a sad, down-turned smile. 'Damn,' she said. 'Life sucks, sometimes.'

They left the den and stood outside in the dusk, breathing in the fresh air, listening to the sounds of the encroaching night. Far off, a low boom drifted on the air, and together Riva and Loretta spoke: 'Bittern.' 'Pérrine Moncrieff.'

'Who?' asked Riva.

'Pérrine Moncrieff,' said Loretta. 'Oh, she was great, fabulous. She wrote the first real pocket guide to New Zealand birds back in the 1920s, and the really wacky thing about the book is that the birds are listed not by order but by size, so you get these crazy pages with a bittern slotted between a mollymawk and a penguin. Imagine actually seeing those birds together, in the wild. It's fantastic.' Loretta took a step towards the lake and cupped her hand over her eyes as she looked out over the water. 'Another thing about her — and this might interest Porsche, I mean Chance — is that she once gave a lecture called "Birds in Relation to Women".' Loretta laughed. 'The talk was about the use of rare and endangered bird feathers in women's clothing. I wish I could have met her.'

The bittern sounded again.

'It must be a late breeding season if it's still booming. We should go and look for it,' said Riva.

'Yeah, said Loretta. 'We should.'

They didn't move.

'How did you come across this woman?' asked Riva.

Loretta pulled a face. 'A couple of years ago I made a map of the South Island, replacing all the male place-names with female ones. It was totally random, as the kids would say. I substituted Pérrine for Nelson, because that's where she settled and spent her life.' Loretta blushed. 'I've also added her to an equally random list of women for a Dangerous Women project

I'm working on. But it's that thing, you know? She's practically responsible for the establishment of Abel Tasman National Park and yet she gets called "the bird woman" because she kept a pet macaw and looked after injured birds. I'm not saying that's dismissing her achievements—'

'I've been called the mad cat lady!' interrupted Riva. "Cause I named this place Tinker, after my cat.'

'Not after Annie Dillard?'

'No. My cat was named after *Pilgrim at Tinker Creek*, but this place was definitely named after my cat.'

'Well,' said Loretta, 'you're definitely mad. I think I'll add your name to my book.'

'Which one?' asked Riva.

'What?'

'I have a legal name and a chosen name. Which one do you want?'

'Both, I guess, but whatever suits you.'

Riva raised her eyebrows and then, adopting a commanding tone, said, 'Ruth Swann. Though my sister used to tease me with "Ruthless Ruth". I dropped the Ruth just before my mother died. She wasn't pleased.'

'I've always liked the name Ruth. It's one of those competent names. I can't ever imagine a Ruth fumbling through her bag for her tickets, immigration card and passport at an airline check-in. Do you know what I mean? She'd know exactly how much her carry-on bag weighed. That's how I picture a Ruth.'

'Yeah, well, that wasn't me. I was more your "never know where I'm heading until I arrive" type.'

In the distance, fainter than before, the bittern boomed and both women turned their faces in the direction of the sound, listening. Minutes ticked by and then once more, quietly, the bird called. A smile crept over Riva's face. 'You know, when I first came here there weren't any bitterns. The first time I heard its call was one of the best days of my life. I was so happy. I knew, then, that I was doing something right.'

She rubbed at her mouth, and her face opened up into a broad grin. 'It was so satisfying. I'd been up to northwest Nelson — *Pérrine*, I should say — and spent some time at Mangarakau Swamp where I learnt a lot about healthy wetlands. Bitterns are a good indication that things are okay: if you have bitterns you should find frogs and fish as well. They're hard to spot, though. If you're keen, we'll have to get going. I've got my canoe tied up over there—' She laughed out loud. 'That sounded weird.'

Loretta looked where Riva was pointing, and for the first time noticed the stern of a dull red Canadian canoe protruding from the edge of the raupō.

'I'll nip back to the den and get my jacket,' she said. 'Won't be a minute.'

It was now dark in the den. The bed, where she had stored her overnight bag, was obscured by shadow and moving towards it Loretta had to take care not to trip on the uneven floor, or slip on the loose skins. She found her jacket easily, but her binoculars seemed to have vanished. She reached into her bag, groped around with her fingers, becoming more and more impatient as she counted the seconds. Removing her hand, she ran her palm over the bed and finally located the cord, following its length to the eyepiece. She placed the lanyard around her neck and was about to stand up when she heard a voice call out, 'Hello?'

She froze.

'Who's that?' asked the voice. 'I can't see you.'

There was a shuffling sound and then a louder thump as a shadowy figure lurched into the den.

'Riva? Is that you?' asked the voice.

Loretta relaxed. She recognised it. 'It's me,' she said.

There was a long silence and the figure came closer, stopping a foot away. 'Ms Reed?' the voice asked. 'Is that you? What are you doing here?'

Before Loretta could answer, Chance continued, 'Wow, you're here. What about Riva? Is she here? Because I think she's having a party. I'm here for a party. Are you? That's great. We can all hang out together.'

The words tumbled out of the girl, one sentence following the other in rapid succession. As she spoke, Chance's voice grew louder, until with a final, 'Let's go find her!', she was almost shouting. She gave a broken laugh, then turned and for a second her silhouette filled the entrance of the den, before she was gone.

Unsure what to do, Loretta followed her. A beam of light suddenly lit up the path ahead, and a moment later Riva stepped into the clearing in front of the den, the flash of her torch striking Loretta full in the face. Chance flung her arms around Riva's neck and laughed, adding theatrically, 'Good to see you, old friend! This is great.' She let out a strangled whoop and then swung back to check that Loretta was listening. 'You, too, Ms Reed. Loved your book! Look at this . . .' She plunged her hands into the pockets of her cargo pants and started pulling out sheets of paper, smoothing them one by one and waving them in the air. 'Look at my notes! Didn't I do well?' She tossed one of the sheets in Loretta's direction and then pressed another into Riva's hand, before throwing the rest into the air. 'Look at all the brilliant research I did.' She allowed her eyes to settle on the sheets of paper as they floated towards the ground. Suddenly, her head jerked upwards, and turning back to Riva she ordered, 'Ask me how it went. Come on. Don't be shy.' She did a shuffling dance step and demanded, 'Ask.'

Riva hesitated, and, in that moment, Chance continued. 'Hey, here's a great question for you, courtesy of my mother. Tell me — a starter for ten, worth $1000 — to get us going. Just to get us off to a good start, before we get into the nuts and bolts of the chat. Just a little warm- up. Who is the implied reader of *The Summer Book?*'

A sickening feeling took hold of Loretta and from where she was standing she could see Riva stiffen as if she'd been knocked in the stomach.

'Come on, you two. Who . . . is . . . the . . . implied . . . reader? Hmmm?'

Chance twirled around, pointing her raised finger first at Loretta and then at Riva. 'Riva? Time is ticking — what's your answer?'

'People who read books?'

'Wrong!' snapped Chance. 'Ms Reed. Over to you. Who is the *implied* reader?'

A ghastly silence settled over the group, broken a second or two later by Chance. 'Come on, I know you're not stu-pid. You should know the answer to this.'

Still, neither Loretta nor Riva spoke.

'Tell you what,' said Chance, her voice growing shriller, 'why don't I make it simp-ler for you.' She paused, raised her hands and clasped them behind her head. Her words came out very slowly and clearly, 'Who . . . is . . . the . . . implied . . . reader?'

'Chance,' said Riva. 'Chance. It's all right. Just come and sit down with us, eh?'

Chance jumped back, almost tripping over her shoes. 'Well, that's interesting,' she said. 'Neither of you know, do you? Clearly, you're not going to win any prizes today. Next question, please? Riva? Ms Reed?' She laughed loudly, 'Did you even *read* the book, Ms Reed? Because it seems to me that you've failed to understand even the most rudimentary elements. Which makes me wonder why we're even here, discussing this *so-called* novel.'

She stopped speaking and bent down, picking up one of the discarded sheets, flapping it in front of Riva's face. Snatching the torch, she said, 'Tell me, what is the point of all these *random* notes if you can't even come to grips with the most *basic* . . .' She trailed off, the sheet hanging limply from her hand. Then she held the paper up and slowly read aloud:

'I really enjoyed this book. I loved how simple the setting and story were, how naturally the events happened and I liked the way nature entered into the story — so that it seemed almost like the characters were really in tune with their surroundings, like there was a real bond between the characters and the island they lived on, even though the island was tiny, smaller than our farm. I loved the warmth of the relationship between the old grandmother and the young girl. I loved how kind the grandmother was, but also that she was cranky but brave and funny. I liked how she sat back and let the girl gain confidence, like the time the girl went in the deep water and the grandmother noticed she was scared but didn't rush to help her. She believed in the girl. I liked how they were close, physically, like when they walked together or slept in the same room. Like they loved one another but didn't need to say it. I liked the simple language and that nothing much happened. It wasn't all fancy but almost like an episode, like a summer holiday story, and it was sweet and loving but not mushy. It felt true and honest. I liked how short the book was. It didn't drag on and on. I thought the grandmother was really cool and it made me think about my own grandmother and how I've never been allowed to meet her and I felt a kind of longing I didn't expect. And I thought about the mother who was dead in the story and I wondered what she was like, too. I wondered if she was also kind and if—'

She stopped, turned the page in her hand and then crumpled it into a ball and stuffed it into her pocket. She took a deep breath, sniffed and rubbed the palms of her hands along the front of her thighs. A moment later she cleared her throat, raised her head and smiled, 'So, what are you two up to? 'Cause I feel like having fun.'

Without waiting for an answer she lunged back into the den and came out with the headdress. 'I've got my costume! What do you think? Do you think I'm onto something, that I'll get rich like you, Riva?' She placed the piece on her head and whooped out loud, followed by a brittle 'Ha, ha, ha.' Raising her hands in salutation, she lifted her knees, jogged on the spot and yelled, 'Man, it's so good to see you, Riva. And you, too, Ms Reed. I'm so happy you're here! This is great.' She stopped, giggled and then sat down where she was, stretching her legs out in front of her, her head resting on her knees, her fingers gripping her ankles. Five seconds later, she was lying flat on her back, facing the sky. Rolling onto her side, she turned to Riva and whispered, 'I had no idea what she was getting at. I couldn't understand a word she said.' She laughed faintly and closed her eyes.

A surge of rage and disgust hit Riva. She pictured herself smashing her fist into Trudy's face, and the fleeting power that image gave her blunted her feelings of pity towards Chance. While she hesitated, Loretta had already crossed to the girl's side, helped her up from the ground and led her across to a fallen tree, where she sat beside her, leaning against the trunk, talking softly and smoothing Chance's hair. Riva saw Loretta, but still something held her back. She turned in the direction of the farm and took a few steps forward but then seemed to waver, as if slowly waking from sleep. She swung around and came toward Chance. She stood to the side, a little behind Loretta, watching but not quite able to close the distance between herself and the girl.

Chance sat still. Her body looked small and vulnerable, the only sign of life the gentle sound of breathing broken every now and again by a long, gulping sigh. As the minutes passed, a primordial calm descended on the group, giving the impression that little by little the small death within each person was, itself, dying, to be replaced by something more powerful, life. The night closed in around them, and nearby a whistling frog began to chirp, its gentle warble fragile: now faint, now louder, on the warm breeze.

'It's a frog,' said Loretta. Her voice was low, barely disturbing the quiet. Her hand resting on Chance's hair, she continued, 'We get them a lot at our house; there's a drain near the back of the section.' She paused. 'I think they live there.' She tilted her head in the direction of the sound and listened. 'When Kit was little he used to take me out to hunt for tadpoles. I'd have to make ponds for them in the paddling pool. They always disappeared or died. Once, I think one of them might have got big enough to grow front legs. I suppose they were whistling frogs, too?'

Her eyes still on Chance, Riva responded, 'Probably.'

'Yes, I thought so,' said Loretta.

They fell silent, neither of them feeling any need to fill the night with words.

'I had a pet stick-insect once.' It was Chance who spoke and she shifted slightly, drawing her knees up to her chin. 'I found it on the washing, when I went to take it off the line. I don't know how it got there. It looked like a stick.'

'Yeah, they do, don't they?' said Loretta. 'There's something magical about them.'

'You liked the book, didn't you?' asked Chance.

'Yes, I did. I liked it a lot. I thought that everything you said about it was spot-on. I felt those exact same things when I read it. You're right, it was true and honest.'

Chance gave a shudder and rested her head on her knees.

'Are you cold?' asked Riva.

'No, not really.'

'Do you want a drink? Or food? I made a cake,' said Riva.

'Later, maybe,' said Chance.

'We used to hear coyotes, when I was in Nevada,' said Riva.

'Really?' said Loretta, her voice rising with exaggerated interest.

'Yeah. We used to go hiking on the city trails after work, and we'd often see them. They're very beautiful. They used to attack small dogs from time to time, especially if it was a drought season and they had pups to feed. You'd see notices pinned up everywhere, warning dog owners to keep their pets on a leash.'

'Were they pests?' asked Chance.

'No. Not to me, at least.'

It was late. Riva estimated that the sun had been down for at least two hours. She felt for the small button on the side of her watch and gave it a press, and a number flashed briefly: 11:31. In another twenty-nine minutes, the anniversary of her sister's death would have passed. Without meaning to, she looked at her watch again and noticed that another two minutes had passed. Panic began to take hold of her, beating against her chest.

'I think I'll get the cake,' she said. She waited, anticipating some response, but when neither Loretta nor Chance spoke, she slipped back to the canoe to fetch it.

Wrapped in a tea towel inside a tin, the cake was still warm. Riva eased her fingers under its heavy base and raised it up into the air, transferring it to a second tea towel laid out on the earth beside Chance. The smell of cinnamon and cloves rose into the air, and mingled with the dry scent of pine and the metallic sweetness of the ground. Riva took a deep breath and then looked around at Loretta and Chance, who quietly sat watching.

'Would you like to try it?' she asked. The penknife she had brought for the job had a small blade, too short for the deep slab, and as she sawed the cake collapsed and crumbled, taking on the appearance of a sandcastle battered by waves. Riva tried to pick up a chunk to pass to Loretta but it fell apart in her palm, leaving a mound of sultanas and crumbs. Riva looked at the mess and shook her head slowly. She'd known from the second she'd muttered 'Rough enough is good enough' as she measured out a heaped mug of wholemeal flour, that the cake would be a failure, and yet she'd made no effort to correct or compensate for her mistake. Indeed, she'd wilfully made things worse by substituting two eggs for three, one quarter-cup of sugar for two, and so on, all the way down the list of ingredients until, by the end, the recipe for coffee walnut cake was unrecognisable, replaced by an approximation of her standard sultana loaf.

Her 'sulk-tana' cakes, as her sister called them, were a source of amusement when Irene was alive. It was okay to ruin the recipe back then; it didn't matter because Irene was still there, and they could laugh about each and every disaster and buy something better from the supermarket. But with Irene dead, the cake did matter. It was the only proof Riva had of her ongoing love and commitment to her sister. It was her cake of remembrance. And, despite its importance, she'd failed to make it correctly.

'Do you like baking?' asked Loretta as she picked at the crumbs that were now deposited in her hand.

Riva was tempted to say 'Yes', but didn't. Her eyes fixed on the crumble, she said, 'You don't have to eat it. It's not very good.'

'No, it tastes fine,' said Loretta. 'Does it have tea in it?'

'Green tea. That's all I had.'

From the corner of her eye Riva could see Chance prodding the cake with her finger tip.

'I always burn mine,' said Loretta, licking her hand and then wiping the remaining crumbs off on her trousers.

'I usually buy mine,' said Riva. 'I only make one cake a year.'

'For your birthday?' asked Chance.

'No. For the anniversary of my sister's death. Irene. She died four years ago today. From cancer.'

'That's such a nice thing to do,' said Chance. She pointed at the mound on the tea towel and asked, 'Can I have another bit? It's so good.'

Riva looked at Chance, and almost cried with gratitude.

'I'd like some more, too,' said Loretta. She took a bite from the crumbly pile and said, 'Here's to Irene.'

'Irene!' chimed Chance.

'Irene,' said Riva, 'I miss you. I wish you were still here.'

All three ate the cake in silence. Balls of dry mixture caught in Riva's throat and, try as she might, she couldn't swallow. She could feel the crumbs moving from one side of her mouth to the other as if being batted, balls that sometimes stuck to her teeth, sometimes collided with the soft pulp of her cheeks. Eventually the food turned to mush, and disappeared down the back of her throat.

She glanced at her watch. It was after midnight. The anniversary was over.

A bird fluttered in the tree above and a short warning 'chink' filled the air.

'Blackbird,' said Loretta.

As she turned her head in the direction of the sound, her cheek caught the light from the moon and glimmered. 'That sound always makes me think of winter in Christchurch,' she said. 'I used to listen to the birds when I was in my hut in the garden and I always associate blackbirds and starlings with frost, and the clinking sound of my father putting out the milk bottles. I know I shouldn't say this, but I actually prefer the song of blackbirds to tūī. It must have something to do with my English background. Some genetic memory.'

As if on cue, the blackbird cried out again, a rapid 'clak clak clak' that faded as it flew off into the night.

'Last year,' said Chance, 'my mum got Dad to lay down new lawn at our place. He sowed a whole ton of grass seed and the sparrows kept coming and pecking at it. I came home from school one day and there were dead birds everywhere. Some of them weren't even dead — they were just rolling around. It was horrible. We didn't know what had happened. My dad thought there must be something wrong with the grass seed and he took it back to the shop. In the end it turned out that Mum had poisoned them. She'd gone out and sprinkled rat poison across the ground because she was sick of them eating the grass seed. Who would do that? They were only sparrows.' There was a long silence and then Chance continued: 'This will sound dumb, but just this second it occurred to me that my mother really is a horrible person. I always thought there was something wrong with me, that I was to blame, but it's not me, is it?' She let out a bewildered laugh. 'That's such a relief. I don't have to try and please her any more, do I?'

Neither Riva nor Loretta replied.

'I'll disown her,' continued Chance, her voice becoming stronger and more animated. 'I can run away . . . I'll be sixteen next spring and she won't be able to stop me.' She laughed again, quietly this time and said, 'I'll come and live with you, Riva. That would be good, eh? And if she comes looking for me, we'll tell her to get fucked, eh? You could do that, couldn't you? I'll tell her: you're a nasty bitch and you can rot in hell, and that will be it. All over.'

Chance's voice was shrill, verging on hysterical. She stood up and started pacing back and forward across the clearing. Her steps were jerky and as she walked she swung her arms: together forwards, together backwards.

'Hey, Chance,' said Riva quietly, 'come back here a minute and sit down with me.'

As if following an order, Chance spun on her toes and went to Riva, plonking herself down on the ground between the two older women.

The frenzied activity subsided, and Chance fell quiet, breathing gently as she snuggled against the log supporting her back.

'Listen,' said Riva. 'Tomorrow I'll go and see Trudy and have a chat—'

'—and tell her I'm going to live with you?' interrupted Chance.

Riva couldn't reply. She pictured tomorrow's meeting with Trudy and felt hopeless. For all her anger and outrage, she wasn't sure if she could help, or make things better.

'It's late,' said Loretta after a moment. 'I'm going to get my sleeping bag and some of the other bedding. We can make a bed up out here, if that's okay with you two.'

She returned with her arms laden and, together with Riva, spread a tarpaulin on the ground, on top of which she placed two foam mats. She disappeared back into the den and came back carrying a bundle of possum furs, which she then layered across the mats. Finally, she unzipped her sleeping bag into a duvet and placed the old sleeping bag from the den beside it.

They lay down together: Loretta and Riva beneath the open duvet and Chance inside the sleeping bag. The air had cooled slightly, but it was still warm, and within a short time the sound of deep breathing could be heard from Chance's side of the bed.

'I'll come with you tomorrow,' whispered Loretta. She shifted uncomfortably, and pulled the duvet across her shoulder. 'Trudy's not going to like us being there . . .'

Riva gave a low, bleak chuckle. 'You reckon?'

Loretta joined in, laughing quietly. 'She'll probably poison us . . .'

'Yikes,' said Riva. 'Just don't accept any food from her.'

'She'll cause trouble and try and get me fired for interfering,' said Loretta.

Riva stifled a yawn and rolled to face her friend. 'We won't let her,' she said.

Above them, the moon eased into view. It was neither new nor full but somewhere between the two, a bright third of light filtering down through the gap in the trees. Riva and Loretta lay awake, following its slow passage across the sky. From time to time their bodies touched and neither moved away, each drawing in the warmth of proximity. They stayed close, lost in their own private thoughts, and, with time, first one then the other fell asleep.

acknowledgments

THANKS TO EVERYONE at Penguin Random House for the quiet, spectacular work on my behalf. In particular I would like to thank Harriet Allan and Tessa King for providing guidance throughout the editing process, and designer Carla Sy for her thoughtful and beautiful design. Many thanks to Audrey Eagle for allowing us to use her wonderful botanical illustrations. Thank you to Anna Rogers for kindly editing this book, and for 'shrugging off' all my mistakes with good humour and grace. Grateful thanks to Pip Adam for encouraging me during the writing of this novel and for sharing some happy days with me in Auckland during 2015. Big thumbs-up to Alex McLellan and Harry McLellan!

Thank you to Alison Ballance for joining me on a wetlands tour of the South, and to Brian Rance for showing us around his (and Chris's) wetlands restoration project outside Invercargill. Frequent visits to Te Nohoaka o Tukiauau Sinclair Wetlands near Dunedin have filled many happy hours during the research and writing of this book, and I'd like to thank Glen Riley and the volunteer team involved in making this wetlands such a wonderful place. Thank you to all the people I have followed through Facebook who are working and campaigning on behalf of fresh water quality, native fish, plant and bird environments. And a final thank you to the builders of the Signal Hill Debacle, a den I 'discovered', visited and enjoyed many times while out walking, for reminding me of the joy of imagination and exploration.

Also available by Laurence Fearnley

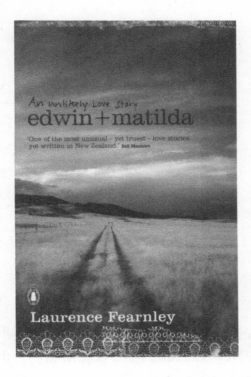

This beautifully written novel by Laurence Fearnley is about finding love in the most unlikely of places. Set in the southern South Island, it describes the unusual bond formed between sixty-two-year-old photographer Edwin and twenty-two-year-old Matilda, as their relationship grows in ways neither could possibly have predicted.

Also available as an ebook.

degreesofseparation
laurence fearnley

On board an aircraft as it makes its way slowly from the Antarctic to New Zealand, three people sit quietly, reflecting on their past summer on the ice. Sally, a composer, has been searching for inspiration. She wasn't prepared for the silence of Antarctica. William, a bird scientist, has been visiting since the 1960s. Estranged from his family, he has just completed his last summer on the ice. Marilyn, a young communications operator, has spent three months at Scott Base feeling isolated and lonely. She has had an affair with a young field-training instructor and now dreads the future. Contrasting the beauty and vastness of the Antarctic with the banality and discomfort of life on the ice, Laurence Fearnley's novel focuses on themes of love and memory to capture the stories of three people struggling to understand their journey.

Available as an ebook.

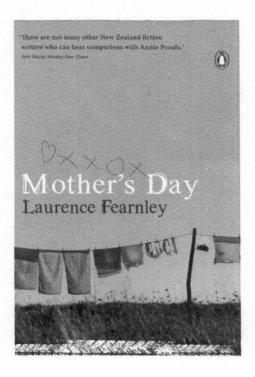

'There are not many other New Zealand fiction writers who can bear comparison with Annie Proulx.'
Iain Sharp, Sunday Star Times

Mother's Day
Laurence Fearnley

Life is tough for forty-year-old solo mother Maggie, a home-help caregiver. Her three children are all giving her a hard time, especially Bevan, who's in trouble with the police. But when she's assigned a musician in a wheelchair to care for, something new enters her life. Maggie's a singer, Tim a fine guitarist. They'll make music together, but tragedy is just around the corner. Then it's Mother's Day, and Maggie and her family gather . . . This touching novel from Laurence Fearnley contains many gems of warmth, affection, love and hope.

Also available as an ebook.

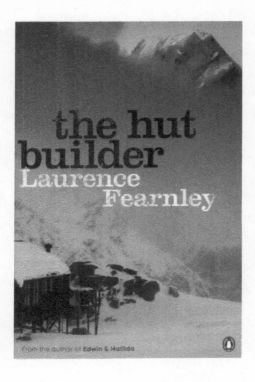

the hut
builder
Laurence
Fearnley

From the author of *Edwin & Matilda*

As a boy in the early 1940s, young Boden Black finds his life changed for ever the day his neighbour Dudley drives him over the hills into the vast snow-covered plains of the Mackenzie Country. Unexpectedly his world opens up and he discovers a love of landscape and a fascination with words that will guide him throughout his life, as he forges a career as a butcher and poet, spends a joyous summer building a hut on the slopes of Mount Cook and climbs to the summit in the company of Sir Edmund Hillary.

Also available as an ebook.

Reach
Laurence
Fearnley

From the author of *The Hut Builder*

Quinn is a successful artist creating new works for an upcoming exhibition. She lives on the coast with Marcus, a vet who left his wife for her and lost contact with his young daughter Audrey as a result. Entering their lives is Callum, a deep-sea diver with a love of the ocean. As the countdown to Quinn's exhibition progresses, each must face challenges and make choices that will test their loyalties and have far-reaching consequences for their future. *Reach* is about risk-taking and the ways in which creativity, struggle and danger empower individuals and enrich life.

Also available as an ebook.

For more information about our other titles visit
www.penguin.co.nz